JOHNNY LYCAN
&
THE ANUBIS DISK

WAYNE TURMEL

Black Rose Writing | Texas

ISBN: 978-1-68433-576-3
PUBLISHED BY BLACK ROSE WRITING
www.blackrosewriting.com

Printed in the United States of America
Suggested Retail Price (SRP) $18.95

Johnny Lycan & the Anubis Disk is printed in Calluna

*As a planet-friendly publisher, Black Rose Writing does its best to eliminate
unnecessary waste to reduce paper usage and energy costs, while never compromising
the reading experience. As a result, the final word count vs. page count may not meet
common expectations.

To Rogine and Annette.
Best. Sisters. Ever.

JOHNNY LYCAN
& THE ANUBIS DISK

CHAPTER 1

Night of the full moon.

The Russian tasted like borscht and cheap cigarettes. Well, his blood did. It's not like I actually ate him—I wasn't that far gone. But with that much blood flying around, some of it got into my mouth and as nasty as it tasted, I licked my lips and felt it fuel my anger.

It was righteous anger, too. The bastards had the twenty-year-old tethered by her wrist to a bed, and she was screaming her head off. She gawked at me, took a breath to shriek some more and yanked on the leather cuff around her wrist like it would magically let go this time.

Good girl, Meaghan. Scream your butt off. Bring the cops so I can bail out of here and let them get you home.

Of course, she may have been more than a little freaked out by her would-be rescuer. Six feet of shaggy, gore-besmirched, pissed-off Lycan will elicit an emotional reaction.

The two tattooed gangsters—*blatnois*, was the Russian word—were doing a fair amount of screaming themselves. The younger one held the shredded remains of his gun hand, staring stupidly at it while cursing me, God, his partner, and his boss for getting him into this. I'm guessing. I don't speak Russian. It didn't matter. He'd pass out in a second and no longer be my problem.

The other guy, Maxim Kozlov—older, meaner, and a lot smarter—held a bloody hand against the wicked scratch I'd torn open on his chest and swore with a lot more conviction than his young partner.

His heavily inked right hand held a commando knife with a serrated blade. The goon was unnaturally calm, muttering to himself as he shifted the handle in his palm to get the balance just right. No screaming. No stupid moves inspired by rage. This was one dangerous son of a bitch. He didn't know or care what I was; he planned to gut me. I had to keep my Johnny side in charge and not let Shaggy run the show. That was a good way to get sliced to pieces.

Meaghan shouted and thrashed on the bed, making it hard to focus. My job was to get her away from her kidnappers and back to her father in one piece, whatever it took. In situations like this, the deal was to get out with a minimum of bloodshed and my hide intact. This time that might be tricky. I whirled and snarled at her. She clamped her jaws together and shut up. While I wanted her safe and alive, all that noise was becoming a distraction I didn't need. At this precise moment, Max Kozlov demanded my full attention.

Roaring as loudly as I could, I snapped at him. The cold-eyed killer just sneered back. I had to hand it to him. That growl-snap-combination thingy was usually all it took to send people into either a panicky run or a fetal position. Not this guy.

I was pretty much screwed.

Kozlov let out a feral scream of his own and came at me, blade held way too high. I grunted with pleasure and swiped a claw at his knife hand, hitting nothing but air. It had been a bluff, and the goon now swung his arm lower and in from the right side. I dodged but felt the white-hot sting of the blade against my body. In this state my hairy pelt blunted the attack, but I still bled. This would leave a mark.

"Ha. You hairy fuck. I'll kill you." With that thick accent, it sounded like dialogue from a John Wick movie, but he left no doubt he meant every damned word.

In no position to indulge in witty repartee, I settled for trying to remove his jugular instead. I swung my left claw at his throat, expecting him to pull away and leaving him exposed to my right. This guy knew his stuff, though. Kozlov tightened and threw his body against mine, trying to knock me down. My blow sailed clean over his shaved head.

I didn't think. I didn't come up with some nifty plan. I just chomped down hard and my teeth met the flesh of his shoulder. This time he screamed. Good and loud.

Despite our reputations, Lycans avoid biting people, except as a last resort. If you're going to use your teeth, you'd better kill the guy. The old legends about turning your victims with a single nip are only partly true. Just a tiny percentage of people can survive an infected bite; most die in agonizing pain from sepsis and whatever germs we carry. I didn't like this guy, but better to kill him outright than be the cause of that horror. Not that he was giving me much of a choice. I drove my jaws into his other shoulder—his knife arm—and tore. This time he collapsed in a shivering, blood-soaked heap.

Through Shaggy's eyes, I watched him hit the ground and knew he wasn't getting back up. Then I turned to the quivering, blubbering woman behind me. She squeezed her eyes shut against the sight of me and pulled herself into a ball.

"Please. Don't hurt me," she sobbed. I couldn't tell her I was a nice guy here to help. Even if my snout could form the words, she'd have understandable doubts. Couldn't really blame her there. Hard to tell the good guys from the bad without a program.

Instead of arguing, I grabbed the strap at her wrist and pulled the steel chain tight. Ignoring her ear-splitting screams, I tore at the leather cuff in a frenzy of teeth and claws until it snapped. The second Meaghan felt it let go, she leapt off the bed onto the floor where she nearly tripped over Kozlov's still-thrashing body. Instead of running or freaking out, she picked up his knife and flailed at me in an awkward two-fisted grip. The kid had guts give her that.

"What are you? Leave me alone." She had no clue what to do with that weapon, and if I meant her harm, it wouldn't have taken much. I crouched low, slowing my breath to calm myself, hoping she'd take the hint and do the same. My elongated jaw made it impossible to form words and tell her I was getting paid to find her and get her away from those goons no matter what it took.

Meaghan O'Rourke was a disheveled mess, but her ratty Korn tee shirt and jeans were still on her, and her red Chuck Taylors. The Russians had done nothing more than grab her, scare the shit out of her, and hold her for ransom. A small blessing, but one that would speed her healing. If the biggest shock she suffered tonight was me, it could have been a lot worse.

Speaking when Shaggy ran the show was almost impossible. I pointed towards the door and somehow formed a growling bark in my snout that sounded enough like, "Go." Whether or not she understood the word, she got the message and slowly circled around me, keeping the blade pointed at my face until she reached the door.

Grabbing behind her, she fumbled with the deadbolt. After a couple of tries, the cold wind blew in. She'd probably regret leaving her jacket on the bed, but pneumonia was the least of her concerns. She wasn't about to stick around. Waving the blade at me one more time, she shouted, "Don't move. Stay." Like I was a German Shepherd or something. Then she slammed the door behind her and ran out into the quiet suburban neighborhood, shouting for help and hoping to wake the neighbors.

A light snapped on in the house next door, and it would only be a matter of minutes until the cops arrived in a very bad mood. I focused on my bloody right claw, closing my eyes and concentrating as hard as possible. My hand shook and ached like a son of a bitch, but after some initial twitching, the razor-sharp nails retracted and the fur receded, leaving a sore and swollen but functional human hand. Using my shirt to avoid fingerprints, I flicked off the back-porch light, turned the knob and slid out into the yard.

Across the fence, the neighbors clucked and shouted questions while Meaghan explained through gasps and tears that someone had kidnapped her. I didn't stick around to hear her version of the rescue. As sirens wailed and the night sky over the house turned red and blue, I hopped over the fence into the alley where I'd parked my car. In a couple of minutes, I'd be human, clothed, and inseparable from nine million fellow Chicagoans.

Just the way I liked it.

CHAPTER 2

I drove wearing just my gym shorts for a few blocks until I was safely out of the investigation zone. Then I pulled my old car onto a dark, weed-infested side street, cut the engine, and laid my head on the steering wheel hoping to still the taiko drums in my skull.

No matter how many times I'd made the change—and I was damned good at it given I was self-taught—coming back to myself gives me a bitch of a headache and strains the crap out of every muscle in my body. It felt like spending the morning after a tequila bender in the weight room, only the pain lasted forty-eight hours. As a rule, it took a couple of days for my muscles to forgive me, but I'd be asleep for most of it. These weren't normal circumstances.

For one thing, my belly was on fire. I looked down, and sure enough, Kozlov's knife had gotten me good. Because it mostly hit coarse hair, the wound wasn't deep. It looked like a nine-inch papercut, but it throbbed and stung and was likely to get infected. I dragged my ragged ass out of the car and around to the trunk where I kept the first aid kit and a change of clothes.

The cold metal of the Charger's trunk felt good against my feverish skin. The old girl was a two thousand and six, black roof and hood with orange side panels. Well, except for the silver fender on the left front that I hadn't gotten around to repainting. Still, I owned her outright, and she worked. Mostly. I popped the trunk.

I'd removed the bulb so no one could see me like this, and it took some fumbling around to grab the plastic kit full of gauze and disinfectant. This wasn't the kind of neighborhood where people paid much attention, and sure wouldn't call the cops if they saw anything, but why take chances? It was far enough away that when the police eventually started searching the area, this far from the stash house, I'd be long gone.

I returned to the front seat, taking with me half a dozen gauze pads, and some of that white tape that never adhered properly to my hairy belly. Even when I was just Johnny, I was a pretty hirsute dude.

Not risking the dome light, I sucked in air and poured alcohol on the cut. Then I tore a handful of strips from a roll of tape and fumbled the gauze against the oozing wound in my side. From the amount of blood and my half-assed patch job, I knew I'd have to have my buddy Bill's grandmother look at it. The old Gypsy woman—his *puni daj* — would give me a tongue lashing along with the cure, but those old folk remedies of hers always did the trick.

I think the old bird enjoyed playing mother hen despite her constant squawking at us. It's nice to think she'd have liked me even if I hadn't saved her grandson's life, but whatever. Neither Bill nor I had anyone else looking after us anymore.

After more or less duct taping myself back together, I lay back in the seat to catch my breath. The clock read one forty-five. It was an hour off, but it was almost time to fall back anyway and I could do that much math.

My old friend the man in the moon was high in the autumn sky and that big face smiled down at me. I gave him a big cheesy grin in return. I hadn't planned for this to go down when I was at the top of the Cycle, but until tonight I had no idea where they'd been keeping Meaghan O'Rourke. Better to be lucky than good. And I'd needed that extra lunar assist with Kozlov. That was one tough Russki.

Most people have misconceptions about the moon and how it affects Lycans. It's not like you're perfectly normal, minding your own business and then *Oh crap, it's the moon. Aaaaooooooo.* Shaggy's always inside me, and technically I can call on him any time except at the new moon where he's completely dormant. It's just that when the moon is low, it takes too much energy. It took the first eighteen years of my life to understand why half the month I felt like I was coming down with a cold, and the other half I was bouncing off walls, getting into scraps and generally driving everyone crazy. One week a month I was a more-or-less normal guy. Somehow my teachers, parents and employers never focused on the positive.

I had to learn all this the hard way. Getting off the Ritalin as soon as I left school helped me learn to control the crazy. Mostly. Of course, it took getting out of the house as soon possible, too. No sense howling over spilled milk.

Before I could get home and have this booboo looked at, there was an important piece of business to attend to. I picked up the burner phone, pushed redial, and waited.

Despite it being nearly three in the morning, O'Rourke picked up on the first ring. "Yeah?" His gruff bark came through the speaker. He might have been a bad-ass bookie and Shylock, but he was also a concerned parent. Meaghan was luckier than she knew.

Attempting with mixed results to sound as macho as possible, I dropped my voice an octave. "She's safe. She's with the cops now. You'll hear from her shortly."

He exhaled and sounded more like his usual miserable self. "She's... okay?" No doubt what he was asking without saying the words. And with Russians, the possibility always existed. But, no, they hadn't assaulted her.

"She's good. Shook up is all." *And she'll probably need a butt-ton of therapy, but that's not my problem.*

"And those pricks? You handle them?" Handle was a fairly vague term for a very specific request.

"One of them will never hold a gun again. The cops have him. The other one won't be doing much of anything." I hoped I sounded like Kozlov bleeding out on the floor was just another day at the office.

"Christ. You've come a long way, kid. Commie bastards had it coming." He might be a smart bookie, but clearly not up on current geopolitics. It didn't seem like the time to correct him.

I tried to ignore the fact he used to be my boss and suddenly a client. *Keep it professional, Johnny.* "There's the matter of my ten percent." Somehow my voice didn't crack like it did back when I was just a big dumb kid who provided muscle. The deal was to get Meaghan back in as few pieces as possible and teach a stern—preferably permanent—lesson to the kidnappers. For that, I'd earn a tenth of the ransom demand. Twenty-five grand made up my take for tonight's adventure. By far my biggest score ever.

If I sounded like I did this all the time, blame Bill as my business manager. I sure wasn't ambitious — or smart—enough to come up with that business model on my own. Left to my own devices, I'd have settled for a couple of hundred a day and expenses. But what I could do added value to the transaction O'Rourke wouldn't find on Yelp.

He took his sweet time responding. Finally, he coughed and said, "Soon as I see my baby safe and sound you can come pick it up."

There was obvious pain and relief in his voice. Even if I wanted to be a hard case about it, negotiation skills weren't my core competency. "Fine. Ten a.m."

"You know where." He let out a sigh. "And... thanks." Neil O'Rourke must have reached halfway up his ass to find that expression of gratitude. I'd known the man over ten years, and for two years out of high school he used me as hired muscle. Over the years, I'd picked up thousands of dollars for his operation and never got more than a grunt. This was practically a soliloquy. A father's love and all that.

"Yeah," I said to the air. He'd already rung off. I snapped the cover off the phone, pulled out the SIM card, and thought about where to go next. My body ached, and my stomach growled. The unpleasant copper-and-beet taste of Russian wallpapered my mouth. But I had one more stop to make before home and bed. I'd have to redo the bandages afterward, but it would be worth it to work Shaggy out of my system.

Chicago is an alright place to be a werewolf, if you have to do it. The weather isn't too hot most of the year—a major consideration when you run around in a fur coat—and thanks to some careful city planning, corrupt Illinois politics, and rich people who'd rather leave their money to posterity than to their ungrateful children, there were lots of parks and green spaces. Out in the suburbs, there were over a dozen Forest Preserves and parks.

It took about fifteen minutes to get to my favorite Country Forest Preserve. Pulling into the lot, I prayed there'd be no sign of a white Ford Explorer. Those patrols were a pain in my hairy ass. The coast looked clear. Finally, a break.

With a wince, I got out of the low seat and conducted one more search for prying eyes. The October wind bit deep and cold but felt good. The air smelled of rotting leaves, distant smoke and... rabbits. Out of the trunk I got a clean set of clothes and set them on the passenger seat, then stripped off.

Since it was a full moon, and the second time tonight, it didn't take long to make the change and Shaggy took over. As usual, I felt better, stronger, more... me, which is precisely the problem with taking this form. Addicts say they're never more alive than when they're high. It's kind of like that, only the drug is in your bloodstream every minute of every day. Scoring isn't the problem. It's not drawing on that stash constantly.

After clawing a hole in the forest floor and burying my blood-soaked clothes, I squatted and sniffed the air. The scents filled my nose, stronger and more plentiful now. My brain exploded with smells. Going from plain old Johnny to this condition felt like that scene in the Wizard of Oz when it goes from black and white Kansas to Technicolor. I freaking loved it.

There were more than just rabbits out there. The forest vibrated with every nocturnal creature you could imagine. Bats fluttered overhead, an obscenely fat possum waddled across an oak branch, and from just over the hill near the pond wafted the unmistakable aroma of venison on the hoof. I needed meat and to burn off some of this energy. That buck would be the perfect solution.

Twenty minutes later I sat licking deer spleen off my hands and groaning at how full my belly felt. At my feet lay the gutted carcass of a young, very surprised buck. The County would be grateful for one less rat with horns, and nobody would ever have a clue I'd been there. Some poor coyote would get the blame, but they've been taking shit ever since the roadrunner cartoons. Screw them.

Back at the car, I slipped a disk into the CD player—one of the few advantages of driving an old piece of crap was equally old technology. My luck held, and it started on the first crank this time. Life didn't suck.

Turning Zeppelin up to not-quite-ear-bleeding, I pulled out onto Dixie Highway. Twenty-five grand would buy me a much sweeter ride, hopefully something with vinyl seats or something easier to clean. I let out a happy howl and pointed the Charger North and East.

The full moon limped across the sky and dawn broke just as I got home.

CHAPTER 3

The sun was coming up over the lake as I pulled into the concrete slab driveway. It looked beautiful, the sky a perfect Fall Blue, but the dawn damn near fried the eyeballs out of my head. My high-cycle heightened every sense. Bright lights just added to the sensory overload and attendant misery, so I had to wear sunglasses, even at dawn, if I didn't want the mother of all migraines.

The building I shared with Bill and his grandmother was a typical red brick Chicago three-flat. They had the main floor. With his disability, the fewer stairs the better. Plus, Gramma owned the building and got first pick of the units. The top floor belonged to a Loyola grad student of indeterminate gender identity named Robin, who we seldom saw. I lived in the "garden apartment." That's the Chicago word for a basement studio with one long, skinny-ass window right at ground level, usually blocked by mud and a hydrangea bush. That was fine. It was dark when I needed it to be, like this morning, and light bulbs were cheap when I needed to see.

The place was nothing fancy, but the rent was stupid-low, and I was a flight of stairs from my only real friend. Plus, since I had a car and none of the others did, I got the building's only parking spot. In return, I'd occasionally drive Bill or Gramma around when they needed it. Parking in Chicago being what it is, and since Bill seldom left the house anyway, it was a sweet deal.

There was nothing more my body craved than to curl into a fetal position and get three hours of blessed sleep before I had to go meet O'Rourke out in the burbs. No such luck.

The annoying *buhdeboop* of an incoming text message went off just as my hand hit the knob.

Come up and tell me.

Bill was either solar-powered or half rooster. The man was up earlier than anyone I ever knew, even as a kid. Taking a step back to look up at the living room window, I saw him. There he was, already dressed and leaning on his forearm crutch. He beckoned me up. I groaned but waved back and tackled the stairs, willing the gauze and bandages to stay in place.

We all had keys to each other's apartments, so I slipped in, kicked off my sneakers without unlacing them, and followed the scent of dark roast coffee into the kitchen. My best friend sat at the little table cradling a mug in his hand and trying to look like he hadn't been waiting at the window like a neurotic shih-tzu waiting for its owner to return from work.

"Well? How'd it go?"

I tried to act like rescuing someone, killing a guy, and turning into a feral night creature was no big deal. "Pretty good. She's safe." It was a mistake to try talking and sitting at the same time. He caught my grimace.

"And... uh, what about you?"

"Shaggy got the worst of it. I'll live. It's just a scratch. Really."

"Uh-huh." Bill took another swig of coffee rather than continue a pointless argument.

It hurt too much to get up again. "You going to get me some of that?" If Bill was determined to keep me up, he could damned well keep me caffeinated.

My buddy struggled to his feet and clomped across the cheap yellow and gray floor tiles, grabbed an oversized mug with his employer's logo on it, filled it to overflowing, and set it in front of me without slopping too much. While he did that, I took two or three deep breaths and got my game face on.

"Who did the work tonight, you or... the other guy?" Bill was the only person on earth who knew about Shaggy—or at least that Shaggy and I were the same thing. Person. Whatever. That didn't mean he was comfortable talking about it. He'd watched me change the night I saved him from that beating. It wasn't soon enough to save his leg from permanent damage, but he could walk with a little aluminum support. The thing was he saw it, told no one, and pretended it didn't bother him. It's what friends do. I'd been keeping his secrets a lot longer.

I closed my eyes and let the strong, black java work its magic instead of answering him. We sat, slurping and looking at the ceiling, then out the window, pretty much everywhere but at each other. He knew if he stayed quiet long enough, I'd crack. Which I did.

"It was bad, but she's okay. And I'm okay. Really."

Bill nodded thoughtfully. "And the money?"

"I'll pick it up later."

"You mean you haven't been paid yet? Jesus, Johnny..."

"Come on. It was four in the morning and he hadn't even seen his daughter yet. He's good for it." If you couldn't trust a bookie to have the cash he says he'll have, what was the world coming to? "Relax, I'm picking it up at ten."

"And then?"

God, he could be a pain in my furry butt, but I dutifully recited the plan. "Bring it back here, break it up into smaller bundles, and take it to the bank a bit at a time." Before Bill became my financial advisor, I hadn't even had a bank account. I was strictly cash only, pretty much living off the grid like some Mexican dishwasher.

Bill's eyes lit up. "Oh, let me show you." He popped up and crutch-stepped as fast as he could into his room, returning with half a dozen printed sheets of paper. "Here are the invoices. All official-looking as hell, if I do say so myself."

Now that I was working for real money, I needed to do things like pay taxes and have a debit card. Bill had drawn up some fake invoices I could use to deposit the money without awkward questions from the bank. They looked good, but the name at the top bummed me out.

"J Lupul and Associates?" I thought we were calling it Vandelay Industries?" My friend gave me one of his snarky "ach" noises.

"That's a lame-ass Seinfeld reference. You may as well put a big neon sign on your door that says, 'audit me.' Honest to Christ, man, you're thirty-one years old. Time to live like an adult."

He was right, naturally. A complete pain in the neck, but correct. And he had the patience of Job with my ADD-assisted ignorance. That time he suggested I get paid in Bitcoin, and both our heads nearly exploding during the conversation, was a case in point.

I focused and studied the papers. We billed parts of my fee to a fictional, innocuous-sounding company. They were for various amounts under ten thousand dollars so they wouldn't ring any bells with Homeland Security or the DEA. I had to admit they looked legit and grown-up. Without my buddy's assistance, I'd still be taking crumbs and shoving them under my mattress, pulling out a fistful whenever the bills were due. It's what I did for years, working construction. With everything done online now, there was no way for anyone to function on a strictly cash basis anymore. Until the Zombie Apocalypse, that is. Bill Mostoy never took my concerns about that seriously.

"So, I've got all your DBA paperwork done, you just need to sign it. And the website's ready to go tomorrow morning, too. I did it all in dollar bill greens and golds. WordPress isn't very sophisticated, but it's got some great widgets, and we only need enough of a presence to pass the sniff test. People who want to hire you won't be impressed by..." He babbled on excitedly, and I did a fair job of pretending to listen. Website, presence, blah, blah blah. He was going to a lot of trouble for me, but what I needed most at that moment was a nap.

"Hey, when this is all done, you think I could get a new ride? The Charger's just about had the biscuit."

His face lit up. "Really? You're ready to ditch that old rust bucket? Hell yeah. If you're going to be an adult, you should travel like one. It'll look more professional when you meet clients. What were you thinking, like an Acura?"

"Um, I was thinking another Charger, just like a 2016 or something. Something with all the fenders the same color. I can pay cash..."

Bill drove an imaginary Samurai dagger into his belly. "I'm trying to make a real company out of you and all you want to do is swap it for a slightly less humiliating version of what you have? It's hard to write a muscle car off as a corporate expense."

The sound of slippers on slick, old linoleum alerted us to Gramma's presence. Bill's *puni daj* was just over seventy but looked ninety. She was an old Romani woman—I'd get the wooden spoon across my butt if I ever called her a Gypsy, although that's exactly what she was—bent and sun-wrinkled and worn to a nub by a hard life of which we knew only the tiniest details.

Gramma Mostoy did what she always did before entering any room I was in. When she didn't think I could see, she pulled her bottom eyelid down to ward off the Evil Eye, then spit on the ground. What she thought I was, she never let on directly. Maybe it was out of gratitude for saving Bill's life, but she never once said anything. Protected from whatever evil I represented, she forced a smile and shuffled into the kitchen.

"You boys are up too early. It's not natural. You should be out late drinking and getting laid, not talking business 'fore the sun's even up."

Bill and I exchanged eye rolls. For all her salty talk and world-weariness, we were both sure she had no idea that her grandson's ideal romantic partner was a-six-foot-tall blonde frat bro, likely named Jason. It was one such specimen and his asshole buddies who jumped Bill for making an ill-advised pass the night Shaggy and I came to his rescue. The beating had left him romantically unattached and with a permanent limp. All the old lady knew about that night, or would admit to, was that I was a good friend who'd saved her grandson's life. For that, I got cheap rent and admission to the inner circle.

"Acting like a bunch of *gorgers,* the both of you." Calling us the Old-World word for anyone who wasn't Roma was the highest insult she could muster. And this from a woman with a world-class colorful vocabulary.

She padded over in those ugly furry slippers and gave her grandson a kiss on the forehead, then looked me up and down. "What'd you do now?"

I fibbed like a five-year-old. "Nothing."

She motioned for me to show her.

I looked at Bill for help, which wasn't coming. He just grinned that superior smirk of his and stared into his coffee mug like there was something fascinating at the bottom. Avoiding eye contact with her, I lifted my shirt. A little blood had seeped through the gauze and crusted, meaning it tore the scab and started bleeding all over as I exposed my abdomen.

She shook her head and said something I didn't quite catch. It didn't matter, the world for "dumbass" sounds the same in any language. She scuttled off and returned with a proper first aid kit.

The crone administered rubbing alcohol, more clean gauze, and a healthy dose of verbal abuse. Finally, she determined I'd live and waved at me to put my shirt down. "God, you're a furry bastard. Any woman you're with would probably cough up hair-balls."

"I haven't had any complaints." Bantering with her was a lost cause, and God only knows why I bothered.

"You haven't had any *anything* in so long you don't remember."

My supposed best friend damn near snorted coffee out his nose, which only put him in her sights. "You should talk. The two of you, honest to Christ."

It was time to make my getaway. I pushed away from the table. "Thanks for the coffee. I'm gonna take a catnap before I go to... my appointment." I gave her a peck on the top of her grey head and retrieved my shoes from the entryway. There was a door leading from the kitchen downstairs to my apartment. We never locked it so I could come and go pretty much at will. Still in my socks, I headed to my room to catch an hour of zees before meeting Neil O'Rourke and the biggest payday of my life.

CHAPTER 4

First day past full- waning gibbous moon.

"O'Rourke?" The kid behind the counter at the cigar lounge didn't even look up from his phone. He just jerked his pierced head towards the small room in the back. I managed not to throw up in my mouth and said, "thanks." On one hour's sleep and a high-cycle hangover, the stench of all that raw tobacco was doing terrible things to my gut. Fortunately, I had a good base of county-provided venison holding everything down. Still, I felt like crap.

Neil O'Rourke had been running his book out of The Golden Humidor since I was in high school. He had some kind of arrangement with Sammy, the Lebanese guy who owned the joint, to claim the back smoking lounge as his personal fiefdom.

It didn't look like much of an empire. An old card table sat ostentatiously in front of the biggest flat-screen TV. O'Rourke held court in an oversized leather chair, occasionally poking fat fingers at a laptop keyboard. The fat Irishman sat there all day, puffing on the longest, fattest, most noxious stogies and taking bets from all the respectable—and delusional—Cubs fans and Northwestern alums who made up DuPage County.

Like most such places, the lounge was BYOB, but it still jarred me to see a bottle of Connemara whiskey and a half-empty glass sitting on the tray at that hour. Despite the peaty blood flowing through his veins, the big man was infamous for keeping a sober head. That made him even more dangerous when crossed, because he knew exactly what he was doing, or threatening to do, and had a memory like a bull elephant.

He scared the crap out of me when I worked for him. O'Rourke had taken me on a year out of high school to intimidate the slugs who fell behind on payments, and I'm ashamed to admit that I dug the feeling of power it gave me. I didn't know what to do with all that lunar rage back then and beating the crap out of deadbeats was an outlet. But there wasn't a moment's doubt that my boss was bigger, meaner and all-around more dangerous than anyone in the room.

This morning, the baddest man in Dupage County didn't look menacing at all. He was middle-aged, fifty pounds overweight and bleary-eyed. His jowls sagged, and there were blood vessels visible in his cheeks with more red lines than a Metra Rail map. I recognized his buzz-cut from the back. He turned just enough to acknowledge my presence, held up his hand until he punched two keys on his computer and hit save. Then he struggled to his feet, put his giant hand on my arm and steered me out the back door into the alley.

After the stale smoke and rolled tobacco, the fresh air felt wonderfully cleansing, or at least as clean as a parking lot off a busy secondary highway can be. A nice deep breath calmed the riot in my belly. O'Rourke's well-manicured hand took my arm and led me to his Escalade and around to the tailgate, out of sight of anyone on the street and the store's lone security camera.

"You don't fuck around, do you, boyo?" I pretended I knew what he was talking about. "Them two are in the hospital and one of 'em ain't going to make it."

My guts churned again. Kozlov was an objectively evil guy, but he was— if barely—a fellow human being. I wasn't proud of myself. I couldn't let O'Rourke know that though, so I struck a pose. "How's Meaghan?"

"She's a bloody mess," he snapped. "I was already paying for rehab and therapy, and this has probably set her back aways. The story she's telling... didn't know you had that in you."

He studied me for a minute, then let out a ragged sigh and averted his gaze. "She'll be fine. And you're right, she's in one piece. Thank you."

"Yeah. We're good." I nodded to the back of the truck like I made this kind of money every day and managed not to drool. "Is it in there?"

He dropped the tailgate and grabbed a knockoff Louis Vuitton bag, pulling it towards us. Twenty-five grand was literally in arm's reach. It was

JOHNNY LYCAN & THE ANUBIS DISK

all I could do not to grab for it. Everyone in town knew that O'Rourke moved bigger numbers than this on a weekly basis, but his hands shook as he opened it. I saw bundles of bills and hoped my eyes wouldn't bug out of my head like a cartoon.

They were hundreds, and the wrapper said there was five grand per. It looked right, but then I'd never even seen five thousand in cash at one time in my life. Picking it up, I pushed one bundle to the side and picked up the second. *Two bundles...*

"You're going to count it right here?" he asked. "You don't trust me?" I ignored him and kept counting. *Three bundles, four...*

"Something you oughta know, boyo."

Four... there were only four bundles. Math had always been my worst subject, but even I knew four times five wasn't twenty-five.

My head throbbed, and I felt my nerve endings ignite. One day past the full moon, my temper was on red alert anyway and it was taking everything I had not to lose my shit completely. The bastard was trying to stiff me on his daughter's reward. When I worked for him, there was never a question come payday. Now this.

"You're light, Mr. O'Rourke."

"It's not what you think. Let me explain." There was something unrecognizable in his eyes. I caught a whiff of his body odor. It wasn't fear exactly. O'Rourke regularly faced tougher guys than me, at least in my human form. There was something else in his scent—something moldy and dank. He avoided my gaze to look down at the cracked blacktop. Then I recognized it. Shame.

"I'm not stiffing you. I promised you, and you'll have it. Hand to God. I know what you did for me and my family."

Just as I was thinking the world was a messed-up place when even loan sharks and bookmakers didn't carry enough cash, a phone rang. It wasn't mine. The generic ring tone was coming from inside the bag.

"You're gonna want to answer that."

"Where's my money?" I barely recognized the growling voice barking out of my mouth. *Easy Shaggy. I got this.*

"Answer the goddamned phone." O'Rourke's brogue dropped to a whisper. "Trust me."

Trust him. After stiffing me on a deal? Did he think I was crazy?

Of course I answered. "Hello?"

"Mister Lupul?" The connection on the discount store phone wasn't great, but the voice was male, high pitched, and barely audible over the sound of some machine hissing and pumping in the background.

"Who's this?"

The mystery man ignored my question. "Don't worry. O'Rourke has your money. I just wanted to get your attention." My eyes drifted to the Irishman who, after miming that he didn't have a gun, pulled the last five Gs out of his inside jacket pocket.

"What the hell?"

"I have a proposition for you. Now that you're a respectable businessman and all, you might want to... leverage your investment. You can turn that last five thousand dollars into ten if you're interested."

I was interested. Additionally, I was scared, confused, nauseated and shaking like a junkie before welfare day. My hesitation didn't sit well with the jerk on the other end of the line.

"I'll give you the additional ten in cash. All you have to do is come meet me this morning. Or you can take the pittance..." the asshole actually used "pittance," a word I'd only ever seen in books, "... Mister O'Rourke has in his hand. I can assure you, I'm good for it. And there's an opportunity for you to make more money than this. A great deal more."

He saw the confusion written across my face in Magic Marker, because the Irishman whispered, "Take the meeting, kid. You'll have to meet with him, eventually. Cromwell doesn't take no for an answer."

Who the hell is Cromwell, and why do I give a rat's ass?

I'd seen a similar look on my old boss' face once before. He'd given a degenerate the chance to walk away from a suicidal bet on the Cotton Bowl. The poor bastard didn't take the lifeline, naturally. I wasn't on the scene when the inevitable happened. It's one reason I found another source of income. He wasn't usually a forgiving man. Stepping off was good advice then, probably still was.

The voice on the phone was getting irritated. "Your, uh, client is right, Mr. Lupul. I am persistent, and this is ultimately in your best interest. Tell you what, he will pay you what he owes you right now. Talk to me and you'll get an additional ten thousand dollars in cash. One meeting. If you don't like what I have to say, walk. Ten thousand dollars is a lot of money to someone like you."

Someone like me. This prick was getting on my nerves. I had my pride. Then again, ten grand was worth way more than my ego, and I was curious as hell. Plus, the look on O'Rourke's face told me I didn't have as much choice as I'd like.

"Where and when?"

"Now we're getting somewhere. I'll text you the address. It's on the Gold coast. In exactly one hour. Don't be late."

I had to ask. "What if I'm late?"

"That would be an expensive mistake. Besides, the way you drive, I'm not worried. Unless that old Dodge of yours finally breaks down for good." The hairs on the back of my neck stood straight up. "Pass the phone to Mister O'Rourke please."

I offered the phone to the other man, who snatched it from my hand and offered a curt, "Yeah." Then he stabbed it off with more violence than necessary and handed both the device and the rest of the money to me.

"Sorry about the drama, kid. Wasn't my idea."

I looked at my old boss and tried not to look eighteen again. "Who is this guy?"

"Someone with more money than God. And no sense of humor."

"So, he's good for the money?" There was no need to ask. Neil O'Rourke was the scariest guy I knew growing up. Even when I was on the payroll, he could freeze my blood with a look, and he was scared shitless.

"Old Man Cromwell does exactly what he says he'll do. Take the meeting."

My crappy flip phone chimed with an incoming text. The bougie address wasn't a neighborhood I'd spent any time in. I wasn't even sure they'd let me in the building, but I had an appointment to keep.

"Johnny…" The Irishman hesitated. I could have sworn there were tears in his bloodshot eyes. "Thank you. For everything. I owe you one."

That phrase was never said lightly in his world. I nodded like it was my right. "You've paid me. We're good."

"Still, Meaghan is… well, you know." We stood there saying nothing for longer than either of us cared to. Then he offered his hand. His palm was cool and smooth against my calluses.

I broke it off and threw the bundle of bills into the bag with the rest of my payday and zipped it shut.

Bill would be ecstatic with an additional ten grand to play with. I'd be happy to just get the money and go home.

CHAPTER 5

About a mile from the cigar store, the news came on the radio.

"… the two alleged kidnappers are in Stroger Hospital, one in critical condition…"

So, Kozlov was hanging in there. My guts churned along with my conscience as I stabbed the radio's button to find a traffic update. Like everyone else in the city, at least those of us who didn't have smartphones, I only listened to AM radio for Bears games and traffic reports. "Construction Roulette," is the unofficial sport of Chicago. Trying to find the least painful way to get anywhere was tough on the best of days, and this morning the clock was ticking. I had thirty-two minutes to get to my mysterious meeting.

It didn't help that my crappy flip phone didn't have GPS or any of those apps. Not having a smart phone didn't matter to me particularly, and my credit and lack of provable income made it a pipe dream, anyway. AM radio and paper maps got me where I was going most of the time. Between that and my taste in music, I was born two decades too late.

Ten K was a lot of money for one meeting. Whoever this Cromwell guy was, he was stupid-rich and powerful enough to frighten Neil O'Rourke. A smart guy would avoid getting in too deep, so I gunned the engine and squeezed into an opening just ahead of a Hyundai with a bashed-in front panel. *Hit me, man. I have insurance. Now.* So, if I was doing so well, why was I so freaked out?

Cromwell's building was an old elegant stone ten-story two blocks from Oak Street Beach. Serious old money. Once I found the address, it was time to pay Chicago's second-favorite party game; Find a Decent Parking Spot.

The drill was always the same. Circle the area three times, find a spot, pull out when you see the hydrant, find a second spot and squeeze in with fewer than three bumper-taps. Then hope nobody tows your car before you get back. Life in the Windy City.

With four minutes to spare, I walked into the lobby. Most of these older buildings were buzzer-entry. If there was a doorman, it was some old black guy who looked more tired than alert. Not this place. This place had a buzzer and, once I was inside, I found myself face to face with an honest to God door guard. Behind a brand-new steel desk sat a huge guy with one of those freaky upside-down pyramid bodies that can only come from the perfect blend of Gold's Gym and genetics. Judging from the haircut and the way he jumped to parade rest when I entered, the goon was probably ex-military.

"How's it going? I'm going up to ten-oh-one." I got about halfway to the elevator when a hand the size of a catcher's mitt damn near crushed my shoulder.

"Name?"

"Lupul. For Mister Cromwell." The former jarhead—he couldn't have been anything else—looked from his clipboard to my face and back again. I was about to pull out my wallet for my ID when I remembered something. I was packing.

"Hold it. Spread your arms, please." The asshole was about to frisk me, and he wouldn't like what he found.

"I have a concealed carry permit." Rather than muscle me, he just held out his enormous hand, smugly expecting me to comply. Which I did. I reached down to my belt and pulled out my cheap Ruger LC. He looked at it and snorted.

Great, a gun snob. "State of Illinois says I can carry that."

"Illinois ends at that doorstep. Sir. If you want to go upstairs, I'll hold on to it. If not, have a nice day."

I flashed through several mental scenarios, none of which ended with me getting to the elevator, and at least three involved having to pull the gun out of my butt before it was over.

"We good?"

He nodded and stepped aside. "Take the elevator to the tenth floor. Sir."

"Yeah, I know how elevators work." He parried my rapier wit with a derisive sniff.

"You can pick it up on your way out. Sir." He said "sir," like it made his gums bleed.

The elevator was small but better decorated than most apartments I'd seen. Fake mother-of-pearl buttons showed each floor, and the brass panel gleamed. The cage smelled overwhelmingly of metal polish and trust funds. The ride up was so quiet I barely realized I was moving before it glided to a stop on the tenth floor.

The panels slid open to reveal a small waiting area and a single door. The penthouse took up the whole floor, and the number on the door gleamed like real gold. It took me a second to find the buzzer, hidden the same color as the molding around the door. They probably knew I was there, though, judging from the small but intimidating camera mounted on the ceiling.

Soon as my finger touched the button, the door opened. "Mister Lupul?"

The woman was a nurse, judging by the old-school white uniform, complete with white seamed stockings and squeaky white shoes. She was a well-preserved fifty I'd guess, although that coal-black bun at the back of her head pulled half her face with it so it was hard to say for sure. Her lipstick was Fifty-Seven Corvette red. It looked like it had been permanently applied and never messed up by smiling. Her lips perfectly complemented those stone-cold green eyes.

Granite-faced, she inspected me from my two-year-old battered construction boots to my jeans and even scoped out the conspicuously empty holster inside my red plaid lumberjack jacket. It was my tough-guy look, worn for my meeting with O'Rourke. She made it abundantly clear I was under-dressed for the occasion.

"Uh, yeah. Mister Cromwell's expecting me."

"Follow me." It wasn't a request, so I obeyed. The door closed automatically behind me and slammed shut. Maybe it just sounded that loud in my head.

I'd heard of penthouses but had never been in one, so I had nothing to compare this place to except the movies. It was all dark wood and leather, with table lamps everywhere. Definitely a man's apartment; no homey, feminine touches anywhere. Across the east wall, I expected to see a million-dollar—maybe five million dollar — view of Lake Michigan. Instead, there were only closed blinds. If I lived here, I wouldn't even invest in curtains, and this guy didn't seem to care enough to look out.

The entryway and living room formed the middle of a giant H. To the left were the kitchen and some other rooms. She led me to the right. "Mister Cromwell's quarters are in here." She said the name like it was supposed to mean something to me.

I tried to notice everything I could without gaping like a kid at the opulence of the apartment. Expensive furniture, three abstract paintings, some odd-looking sculptures that looked ancient, were obviously pricey, and more than a little creepy. There were no family photos of any kind, though.

At the end of the hallway, she rapped on a solid-core door.

From the other side, I heard that same *thump-hiss-thump* I'd heard on the phone. A nasal voice said, "Come in, Miss Ball," between hacking coughs.

She opened the door and waved me in, then closed it without joining us. That clicking sound was getting on my nerves. A lot of doors in this place closed without giving me a choice in the matter, and I didn't much care for it.

I sniffed the air, picking up the aromas of Lemon Pledge and ammonia as my eyes darted around the room. It looked like the old-fashioned office of any obscenely rich CEO or Bond villain, except for the hospital bed in the corner farthest from the window.

In that bed was an oldish man in a very expensive looking, jet-black housecoat. He was somewhere between sixty and a hundred and six. When people are sick, it's hard to tell. He was short—maybe five-five and about a hundred and thirty pounds, with half a dozen hairs clinging to life on top of a liver-spotted scalp. His eyes were clear, though, and focused right on me.

"Mister McPherson, come in. I'm Malcolm Cromwell."

I'd stuck my hand out to shake his like a professional, but withdrew it slowly and stuck it in my pocket. Nobody had called me that other name in a long time. "It's Lupul."

He swatted my objections away. "Legally, it's still McPherson, isn't it? You haven't changed it officially. In fact, you only started using Lupul after your parents died."

I knew my mouth was open, but nothing came out. The only sound in the room was the pumping of the machine beside him. White plastic tubes led from whatever that was under the sleeve of his robe. I wondered what that was about.

"Do you really want to do this, or will you just accept that I know everything I need to know to hire you?" I clenched my jaw and flexed my hands into fists and back. I already hated this old fart and was close to losing whatever cool I had left.

Cromwell rolled his eyes at my lack of decorum. "Fine. You don't know me, so cry uncle when I've proven that I know you. Born Ioani Lupul in Romania in nineteen eighty-seven. Adopted in ninety-two by Jim and Eileen McPherson, who died two years ago in a car wreck on the Kennedy. You went back to using Lupul right about that time. Interesting."

"Is it?"

The old man shrugged. "Not as interesting as the orphanage in Cluj, I grant you. They kept you with the AIDs cases, but you showed no sign of HIV or any virus. Why do you think that was?"

I remember nothing before coming to Chicago, but Shaggy sometimes has flashes of cribs and children with bony ribs and huge eyes staring between the slats of cheap bed like in those photos that made all the papers. Romanian orphans were hot in the early nineties, like Beany Babies, only white and with very little paperwork. Unfortunately for the McPhersons, there was a stringent no-return policy. I'm sure they checked.

Cromwell rattled on. "Graduated Downers Grove North, nothing very interesting there aside from some behavioral issues... You worked for our mutual friend for a few years, at least you had the good sense to avoid any real unpleasantness. No criminal record, which is a little surprising." *Comes as a surprise to a lot of people, you dick.* "You then took off to work construction for an outfit building franchise restaurants around the country until your parents' accident."

"Waffle Shacks. Just so your files are complete. Why am I here?"

He scowled like I'd ruined his little game, but I didn't much care.

"Because I admire what you did for my associate."

"Associate? O'Rourke works for himself. Always has." Everyone knew that the Irishman was unaffiliated, a fact that drove the various mobs crazy. Even the Italians knew to leave him and his book alone. Meaghan's kidnapping was an attempt to get him to play ball with the new Russian *blatnoia* gangs. How'd that go for them?

Yet he'd knuckled under to this Cromwell dude.

"He did. I've recently, uh, invested in his business. I'd like to be J Lupul and Associates' first official client."

"I have-"

"I'm going to put you on retainer. How does a hundred thousand dollars for the first year sound?"

The room spun, and I had to pee. "A hundred grand? To do what?"

He gave me a superior smirk. "The same thing you did for O'Rourke. Location and recovery work, if you have to call it something to keep the IRS happy. Going legit is a great idea, if a tad limiting for someone with your talents. I admire your ambition."

"I don't know what you think I am..." Cromwell's smug grin told me he had a fair idea.

"This is all perfectly legitimate. I pay you a monthly stipend to keep you available when I need you. Billable hours and expenses above our agreement are extra. At a fair price, of course. You can still have your other clients, but I get first rights to your time. If I have no work for you that month, the money's still yours. It's how lawyers and accountants work. Ask Bill Mostoy."

I hated hearing my friend's name come out of that mouth. "What exactly do you do?"

He groaned and sat up. His bare feet, uncut toenails like old ivory, dangled over the side of the bed. "I dabble in a lot of things. Real estate mostly these days. It pays the bills." It must have been a rich guy joke because he barked out a laugh that turned into a coughing jag.

"Look, I'm a sick old man. This dialysis, if it keeps me alive, restricts my freedom and keeps me stuck here. A man's got to do something to keep himself entertained. Over the last few years, I've developed a passion for unusual artifacts. Sometimes getting and keeping them requires unusual methods. You have a rare talent, and I want to pay you to use it. That's all you need to know."

"Like hell it is. I'm not a thief." *I've been a bagman, a leg-breaker, a lousy framing guy, and a werewolf, but I have my standards.* "I won't go around stealing for you."

The look on his face said he didn't appreciate my suddenly developing backbone. "Don't get your nose out of joint. I'm not asking you to steal, exactly. But some of my things are precious, and I need to keep them safe. That's what you do now, right? Personal and property location and recovery?" Those were the exact words from my DBA application. Not at all creepy. "... Well, I have things I need to be located and recovered."

That sounded a little less like it would land me in prison. "What sort of things?"

He studied me for a second too long before pointing a bony finger at the bookshelf behind his desk. "What do you think is the most valuable thing on that shelf?"

I had no fricking idea. Some of those old leather-bound books alone were worth more than my car. On each shelf was some kind of object. There was an antique bowl with some crude etching on it, a figure of a cat with slits for eyes made from a kind of green rock, and something that looked a little like a Buddha, only creepy as hell and so worn down the features were barely recognizable.

"The cat?" I guessed. Maybe that was jade.

"A fair guess. Each of those three items is practically priceless, but if I had to put a price on them, I'd say the bowl is the most valuable. It's an actual scrying bowl." He waited for me to pretend I knew what that was. I didn't.

This guy loved to lecture. "Ancient cultures used them to read the future or find lost objects. This one works better than any I've ever seen."

I breathed a sigh of relief. Bill's grandmother had at least three "real" crystal balls she used back in the day to scam people when she told their fortunes. Cromwell was just as superstitious and gullible as the rest of us—just a desperate old man. I could just take his money and relax.

"It doesn't look like much."

"Not if you don't know what you're looking for. See, I like things that have a spiritual or occult significance, Johnny. The more unusual, or the more authentic, the more I need to add it to my collection. There are a few of us out there... rich hobbyists, a few true believers. And not everyone wants me to have these items. Or keep them. It's silly, I grant you, but the older you get the more you want assurance that there's more to life than just... this." He gestured around the room.

I'd gladly settle for a tenth of what he dismissed as "this." But everyone had their thing.

He held up a finger to stop me from saying anything else. "I promised you more money for coming out here today. It's in the top drawer over there, if you would. Consider it a down payment."

In two strides I stood behind his football-field-sized desk. Sliding open the top drawer, I saw two bundles like the ones O'Rourke had given me. Cromwell probably had this much between the cushions of his couch, but ten grand was a lot of money, to a guy like me at least. A hundred Gs was even more. Taking the cash would obligate me, but I picked it up and slipped the bundles inside my jacket.

Right on cue, Nurse Ball came in unannounced. I'll see you out, Mister Lupul." She held the door and gave me a look that said if she had to count to ten, I'd be in trouble.

"Keep the phone, Johnny. Consider it a hotline. I'll be in touch with your business manager about the legalities. We'll want to make sure everything is above board. Thank you for your time."

He held his shaking hand out again and this time I took it, amazed at how someone dressed so warmly could have such a cold grip.

"I look forward to working with you," he said.

That made one of us.

CHAPTER 6

2 days past full- waning gibbous moon.

"Who the holy hell is Malcolm Cromwell?" I opened one eye to find Bill standing beside my bed brandishing a piece of paper at me.

The downside of having a door between our apartments is that it opens both ways. My buddy tended not to pay attention to niceties like personal space, especially when he got worked up. He was currently amped up to about an eight and a half—ten being either an orgasm or cardiac infarction.

My high-cycle hangover was in full bloom and I was in no mood for histrionics. I pulled myself to a sitting position and glared at him. "He's a guy I met yesterday. How do you know about him?"

"Because he sent a contact message to your website." By the way I snarled at him, it was clear I didn't understand what that meant or why it was sending him into orbit. "Ugh. The site that became live exactly ten minutes ago? The one that isn't even showing up on Google yet? And he addressed it to me. By name. Do you know this guy?" His voice got higher and bitchier with each sentence.

"Yeah. Chill. I know him. Jesus, I was gonna tell you all about it when I woke up." After my meeting with Mister Big Bucks, I'd come home to take a post-full-moon power nap. Apparently my siesta had lasted thirteen hours.

"Where'd he come from?"

Good question. But let's not freak my manager out on the first day. "He was a referral from O'Rourke."

"He says he wants to pay you a hundred grand. Any idea why?"

Apparently, nap time was over, so I sat up. "He's a fan of my work."

Bill was unconvinced. "Is it legal?"

"Far as I know. He called it a restrainer. Said you'd know what that was."

"Retainer, you moron." Bill's face gradually returned to its usual pasty color as he paced back and forth, the rubber tip of his crutch thumping on the fake hardwood floor. "Or course I know what a retainer is. When were you going to tell me?"

"When I was awake. Jeez. Is your gramma upstairs?" Bill shook his head.

The deer meat had long since worn off. I needed pancakes and eggs, stat, and wasn't about to subject myself to my own cooking in this condition. "I'll tell you about it at the Saddle."

Twenty minutes later, two cups of black coffee down, and my Lumberjack Special ordered, the tank held sufficient fuel to tell Bill about my meeting with Cromwell. He listened, stone-faced, as I laid it all out: the creepy penthouse, the money, the way he scared the hell out of O'Rourke and did the same to me.

"But you got the money, right?" The accountant gene was dominant in his DNA. "Where is it?"

I flinched at the coming response. "The car. In the trunk, under the spare tire. I know, I know..."

He waved me off. "That piece of crap is the best anti-theft device there is. Nobody'd think to look in it for anything valuable. Give it to me when we get home. So, are you going to take the money?"

It was a rhetorical question. I'd probably regret it, but I was sure as hell going to take it. I leaned back and winked at the tired-looking Polish waitress as she dropped my giant breakfast of eggs, ham on the bone and pancakes in front of me with a smile and a side of ancient cleavage. She threw two pieces of toast and a cup of Earl Grey at Bill.

My eyes drifted over her to the TV above the counter. The local news was on, and the anchorwoman I'd lusted over since I was a kid was blathering on about something. Over her right shoulder was a blue and red square with "*Russian Gang Attack*," written across it in fake Cyrillic letters.

"I can do the invoices and submit them..." I shushed Bill and even with my Shaggy-assisted ears strained to hear the news above the clank of dishes.

"One of the two suspected Russian kidnappers arrested two days ago has died..."

So, Kozlov finally gave up the ghost. I tried to still my conscience by feeding it half a flapjack and wished whatever soul the asshole had a safe trip. I nearly choked it back up when she continued.

"Nicolai Danilov died of wounds sustained in a gangland attack. His associate, Maxim Kozlov, has escaped police custody. He is severely wounded but authorities consider him dangerous and authorities ask the public not to..."

Crap.

"Hey, are you even listening to me?" Bill's lecture on amortization and quarterly payments was falling on deaf ears, and he hated being ignored.

"Yeah, I'm fine. Just a headache. That time of the month." He never got tired of that joke. He half-snorted, then carried on telling me about my business. I pushed the plate away, letting him drone on for another twenty minutes. I understood most of it. So, progress.

I tried to forget about Kozlov and wrap my head around the whole retainer thing. "He pays me like, eighty-three hundred a month, and I get to keep it even if I don't do any work for him?"

"Yup, that's the beauty of it." Bill examined me over the rim of his teacup. "Is he the type who'd pay for something and not use it?"

I didn't even bother to answer. Bill nodded and continued the lecture. "Then we figure out a billable rate, and if it goes past what he pays for we charge him the balance."

"You mean I could make even more?" A guy could get used to this retainer stuff.

Say this for Bill, he's good with money. Most people would call that cheap, but he could decode finance better than anyone I knew—admittedly a small sample size. That's how he landed the work-from-home gig for a big accounting firm. It's also how he'd made his grandmother pretty well off, despite the fact she dressed like a bag lady. To his horror, she still read fortunes when her old clients asked for them. The politically correct word was Roma, but he still felt the sting of being called a Gypsy, and Gramma's business didn't help his self-image any.

"Tell me exactly what he said, again. Anything you think I should know."

I obliged. As we strolled around the block letting the weak October sun do its work, I explained about the condo, the weird nurse lady and what little I could suss out about Malcolm Cromwell. Bill limped along beside me and took it all in. Google would get one hell of a workout this afternoon.

The walk was good for him, but I hated to see him hurting. A block was about as far as Bill's leg could comfortably go, so we swung north on Pulaski and headed for home.

The squared-off end of my car peeked past the side of the building. Someone in a red sweatshirt was bent low peering in the passenger window, then stood up and backed out of view.

I picked up speed, trying to keep whoever it was in sight. The sun was killing me, and I held a hand up to shade my eyes.

"Hey," Bill whined.

I yelled over my shoulder. "Sorry. I think someone was poking around the Charger."

"Bank. Today. Get it? The rest you can stash in Gramma's storage locker." I slowed so he could catch up. "Maybe it was just Robin from upstairs."

"Yeah, maybe." It wasn't.

Whoever it was, they'd gone by the time we reached the driveway. For a second, I panicked and popped the trunk. Bill damn near had a stroke when he saw me rifle through the bag. "Jesus, Mary and Joseph, that's a lot of money."

He reached a trembling hand to caress the bag. Like a jerk, I pulled it away from him, laughed, then let him touch the cheap pleather. "This is doughnut money for the guys you work for, isn't it?"

He never took his eyes off the bag, like it hypnotized him. "Yeah, but those are just numbers on a screen. This is like... cash. I've never seen twenty-five thousand dollars up close like this."

"Thirty-five. Remember Cromwell's ten? Kinda cool, isn't it? How about the three of us go out for dinner tonight? I'm buying."

"Damn right you are. And someplace with forks and knives, you heathen. If you're going to make big boy money, you'd better get used to living like a civilized person. I'll make reservations somewhere nice." Nice meant somewhere downtown with a chef he'd seen on TV. It would be expensive as hell.

Feeling like a big shot, I grabbed a stack and held it out to him. "An advance on your commission." He grabbed it a little quicker than he wanted to, but I grinned at my friend's excitement. It felt great, and I forgot all about my headache, the bright afternoon sun, and the possible car thief.

It was the perfect moment. Except that Max Kozlov was out there somewhere.

CHAPTER 7

4 days past full- waning gibbous moon.

"Not a very promising start to our business relationship, is it Johnny?" Cromwell sat behind that aircraft carrier of a desk, fingers pushing against each other like he was about to ask me where the steeple and the people were. My one-and-only client was pissed at me for not being there sooner, even though it hadn't been three full days since our last meeting.

Four days on from the peak, I was in a decent frame of mind to take the tongue-lashing. I wasn't so jumpy and my senses had quit overreacting to everything I smelled, saw, or heard. Finding my happy place, I let him chew me out.

First, he'd texted me on the burner phone, but I hadn't seen it. In my defense, I was busy recovering from my lunar activities. Plus, I left it under a pile of clothes and forgot all about it. Then came the snarky email through the website. So now I had both my client and Bill riding me. I was summoned to his office. Not asked, not requested, not even told. In my whole life, I don't think I'd ever used the word summons in a non-courtroom way, but that's what this was.

Every feeling of being back in the principal's office came rushing back. "No sir, it's not. I'm sorry," I said, hoping to strike the right balance of apologetic and not defensive. A day or so ago this wouldn't have gone so well but I was on the mellow down-hill side of my cycle.

Cromwell said nothing for the longest time, letting me marinate in my own juices. Settling in, I blinked back at him. I'd been playing the stand-off game since middle school. This was nothing new. Eventually, he gave a heavy sigh and pulled open the drawer to his left. Removing a beat-up manila envelope, Cromwell slid it across the glossy desk surface.

"I need you to track something down for me. If you're not too busy."

"I think I can fit you in. What is it?" Inside were half a dozen paper-clipped sheets, which I thumbed through like I knew what I was looking at.

"This was supposed to arrive two days ago. The delivery company's records say the delivery came at two-fifteen. That's not the case. It never got here."

The top sheet was a copy of a copy of a photograph. The item it showed was round and metal with markings all around the outside. An image of what looked like a guy in a skirt with a dog's head was in the center, along with some symbols I couldn't read.

"That's Anubis. The Egyptian god of embalming and the dead. The deity who guided souls to the Field of Reeds. He has the body of a man and the head of a jackal. Fascinating, isn't it?"

I fought back a shiver at seeing something half man and half something so wolf-like. *Was Cromwell trying to tell me something?* Whatever the creepy thing was, it looked maybe five or six inches across. The other sheets were just shipping forms and custom sheets. The final page had three names and addresses on it.

It looked like a simple retrieval job. That made me feel better. "Okay, but what is it?"

The old man leaned forward and pinned me to the chair with those watery eyes. "What it *is*, is mine and I want it back." He made it clear this was none of my business, except it kind of was since it would be hard to find if I didn't know what I was looking for. Once he'd established he was the boss, Cromwell thought better of being such a dick and sat back in his chair.

"The Anubis Disk is Egyptian. I purchased it from a dealer in Libya last month. A fanatic Egyptian cult used it in a religious ritual."

"Why's it so valuable? Is that gold or something?"

He sniffed like he smelled something rancid. "No, it's bronze and not particularly good quality. As jewelry, it's almost worthless. It's not even Ancient Egyptian—it's a nineteenth-century fake made for the fanatics who fought Napoleon at the Nile. A common thief wouldn't even know what to do with this. Somebody was looking for this exact piece."

"Do you know who took it?"

"The last page." I pulled out the yellow sheet of paper as he continued. "There are only three people in Chicago who know what this is or its real purpose. Besides me."

The names were all foreign. One looked Spanish. The second name was "Nasrallah," so some kind of Arab, possibly Egyptian. The third looked Russian. None of the names meant anything to me. The addresses were all on the North Shore and out of my price range.

It's always a safe bet the client knows more than they're telling. "Who's your bet?"

Cromwell shook his head and said something I'll bet rarely crossed his lips. "I don't know. Nobody else was bidding, and I thought I'd kept it a secret. Nobody was ever supposed to know it was en route. I paid... No. I pay—for discretion."

Wow, that was subtle. "What makes you think it's one of these three?"

"Sanchez specializes in Meso-American art, but lately he's been bidding heavily on Egypt as well. Something about all the world's pyramids being linked or some such thing. He's one of those true believers—alien architects and all that bullshit," That was a little harsh coming from someone who believed in bowls that could tell the future, but I kept my trap shut. "... Nasrallah is Egyptian, so he'll buy anything from the region. Spends half his time suing museums to reclaim plundered loot when he's not gaining it in other ways. Vladimir Spitzov is a Russian oligarch. One of those nouveau riche types, you know, who'll buy anything someone else wants just to drive up the price. His methods tend to be more unorthodox than the others."

Unorthodox, says the guy who hires a werewolf.

"I'm guessing there's no police or insurance report?" I knew there wouldn't be, but it sounded like the kind of professional question a guy should ask.

"No, nor should there be. We especially don't want the police involved."

No, "we" sure didn't. I had him walk me through the shipping arrangements and the timeline, all the way from Libya to when it was supposed to arrive. Near as I could make out, it disappeared sometime between leaving the shipping company's loading dock and Cromwell's apartment. That should make it easier, even if it meant talking to the walking Humvee at the front desk. "Is there anything else I need to know?"

"Such as?"

"Is this thing dangerous at all?" The follicles on my neck wouldn't lay down until I had an answer.

"No. At least not in its present state. There's a whole mumbo jumbo religious ritual that has to go with it, assuming it is the real thing... I don't suppose you speak ancient Egyptian?"

"Nope."

"Then it's just an interesting bronze disk. Find it, give it to me, and you'll complete this month's contract. Do whatever you need to do and let me know when you've located it and I'll arrange a pickup. Yes?"

A matronly voice came from over my shoulder and startled the hell out of me. "Shall I show Mister Lupul out now?" There stood Nurse Ball in her spotless starched uniform and stone-faced glory. Even with those ugly nursing shoes, she shouldn't be able to sneak up on me that way. A slight curl of her lip told me she was well aware of my discomfort and rather dug it.

"Yes, I think we're done here. Aren't we Johnny?" Knowing a dismissal when I heard one, I rose to my feet and shoved the papers back into the envelope. The woman unnerved me, and I fumbled a bit before putting them away.

"This way." Miss Ball said it like I'd never find the door without her. The hand she put on my arm was cold, even through my clothes. I looked back to see her shut the door to the old man's study and glimpsed—*sweet Jesus, is that a garter?*—holding up her white stockings. Naturally, she turned around in time to catch me creeping on her but said nothing and brushed past me towards the door.

I had to ask. "Why do you wear that uniform?"

"What do you mean? I'm a nurse. This is a standard nurse's uniform."

"Yeah, if it's nineteen sixty-two. Every nurse I know just wears scrubs. You know, with Care Bears and stuff on them."

The nurse sniffed like I'd just let a fart rip. "Do I strike you as the Care Bear type?" She gave me a moment to wallow in my stupidity, then added, "Mister Cromwell likes a more traditional look in his home. You get used to it. A lot of women need to wear a lot worse in this world. And you may have noticed that I do... add a personal touch to it."

I honest to God blushed. This woman was twenty years older than me, and she'd caught me scoping out her legs. It was definitely time to reestablish some professional credibility. "How well do you know the guy at the door downstairs?"

"Exactly what do you mean by how well?" I realized how it sounded and the blush burned my cheeks even hotter and the words disassembled in my mouth. I managed to put them back into something sounding like English. "Christ, no. I... I mean, how long as he worked here? Do you trust him?"

"Justin? He's been here two years. And he's been completely vetted."

"So there's no way he would have... intercepted Mister Cromwell's package?"

Those painted lips formed something close to a smile. "That boy follows orders well, and he looks imposing, I suppose, but he's the sort that follows orders to the letter. Not much on initiative, though. No, if he says it didn't arrive, I'm sure it didn't."

That made sense, although it would have made my life a lot easier, and a lot more satisfying, if the big door guy had done it. I'd have to ask him some questions and he wouldn't like it much. He knew why I was there, though. Maybe he wouldn't take it personally.

Nurse Ball reached past me to open the door, leaning into me as she did so. Whatever encased her breasts had no give to it. I got a whiff of hand sanitizer, hair spray, and cinnamon gum as she said, "Anything else I can do for you, Mister Lupul?"

"No ma'am, I'm good."

Her eyes were colder than Clark Street in January. "Good luck. I'm sure we'll see you soon." The door closed in my face before the sentence was complete.

I rode the elevator down, trying to put something like a plan in place. First, I'd have to talk to Justin the Hulk and get whatever information I could. Then there was the small matter of which of the three suspects actually stole the—whatever it was. I'd probably need to talk to the delivery guy. Oh, and I'd have to get the damned thing back, preferably without committing a felony.

The door dinged, and before I even stepped off, the door gorilla had my Ruger extended, butt first. He didn't even glance at me, just grunted what sounded like "*hafagudayzir.*" I slipped it into my belt.

"Justin, right?" He looked up, amazed that I'd spoken to him at all, let alone used his name.

"That's right."

"I'm Johnny."

"Yeah, I know. It's on the sheet." That officially doubled the number of words we'd spoken to each other. I watched him try to figure out my game. He hadn't tried to snap me in half yet, so we were off to a good start.

"Look, I'm working for Mister Cromwell. You know, that, right? I'm trying to track down that package that went missing the other day."

His spine stiffened, and his eyes turned cold. "I can't talk about the residents. With anyone."

"I get that. You're a pro. Not like most of the other mooks who sit in lobbies. You guard..." I reached for the military-sounding word. "...high-value assets."

It must have been the right buzzword because his muscles relaxed just a tad. He spun his chair towards me.

"I need to ask you a few questions so I can do my job. I won't ask about any other residents or anything that isn't relevant. Fair enough? Just one professional to another."

Justin laced his fingers together and placed them in his lap. "Only about Mister Cromwell. Shoot."

"This delivery company, North Coast Couriers? They deliver here often?"

He took one of his kielbasa-sized fingers and stabbed at the logbook on his desk. "Nearly every day. They do high-dollar deliveries when the residents don't trust FedEx or UPS. Contracts, cashier checks, that kind of thing."

I stole a peek over his shoulder and noticed the company name and three different signatures. "Do they use different drivers all the time?"

"No. It's always Darrell. The same guy as long as I've been here."

"But this week you've had three different people."

He knitted his eyebrows and read over the ledger. "Tuesday, we got nothing at all. Looks like Wednesday and Thursday were different drivers. That's weird."

Yeah, it was. Tuesday Darrell should have brought Mister Cromwell's thingamajig and never showed. Then Wednesday and Thursday, no Darrell. That didn't sound right. I would have to talk to the man.

"I appreciate your help. How long were you in the service?" As long as we were bonding, I figured I'd invest in the relationship a bit.

"Twelve years."

"Where'd you serve?" I probably wouldn't recognize it, but it always worked in bars to get guys on your good side.

"Three tours. Two in Afghanistan."

"Jeez, that must have been some shit. And the other?" My question earned me an icy stare. I'd seen that look before. It came just before they said if they told me they'd have to kill me. "Oookay then. Well, thanks for your service. You have a good day."

"You too. Sir." I offered a mock salute and was halfway to the door when something occurred to me.

"You've been here what, two years? Has Mister Cromwell ever had anything go missing before? Anything weird?"

Justin's eye twitched twice before he got it under control again. "Not on my watch."

"Yeah, I mean you're a pro. Although just between us, he's kind of an odd duck, isn't he?"

The guy's face turned to granite, and he looked at me like I'd sprouted a second head.

"Right. Well, you've seen worse than this place can throw at you. Have a good one."

I had my hand on the knob when I heard him say, "You too. Now that nurse chick. Miss Ball? She scares the crap out of me."

So it wasn't just me.

CHAPTER 8

7 days past full- waning gibbous moon.

When a guy really knows how to handle a gun, he doesn't make a big show out of having one. As Darrell stepped out of the delivery van he planted both feet, put his hand to his hip, and looked around with his jaw stuck out like "what are you going to do about this?" I breathed a sigh of relief. He was an amateur.

Like on the half dozen other stops, he pulled an envelope from the seat beside him and took it inside the building. A minute later he came out. Another pose by the door, then back to the van.

From my parking spot on the next block, I could see he was trying too hard to look tough. Darrell wasn't looking for trouble—he was just a guy who'd been jumped and was still salty about it.

I followed him for four more deliveries. Each time the same routine: park and put the flashers on, get out, show the world he was an armed badass, then deliver his package. Marching in, his eyes darted everywhere, riding the edge between alertness and paranoia. On the way back to his van he whistled and walked with a looser stride, relieved to be one more burden lighter.

He seemed like a good guy. I hated that I was about to ruin his first day back.

On the sixth or seventh stop, he hopped out, struck his pose, then marched across the street. Darrell held the door for a lady with two shopping bags before disappearing into a three-story office building. The longer he went without a problem, the less worried he looked. Sucked for him. He must have dropped the package off at the front desk because I had just enough time to park my butt against the front fender, fold my arms across my chest and try to look casual before he came out.

The look on his face when he saw me was comical. He stopped in his tracks, rolled his eyes to the sky. Then his lips formed what looked distinctly like, "fuck me," before straightening himself and lowering a shaky hand towards the pistol on his hip. He took a deep breath, gave his neck a crack and stepped towards me. Darrell halted in the middle of the street.

Before he could go full Security Guy on me, I held my palms up in what I hope he'd recognize as a gesture of peace. "Hey, Darrell."

"Can I help you?" A moving van bore down on him and he had to decide if he would get closer or not. Deciding I was less dangerous than the truck, Darrell stepped to the back of his van, keeping me in view with his hand on his belt.

"Names Johnny Lupul. Can I talk to you about the other day?"

"You a cop?"

"Seriously dude? I look like a cop?"

He ignored the question. "What's it to you?"

He hadn't freaked out and shot me yet, so this was going pretty well. "Can I put my hands down?" I knew if I did, my jacket would open and he'd see my gun. This was no time to make him nervous. "I have a permit for this... and I won't show you mine if you don't show me yours, okay? I just want to ask you a couple of questions about what happened. I work for Malcolm Cromwell, the guy that got ripped off."

He looked away for a second and sucked his teeth. "Can't talk about that. Company policy."

I was never a "company policy," kind of guy, but I had a grudging respect for those who were. The ability to take the boss's crap and keep coming back day after day for a paycheck was not a skill I possessed. Darrell looked like the sort of guy who not only took it but did so in exchange for maybe making Supervisor one day. God love him.

"Yeah, fricking bosses and their rules, right? I don't want to get you in trouble, man. Just trying to help Mister Cromwell get his package back. Just doing my job, ya know?"

"I hear you, but I still can't talk about it. They wouldn't let me call the cops, said they needed to maintain client confidentiality. Like they're lawyers or something."

Poor guy was getting it from all sides. He didn't need me piling on. "How much of a sling is your ass in?"

"Whaddya mean?" He leaned against the side of the van now, hands across his chest. Gotta love de-escalation.

"You got ripped off and lived to tell about it. They're probably pissed you didn't go down in a blaze of glory. Am I right?"

"Hey, I'm no coward, but I'm not taking a bullet for twenty bucks an hour." Darrell was a good guy but not a fanatic. Perfect.

"No shit, twenty an hour? With benefits?"

He grinned. "Full medical."

"They hiring?" Two weeks ago, this would have seemed like great money.

Traffic was picking up, and the temperature was dropping. Over Darrell's shoulder, I saw a little family-run doughnut shop. "Listen, can I buy you a cup of coffee and ask you some questions? Sooner I get this done, sooner you can get on your way and I can stop bugging you."

"No man, the company…"

"… is probably giving you a metric crap-ton of grief because of my boss. Old man Cromwell is threatening to sue their asses off if he doesn't get his, whatever the hell it is, back. Help me recover it, they don't get sued, and they're off your back"

He rubbed his arms for heat but decided coffee was better. "Ten minutes, that's it. If I'm late, it's your ass."

"Great. I'm buying."

"Damn right. Ten minutes."

A minute later we sat with styrofoam cups in hand, watching the late afternoon traffic go by. For someone who didn't want to talk about it, once Darrell got started there was no shutting him up. I tried writing stuff down in my notebook, but he was going way too fast for my clumsy fingers, so I just listened.

"So, I'm in front of your—Cromwell's building, right? I park and before I'm even out of the van, two guys pull the door open and have guns in my face. I said 'hey, take what you want', but the one guy…"

"What'd they look like?"

"Oh, right. One was white, about your size. The other guy was black. Like, Africa black. Tall, too. NBA tall. And skinny as hell. Big scar down each cheek. I think he was the boss."

"Why's that?"

"Cause the white guy did all the talking but kept looking to the big guy for everything. Like, he'd say 'don't move' and then look to see if it was okay. Almost like he was a trainee or something. You ever get a waiter who's just started, and they do all the work, and the other guy just stands there and watches? Like that. Weird"

Darrell was talking faster and faster, but I still had a lot to learn and the clock was ticking. "They knew what they were looking for, huh?"

He nodded. "Asked for the package for Cromwell."

"What was it?"

"Hell, I don't know. It was a box. About yay big..." he held his hands about a foot apart, "... by yay big. Wait a minute, you don't know what it is either?"

I shook my head. "No goddamn idea. Company policy, you know."

He toasted me with his coffee cup. "Heard that. Anyway, I give the white dude the box and the tall, scary guy tells me to just make my other deliveries and forget this ever happened. But in this deep voice, with an accent."

"What kind of accent?"

"Sounded Nigerian maybe, or some kind of African. Wasn't American, that's for sure. You really don't know what's in it? How the hell are you supposed to find something when you don't know what it is?"

"Welcome to my life."

"Well, be careful. It had a hazmat logo on it. Anything else?"

A hazmat logo. That would've been good to know. "You sure they're not hiring?"

The driver gave me a grin. "Good luck, man, hope you find them. Take care of yourself. I gotta go Getting robbed is one thing, but they have zero tolerance for being late."

"You too. And thanks, I owe you one." He never looked back, just offered a dismissive wave. A blast of bitterly cold October wind blew into the little shop as he exited.

I studied the chicken scratch I'd put in my notebook. Two guys who knew what they were looking for, one white and probably American, one black and definitely not. Maybe African, but he was the boss. The package was about a foot across and—*oh yeah, thanks for telling me Cromwell*—probably dangerous.

I pulled the papers Cromwell gave me out of my inside pocket. Sanchez... Nasrallah... Spitzov... Then a crazy idea occurred to me. I might not know what I was looking for exactly, but I had a fairly good idea of where to start. If it was one of these three names, I knew which one to check out first.

CHAPTER 9

Nine days past full- waning gibbous moon.

Bill was all green and black and creepy through the night vision binoculars. He looked eerier when he scrunched his nose up in complete distaste at my childishness and put his hands on his hips like an old lady.

"Are you done screwing around?"

I wasn't but knew better than to get him all pissy with me. I placed them back on the table and blinked at the glaring light in the kitchen. "These are great, how d'you get them so fast?"

"I paid for the overnight shipping like a real person. You have the money now; you don't have to live like such a... a peasant."

Disposable income took some getting used to. Thanks to the fee for rescuing Meaghan there was no more having to find everything in second-hand stores, or running all over town clutching a wrinkled, expiring coupon. Need a piece of surveillance equipment? Click a button and presto—someone making less money than you magically brings it to your front door.

I still didn't have a credit card. I had money, but I lacked, as Gramma liked to say, "the brains God gave a goat." Whether I could be trusted not to go crazy with the plastic was an open, ongoing discussion.

I was fine with the arrangement. Bill thought like an accountant, not me. I thought like a guy trying to find something that didn't want to be found, and my friend couldn't wrap his brain around that, so we were even. Teamwork makes the dream work.

"Tell me again why it's this Nasrallah guy and not the others?" He took a long slurp of his coffee, placed his cup in the saucer, folded his hands in his lap and gave me his best bean-counter glare. Usually, by the time I could explain something to his satisfaction, I had my facts down.

There was a game we played in high school. We called it "Sherlock." The idea was to explain something to the other person like you were solving a crime. It was lame, but it always amused us, even if he was far better at it than me. It made having to show my work in math class a little less agonizing.

"Elementary, my dear Watson," I said. "The African. He's the key." From the other side of the table, I could tell Bill was skeptical.

I took a breath and held up my index finger. "One. Sanchez is Mexican. They don't hire anyone who can't speak Spanish. It's like their superpower, so we Anglos don't know what they're talking about. You have a white American, probably doesn't *habla espanol*, and some tall dude from Africa—not exactly a hotbed of Latino culture, right?

Bill granted me a slow nod, so I help up the second finger. "Number two, we know it's not Spitzov.

"Because?"

"Because Russians are racist as fuck, and they'd never put a black guy—especially an African—in charge of anything. Not when there's a perfectly good white guy right there. Ergo," I grinned at using the word and dropped my index finger leaving my middle digit pointing up at my friend, "It has to be Nasrallah you suspicious bastard. You know I'm right."

"Humph. Not exactly scientific, but I'll give it to you. How are you going to prove this intriguing little theory?"

I picked up my new toy. "Good old-fashioned surveillance. I need to see if there's a connection between this Egyptian and the two goons who intercepted the package. Since I have no idea where they are, I'll start with what I have. Which is where these come in." I lifted them to my eyes again. An olive-green shadow appeared in the doorway behind Bill.

"You two idiots eat today?"

"Yes, Gramma." We said in unison. The old girl muttered her disbelief.

Bill ignored her. "Where are you going to start?"

"Cromwell gave me Nasrallah's address up in Deerfield. Figured I'd start there."

The old woman harrumphed. "Oooohhh surveillance. Fancy. You wanna watch something, start in the alley back there. Something was banging around the garbage cans last night. Woke me up." She scooped up our empty coffee cups and refilled them, plopping my mug on the table and placing Bill's gently in the little chipped saucer and ruffling his hair.

Like most old people, she was awake half the night anyway, and constantly imagined she was being targeted by prowlers and evildoers. Being a good Romani, she also had a list of supernatural beings that could have been rummaging through the trash. Still, it could be whoever was in that red hoodie prowling around. I told her I'd take a look-see.

My arms hugged myself for warmth as the bitterly cold wind whipped up the alley. Like the back of every building in Chicago, a line of cracked, pot-holed pavement with grass poking through it ran between rows of mismatched fencing and dented trash cans. Half-hearted, I kicked at the muddy ground. Yesterday was garbage pickup day, so at least the can was empty. The city garbage crew had done their usual bang-up job, because they dented the plastic tub on one side like somebody punched it. Most likely the Sanitation guys banged it against the side of the truck to shake everything loose. They'd also managed to put three long scratches in it, the white plastic showing through the blue.

I beat on the inside of the tub a couple of times to bounce it back into something like its normal shape. That's when I saw the two rats. Well, rat and a half. The live one, a robust specimen, sat up on his hind feet next to the battered fence and sniffed at me. The dead rodent, or what was left of it, lay stiff and headless in the muck beside the trash bin. Something—probably a coyote or a feral cat—had taken its head off.

The healthy critter squeaked his annoyance at me.

"Don't look at me, I didn't do it," I told him. The fat rodent gave me a disbelieving sneer and darted off under the fence into the neighbor's yard.

I grimaced, held my breath and picked up the dead rat by the tail and dropped it into the bin. Since I was about a week into the downward cycle, my tolerance for nastiness wasn't what it should have been. I choked back a gag as I threw moldy handfuls of whatever-the-hell-it-was strewn around the alley back into the trash and made sure the lid was tight.

Gramma yelled from the back porch. "D'ya see anything?"

"It's Chicago. Garbage and rats is all. Nothing unusual." I paused, then asked her, "Hey, have you seen anyone hanging around the last day or so? Maybe wearing a red sweatshirt?"

"Don't think so, but I'll keep an eye peeled. Anything I should worry about?"

The garbage and muck were under my fingernails and I'd need to clean up before heading to the Northern Suburbs. "No, it's all good."

"Would you tell me if it wasn't?"

"Probably not." She waved both hands at me in frustration and shuffle-stomped back into the kitchen.

The burner phone in my pocket chirped. I flipped it open and wrinkled my nose. Partly because it was Cromwell, but mostly because my hands smelled like garbage. "Lupul."

The hissing of the dialysis machine was in the background and his voice sounded weak. "What have you learned? Anything?"

Nice greeting, dick. "I'm pretty sure it's Nasrallah."

My client took a deep breath. "I'm not paying you to be 'pretty sure'. When will you know for certain?"

Never show the boss how annoyed you are. You're a big boy now. "Tonight, I hope. I'm heading up to look around and see if I can't connect some dots."

"Which dots are those?"

I looked up at the sky to ask for patience, but nobody answered me. "I have a lead on the guys who stole the box. I just need to connect them to the Egyptian dude. Hey, I thought you said this thing wasn't dangerous? They marked it hazmat."

"I put it in a biohazard case so nobody would mess with it."

That made a strange kind of sense, actually, even if it didn't work. "Okay fine, I'll let you know when I know something definitive."

"I hope it's sooner rather than later." That made two of us. "Oh, and Johnny, it's perfectly harmless, but whatever you do, don't get any blood on it." Then he hung up.

Yeah, that wasn't at all weird.

I stared at the phone in my stinky hand.

CHAPTER 10

10 days past full—last half moon.

Depending on whether you're an optimist or a pessimist, the moon was half-full in the afternoon sky. For me, it was the best time of the month. Shaggy had gone more-or-less dormant, and I felt great—strong but not hyper. My energy would start taking a serious dip in the next day or two as the moon waned to nothing, but for the moment it was all good. I had cash in my pocket, a case to work, and old-school Styx blaring on the Charger's cheap speakers exactly the way God meant it to be played. That renegade, he had it made, and my steering wheel made a satisfying thump as I drummed along.

On top of everything, the traffic gods were throwing me a bone. I made decent time up the Kennedy to the Northern Suburbs; land of insurance companies, medical devices, and big-ass houses. Somewhere between the tollway and the lake, the houses and their lots got bigger and further from the road.

Crap.

I was used to following people in the city where there was a lot of traffic to hide in and front doors were just a sidewalk away from the road. Here in the burbs, I sat in my idling, orange and black muscle car on the shoulder of the road watching white SUVs and forest-green Subarus whiz by. Dozens of them. With all the money in the world, everyone out here chose to drive the exact same cars. The Subaru drivers, in particular, gave me dirty looks as they drove by. Even in the fading October dusk, I stood out like a balloon at a funeral. If the first rule of surveillance is to be inconspicuous, I was failing miserably.

That wasn't my biggest problem.

Wafik Nasrallah's house was a square red-brick and white-trimmed monstrosity standing behind a six-foot-high brick wall, a row of trees, a wrought-iron gate with a security cam, and a hundred yards of manicured lawn dotted with ugly white garden statues and one big oak tree. There was a huge empty lot across the street that provided no cover, despite the dead brown weeds and grasses. From my position, I couldn't see much of anything—which was probably the whole idea. Meanwhile, anyone taking even a half-assed peek out the windows saw me sitting out in the open.

When a cop car did a slow drive-by, I knew I'd have to try something that didn't draw so much attention. Once the cruiser disappeared over the hill, I pulled out my old Thomas Guide and studied my options. There was a forest preserve about a quarter-mile up the road. Parking would be easy, and not much of a hike back. Besides, it would be dark by then. It was the best I could do. No sense whining.

Half an hour later I was wedged securely into a corner between an arborvitae bush and the brick wall at the far edge of the property. In my backpack were the night vision binoculars, a notepad, my phone and, most important for a stakeout, half a bag of generic cheese puffs and a bottle of store-brand diet pop.

The hidey-hole was darker than a landlord's heart. A few amber lights lined the fence, but with the trees, the distance from the road and the cost of utilities, Nasrallah had bothered little with this corner of the property. If there were cameras trained here, they wouldn't see much now that the sun was down.

I strapped the binoculars to my head and switched to night vision to test them. I took a long, sweeping look at the road and nearly blew out my retinas as a car—another white SUV, of course—whizzed past with its high-beams on. I ripped the equipment from my head and blinked until my vision cleared.

There were lights on over the garage door, but the house was dark except for one window. It was on the top floor, dead center between a room with girlie-looking curtains and bigger windows that were probably the master bedroom. Everything else looked dark and dead. Zooming my binoculars to the top floor, the only signs of life were shadows moving in the one room. Someone was home, and it was obviously some kind of office. By the lamplight inside, I made out the tops of bookshelves, but from this angle not much else.

That was about all I could make out from there. Maybe more than one person was in there, but it was hard to tell. The rest of the property was dark and deserted, so it seemed unlikely. The angle would be better further along the wall, but that would involve surrendering my cozy little den.

A good vantage point would be atop the wall. Better yet, a high branch in the big oak tree that stood between me and the house. The problem was there were probably laser triggers all along the perimeter and it would be hard to explain my presence if the alarm got tripped.

Trying to concentrate, I pulled my goggles off and rubbed where the line of sweat formed despite the cold night. It's hard to see red, especially LEDs, through those things. Standing on tiptoe, my eyes followed the top of the fence to the corner. Sure enough, a tiny red dot blinked at me. A twist of the head the other direction and its partner blinked back from the far end. Okay, there was an alarm. But how sensitive was it? I inched closer to the first beacon and blew a cloud of dust and dry leaves into its path, then dropped out of sight and held my breath. There was no motion or noise from the house.

I slowly exhaled. Most alarm systems are set too sensitively at first, but after enough false alarms caused by branches falling across the beam and horny squirrels chasing each other along the property line, people over-correct. I wasn't stupid enough to think it wouldn't pick up a grown man crossing the perimeter, but at least it would be hard to trigger by accident.

The hard part would be getting over the fence and to the base of the tree without announcing my presence. The second bit would be a breeze. The old oak was what we called "a good climbing tree," when I was a kid. Solid branches within arm's reach, a simple leap, and haul my butt off the ground. Easy-peasy. The bitch was, I had to get to it first.

Tossing the goggles into my backpack, I scouted for a way over the wall. I'd need to clear the laser beam by about a foot. Break that red line and all hell would break loose, but if I got over it clean, there'd be no problem. If it was the full moon, Shaggy could have done it from a standing start. Tonight I was left to my own devices.

I stumbled along in the dark along the eastern side of the wall towards the back of the property and away from the main road. Dry, knee-high grasses grew alongside the bricks, but there was nothing to use as a ladder. Maybe I should have had Bill order me an Official Batman Utility Belt instead of the goggles.

About to give up and come back the next night, I almost tripped over some old lumber laying in the grass. A quick inventory showed three or four grey, worm-eaten two-by-sixes and three sheets of cracked, badly damaged plywood that had once served as a "keep out" sign. All of this was useless for climbing, but might make a decent ramp.

Strategic planning was never my strong suit, but all I needed to do was get over the wall with no one seeing me. If the alarm got tripped on the way out, it wouldn't matter much because I'd be on the road and gone by the time the alarm company or the cops showed up.

I leaned the boards against the brick wall and wedged them under the top bricks. Then kicked the bottom into the muddy dirt as firmly as I could and laid the plywood over top. I'd have given my left gonad for a handful of nails; if this didn't hold, I'd do a full Wile E. Coyote face-plant into the wall. But if I got a good enough run at it, I should be able to clear the beam into the yard. The landing wouldn't be pretty, but screw it.

Backing up a few yards and looking at my jerry-built ramp, it seemed doable. Wearing work boots didn't seem like such a great plan now, and I wished I had a little more Shaggy-power at my disposal. Fortunately, I was in decent shape on my own. A few more days and I wouldn't have the energy to make my own bed, let alone a jump like this. But with a little luck... *Yeah, because I have so much of that.*

I made sure everything was secure in my backpack and zipped it closed. Taking about ten steps into the long grass, I looked around to make sure nobody was watching, took a deep breath, and charged as fast as possible at the ramp. Three-quarters of the way up I launched myself, hugging my knees to my chest. The plywood slipped off the boards under my boots, sending me off at an awkward angle, but I cleared the top of the wall by a good foot and a half.

My brain envisioned a graceful gymnast's tuck and roll through space. The reality was an ugly, flailing blob of humanity that plopped onto the soft turf, knees and elbows first. I rolled onto my back, gasping for air. Then came a quick inventory of my body parts. Everything seemed to be intact except for my dignity, which wasn't required for this job.

I rolled onto my knees and lifted my head to study the house. Nothing moved. No lights came on, and there was no sign that my grand entrance drew anyone's attention. Staggering to my feet, I wiped mud from my knees and palms and listened. Whoever was home wasn't paying much attention to the outside world.

First, I ducked low against the bricks, then dashed across the open lawn. It only took a few seconds to reach the base of the big tree, where I reached for the lowest limb and gave a quick test pull. It was sturdy as—well, as oak— and I grinned at how smart I was and how easy this was going to be.

Big mistake.

Whenever I get cocky, it's like flipping God the bird. Bad things were coming, often in bunches, and they didn't take long. In this case, before I could pull myself up onto the first branch, my ears detected my least favorite sound in the world.

A low, bass growl rode the wind from my right along with a scent I knew all too well. I slowly turned, knowing what I'd see, but it was worse than I imagined. A bull mastiff, black and big as a Buick, looked at me and lowered its back legs to charge.

I hate dogs, but not nearly as much as they hate me. All canines, from Chihuahuas to Great Danes, seemed to know instinctively what lay inside me and didn't care for it one little bit. This one gave a bark that was more of a roar and charged.

Fuck me sideways.

Grabbing the branch, I pulled and jumped as high as possible, wrapping my arms around the limb and kicking my boots against the tree trunk. It was barely enough. The monster missed me by inches. Tumbling to the grass, he jumped up to take another run at me. The beast roared and barked and carried on. I scrambled up three more branches and hugged the trunk. The good news was I was out of range of those chompers. The bad news, I was well and truly screwed. There was no way out.

The shadows in the office finally moved. There was definitely someone there. Two someones. A lone male figure stood at the window, holding a hand over his brow to see what all the fuss was while a second, taller, shadow played on the wall behind him. I wouldn't have to wait too long before the ravening beast below me had human company, and that wouldn't be pleasant.

"Shut up, you stupid bastard." Shockingly, it didn't listen and kept jumping and snapping. "Oh, come on."

More lights came on now. Reinforcements were on the way. I couldn't outrun the dog which meant there was only one thing to do. This would hurt like a sonofabitch. For both of us.

At the half moon, Shaggy is awake but not paying much attention. That didn't mean I couldn't wake him in case of emergency, and this certainly qualified. Squeezing my eyes shut, my mind focused on my right hand. It took a moment, but finally, the tendons stretched and popped. I only needed one hand for this trick, which was good because it took every resource I had to manage even this much. Whatever change was going on inside my body was obvious to my opponent as well, because he went from angry to bat-shit crazy. The mastiff jumped higher and higher, getting closer to me each time. I needed to stall a few more seconds for my hand to morph into what I required: a weapon.

When the dog landed on the ground again, I dropped one branch lower—closer to the leaping monster than I wanted to be, but well within range. He leaped, and I pulled back. The mutt was fast, but now I had his timing. A second attempt, closer this time. I heard the snapping of his jaws and smelled the dog food on his breath. He ate better than me.

On the third jump, I had him. As he rose towards me, teeth first, I swung my arm from the shoulder. When my claw struck his throat, the impact shivered all the way up my arm. The damned thing was solid muscle, and for a second I wasn't sure I'd done it. Then a combination whine, howl, and whimper filled the air as the big body hit the grass.

From the house, a voice called to the dog. "Nestor, what is it?" Why do people talk to their dogs like they can answer? This one sure couldn't. Old Nestor lay on the ground, legs flailing in an attempt to regain his feet and continue the fight. It wasn't going to happen. The blood squirted from his throat, then oozed, then stopped completely.

There was no time to feel bad about it. I dropped from the branch and was pumping my legs before my boots even hit the ground. Four strides carried me to the wall. My claw-hand gripped the top brick, and I pulled myself up, boots kicking at the bricks until I straddled the top. Only then did I take the time to look back.

What remained of poor Nestor lay lifeless on the grass. From the doorway of the house a short, middle-aged man with a thick Middle Eastern accent shouted into his phone. Coming my way at a dead run, gun in hand, was the answer to at least one of my questions.

The big African guy definitely worked for Nasrallah.

He lifted his gun. Even from here it looked like a cannon. I rolled over the fence to safety, landing in a heap in the grass. My hand burned and throbbed as it reverted to normal, but there was no time to think about that. The blinding pain didn't prevent my running as fast as I ever had towards the safety of my car.

Dizzy and sick with panic, it took two tries to fit the key into the lock. I hurled my backpack onto the passenger seat and nearly slammed the door on my ankle as I scrambled in. On the third crank, the motor caught. I peeled out onto the side road, my faithful Charger fishtailing on the gravel shoulder, and headed for home.

CHAPTER 11

My right hand felt like it had gone through a meat grinder. It twitched and cramped in my lap while steering with my left. My vision was so blurry I didn't dare take the tollway home. The periodic *thumpthumpthump* of tires on the gravel shoulder meant I needed to make a pit-stop until my condition improved. I didn't want to kill anyone or anything else.

Miraculously, I pulled into the parking lot of a Greek diner on Milwaukee Road without hitting someone. I turned off the car and laid my head back against the seat, willing my veins to stop pulsing and my eyes to focus. That felt good for about thirty seconds until I felt the need to hurl. With barely a second to spare, the Charger's door flew open, and I dry-heaved onto the blacktop until the world stopped spinning. The chilly air helped a lot, and I sucked in big heaving gulps of oxygen.

My stomach couldn't decide if it was queasy or ravenous. This looked like as good a place as any to settle it down. It also provided a chance to think about what a giant botch I'd made of things. More or less upright, I entered the joint and plunked my ragged ass into the nearest cracked vinyl booth.

After grunting out a plea for coffee along with ham and eggs, I heard a buzz like a drunk hornet. It was Cromwell's phone. I fumbled through my backpack, cursing under my breath. My right hand still hurt too much to even flip it open, so I used my left thumb to reveal a text message.

What did you learn?

The old bastard didn't waste any time, but it was his money. I slowly finger-poked out a response.

Nasrallah took it.

The reply was instantaneous.

Does he still have it?

Did he? Between dodging bullets and dogs, I never had time to make sure one way or the other. If he did, would he be crazy enough to keep it in his house? Or maybe he had a rich guy's arrogance and just left it on his desk to admire. I had no damned idea. With more energy than it should take, I summoned the strength to respond.

IDK

This time the answer was long in coming. When it arrived, I could practically hear the acid in his voice.

You're not thirteen years old. Please type in proper sentences. Does he still have it?

Proper sentences? One-handed on a flip phone? It took several tries and a lot of backspacing, but I finally told him:

Driving. I will call you with the details in the morning. Will that work for you?

After making sure the period and question mark were in the right place, I hit send. Then I snapped the phone closed and stared at it while it buzzed one last time. I hoped he said, "okay" or I was out of a job.

By the time my late-night feast was nothing more than two streaks of hot sauce and three sad shreds of grated potato, I felt mostly human and capable of thinking things through. My right arm ached from elbow to wrist too much to write anything down, but I ran down a mental checklist.

The African—or whoever, it wasn't like I checked his passport—worked for Nasrallah. And he was in the house after-hours, so likely he was personal security instead of some random goon. That fit. The little Egyptian didn't seem like the type to let part-time help hang around the house.

That being the case, Nasrallah had the Anubis-whatever in his possession at one time. I honestly didn't know if it was in the residence or not. Odds were fifty-fifty at best. Now that it was fed and content, my gut said it was in there, and that was a decent working theory. In theory, if it was important enough to take from a guy like Cromwell, Nasrallah would keep it close. But I couldn't be a hundred percent sure, and breaking and entering wasn't part of J Lupul and Associates' portfolio of services. Unless it had to be.

Then I thought about old dead Nestor and the bullet holes in the brick wall. Nope, burglary was not on the table.

After another thirty minutes of Styx and self-loathing, I pulled into the driveway at my apartment. All I wanted was a bed. What I got was Bill's grandmother screaming out the bedroom window.

"Good. Glad you're home. Can you make yourself useful and throw this garbage out for me?"

I cussed under my breath, then shouted up, "'Course. Be right there." Bill wasn't home, and that was too bad because I could have used someone to talk to about my night. I walked around back then up the stairs to the kitchen door where I was met by an old lady in flannel pajamas, a cigarette in her mouth, and a leaking bag of Christ-only-knew-what.

"Thanks, honey. I appreciate it. Can't get that boy to leave the house all day, then when I need him, he's out doing God knows what. Something about work, probably." I don't know how the old gal managed to make the word "work," sound like it hurt her teeth. She stopped, looked me over, leaned in, and sniffed. "Whew, you're a damned mess. What have you been rolling in?"

"The job got a little messy. I'll take this to the trash for you. G 'night Gramma." Without another word, I took the bag and managed not to leak any of the nastiness on me on the way to the trash cans. My mind was still back up that damned tree, so it wasn't until I deposited the trash and put the lid back in place that I looked down at my feet.

Four headless rats lay in the alley. Not that anyone would miss the creepy little shits, but it still made my skin crawl. Because my night hadn't been lousy enough, I picked each one up by the tail and dropped it into the bin and put the lid on extra-tight. My hand was working again, so that was good.

After handling vermin, that hand needed to be scrubbed and sanitized, along with every square inch of me. A shower sounded like the greatest idea ever. I came around the corner of the building to retrieve my backpack from the car when I heard sneakers smacking concrete. Our block only had one working streetlight, but in its glow, I spied a skinny figure in a red sweatshirt. Whoever it was had the hood pulled up over their head. The figure paused, looked back at me and took off around the corner.

I thought about chasing him, but my body vetoed the idea. It was all too much: needy clients, rat-gobbling critters prowling in the alley, and someone sneaking around for reasons I couldn't imagine. My poor brain tried to wrap itself around all of that, then shut down. I needed a shower, a bed, and eight solid hours of sleep.

I was just about to plug my key into the door when a flapping piece of paper caught my eye. It was jammed into the crack around the doorbell and probably would've blown away in a few more minutes. Maybe my mysterious stalker put it there. Or a bill collector. Odds were about the same.

There were three words written on it. The first word, "*who,*" had been written in blue ink, then scratched out so hard the paper tore a bit.

The new sentence read:

What are you?

CHAPTER 12

It took every ounce of energy to shrug my backpack onto the bed before collapsing beside it and staring blankly at the ceiling. I stunk, looked like hell, my whole body ached, and the shower was waaaaaay over there.

My body hitting the mattress jostled the bag, and my ears detected the unwelcome sound of broken glass crunching.

Crap.

I knew what I'd find before even opening it. My fancy new night-visions were toast. One whole lens had pretty much disintegrated, and I cracked the frame, likely from landing on my back when falling from the tree. Then again, it might have been coming to earth awkwardly after jumping off a brick wall twice, or even the subtle way I hurled it into the car while dodging bullets. It had been quite a night. Cringing, I dumped the broken electronic corpse, along with the bag's other contents, onto my bed in a sad heap.

My only thought at that moment was how pissed Bill would be. Fortunately, I didn't need to face him in this condition. I stripped down, turned the shower on and let it run for a while. Like most old Chicago buildings, the water in Gramma's building only had two temperatures—so cold penguins would complain, or water you could make tea with. It's a good thing I liked it scalding hot.

Placing my hands on the tiles, I leaned forward to let the steam melt away layers of grime and failure until my skin glowed lobster-red through my dark body hair. Usually, I did my best thinking in the shower, but this time it blessedly worked in reverse. My mind went blank and my breathing, stomach, and abused muscles all returned to something close to normal.

After putting on a tee shirt and clean boxers, the steam cloud parted, and I walked into my room.

"See, this is why you can't have nice things." Bill stood at the foot of the bed, leaning on his crutch and holding a big plastic bag from an electronics store in his free hand. His face bore a look of parental disappointment and disapproval.

"Yeah, sorry about that. Didn't you buy an extended warranty?"

Bill sniffed. "Extended warranties are a scam. Usually. Besides, I doubt it would cover getting hit by an asteroid or whatever the hell you did to it. What did you do to it, by the way? Are you okay?"

I sank into the old leather chair in the corner. "I'm fine. I don't think our one and only client will be thrilled with me, though. What's that?"

He looked at the bag. "Oh, I brought you a couple of things you need for the business, but that can wait." He set the bag on the floor and perched on the corner of the bed, facing me with his hands on his knees, awaiting an explanation.

Bill Mostoy was the only person on the planet who ever got the real truth from me about anything, and even then I only gave him most of this story. He listened in accountant mode, nodding occasionally and interrupting with questions like, "what do you mean you *handled* the dog?" until he had a reasonable picture of the evening's fiasco.

"I didn't know you could even make the change this far past the... time." Even after all these years he still couldn't bring himself to say, "full moon," but I knew what he meant.

"I can, but only partially, and it sucks. Hurts like hell. I puked a bit."

He resisted the urge to offer a hug. Instead, he straightened his back and got back down to business. "What are you going to tell Cromwell tomorrow?"

"What I still don't know is does Nasrallah still have the thingamajig with him or not? Gotta find that out. I think I know how to do it, but it'll depend on if Cromwell's willing to help." The badly deformed germ of an idea occurred to me while I was at the diner, but it was a long way from complete. Maybe it would make more sense in the morning.

I nodded at the bag Bill brought with him. "What's all that?"

His face lit up. "Stuff for the business. Now that you're flush, there are some things you've needed for a while. As your business manager, it's time we made some investments."

"We?"

"Okay, you. And that was before I knew we'd have to replace certain—uh—equipment."

"So, what did I invest in?" He had me curious now.

My friend and business guru dug into the bag and pulled out a box that he held up triumphantly. "Ta-DA! A real grownup smartphone. No, don't friggin' look at me like that. You need this."

"Why? My flip phone works just fine."

"Yeah, for calling other Neanderthals. There's stuff you need. GPS, for one thing. Not to mention the ability to look stuff up on the fly. And pictures—you can record video on this and don't need a separate camera. Which you'd probably break, anyway." He fumbled the box open and handed the device to me. I took it from him like he'd offered me a live cobra.

"It's fine, Johnny. I've already set it up with everything you need."

The home screen sported a nice version of my company's logo. It did look kinda sweet. Very professional. Compared to everyone else's phone, there were only a few apps on it. A browser, a couple I didn't recognize, Grindr... "Whoa, what the hell is this?"

Bill howled. "In case you get lonely on a stakeout. I set up an account for you. Username is Furry Guy 1. You'd be surprised how many guys like a little pelt. Not my thing, personally, but..."

"You asshole."

He shrieked with laughter. "Dude, you should see your face. I just put it there for laughs. Just delete the icon." His hilarity died down a bit when he had to show me how to push on the icon and drag it to the trash bin. I don't think he fully appreciated what a technical idiot I truly was.

"Fine. But I'm not doing Twitter."

"No, you want to keep a low social media profile. It's part of your brand—the whole man-of-mystery thing. What you really need is this one." He pointed to what looked like a green thought bubble from a comic book. "That's an encrypted messaging app. We can text back and forth without anyone being able to intercept them."

"Do I need that?" Seemed like overkill.

"Clients like Cromwell? They have secrets. You're going to be working with a lot of things people don't want anybody to find out about. Oh, one more thing…"

He fished around in the bag, then pulled out an envelope which he tore open with great ceremony. Handing over a three-by-two rectangle of plastic, he announced, "Today you are a man."

It was a credit card in the name of J Lupul and Associates.

"This is mine?"

"That reminds me, you have to quit dicking around and get your name change done. But yes, you need to have a credit card like a real grownup person."

I felt unexpected tears well up. "Wow, you shouldn't have."

"Technically, I didn't. You paid for it, it's your company."

That brought me back to earth in a hurry. *How much was this all going to cost me?* "And I can use this for anything?"

"With the approval of the signing officer, which is yours truly. And there's a three-thousand-dollar limit. I'm not an idiot."

Fair. Bill was determined to make an adult out of me, even if I went kicking and screaming. This time I got out of the chair and gave my friend a hug which he broke after two awkward shoulder pats.

After the embrace, Bill looked around uncomfortably. That's when he found the note. Picking it up from my bed, he studied it, eyebrows raised.

"It was on the door when I got home. I think the red hoodie guy left it." That started a whole new discussion. No, neither of us had any idea who it might be. No, his *puni daj* didn't suspect we had a stalker, or she'd have said something. Yes, it was creepy as hell.

"But you think this guy knows… about you, I mean?" Bill never had a problem saying what was on his mind unless it came to my condition.

"I don't know what anyone knows anymore. You're the only one I've ever told." I didn't add what I was thinking. *And the only one who's ever seen me change and been able to talk about it.*

Shaking off that thought, I went on like it was a perfectly normal conversation. "Cromwell acts as if he knows more than he does. At least I hope so. For sure, he knows more than I'd like. He kept dropping all kinds of hints but didn't come right out and say it."

My friend looked at the floor like he always does when he's thinking. For a long time he said nothing. Then, "Are we... is Gramma in any danger?"

"I don't think so, man. But I need to know who this guy is and what he wants. We need to ask him a few questions.

Bill waved his crutch at me and put on a tough guy face. "Yeah, I'll just run him down and give him the old one-two." We chuckled at the notion of him threatening anyone, then his face fell. "You look like shit, buddy."

I felt like it, too. "Just tired. I need some sleep if I have to face old man Cromwell in the morning."

"Okay. G'night." Bill turned towards the stairs. "Oh, have you seen anything weird in the back alley? Gramma says there's a big old coyote or something rummaging around back there."

The picture of half a dozen decapitated rodents played across my brain. There likely wasn't anything there to worry about. Not with strangers hanging around, and odds were that hoodie-boy wasn't killing rats with his bare hands.

"Nope. Nothing at all."

CHAPTER 13

11 days after the full moon- waning crescent.

After a good night's sleep, the world looked a bit better, but I still resisted facing the day. The sun clawed its way through my mud-caked window with mixed results, but the lone ray that penetrated found my eyeballs. I groaned and flipped over to postpone the inevitable.

My hand was swollen and still ached when I flexed it but didn't seem permanently damaged. With all the stretching and straining my ligaments do during a change, my best weapon was a limber body, or it could lay me up for days. Being hairy and stocky, people are surprised by how bendy I am. I work at it. Every day I stretch until I think I'm going to tear my arm off my shoulder. Not that I do any formally recognized yoga poses. No *downward-dog-kama-sutra-third-eye-blind nonsense*. Like almost everything else about my body, I learned that the hard way and on my own. I knew what muscle groups were most affected when Shaggy took over by where the pain was the next day. It was simple. The more I stretched, the less it hurt.

Before facing Cromwell's inquisition, I needed to do my thing. Just like the moon itself, I was a little weaker than yesterday. That didn't impact my exercises at all, just the will to drag my ass out of the sack and do them.

I stood in my boxers, bent at the waist with my head touching my knees, groaning like an old man which may explain why I didn't hear Bill come down the stairs.

"If I could bend like that, I'd never leave the house."

"Can you knock first?" I said into my kneecaps.

"Seriously. Have you ever tried to... you know... yourself? Just saying..."

I slowly straightened, exhaling as I rose, then spoke before he painted any more mental pictures that couldn't be unseen. "What do you want?"

"You've had a few requests."

"Really? Anything good?"

Bill shrugged. "Depends on what you call good. Two missing dogs and a little help collecting a debt from a family member."

It sounded like Cromwell would be my only client for a while longer. Any dogs I rescued wouldn't be happy to see me, and I'd had enough of collecting debts when I worked for O'Rourke. Enough that I quit to build Waffle Shacks around the country with a shady construction company for two years. And how messed up did your family have to be to send hired muscle to go after your brother-in-law? No thanks. Long as I was flush, I could afford to be picky.

"Okay, I'll send them a thanks-but-no-thanks. Oh, Cromwell wants you there by ten. And his email sounded grumpy."

I'd planned on nine, so if he was giving me till ten I guess I wasn't in that much trouble. An idea occurred to me. "Do you wanna come with? Seems you're in touch with him more than I am. And you are the business guy."

Bill looked like I'd offered him a live grenade. "Hell no. I work from home because I don't want to see my own customers. Why would I want to hang out with yours? Besides, this guy sounds awful. And hospital beds still give me the creeps."

My boy had seen enough of those to last a lifetime, so I got it. "'Kay then. I'm going to shower and head out. Did Gramma hear anything again last night? In the alley?"

"Not that she told me. Have you figured out what you're gonna do about your stalker, dude?"

A half-assed idea had occurred to me, but I'd need help. "Can you walk a bit without that?" I pointed to his crutch.

"Of course. I only use it because it's so damned attractive. Yeah, I can walk a bit these days, but I'm not chasing anybody, that's for sure."

"I mostly need you to stand there and look pretty." What I needed was a decoy for a few minutes, but I could tell by his face it made no sense to him. He wouldn't care for it, but it wasn't my worst idea ever. "Let's talk about it tonight."

He knitted his brows for a moment. "Hey, I'm happy to help and all, but you know I'm not much use when it comes to physical stuff. Is Gramma okay? Do we need to worry?"

"Let's talk about it tonight."

"Yeah, we probably should." He mumbled.

After shooing him up the stairs, I showered and put on a clean shirt. Then it was off to Cromwell's place, where I nearly got my head blown off before I made it to the elevator.

To be fair, it was my fault. As soon as I entered the lobby, I reached for my Ruger to hand it over to Justin at the desk. I didn't think he'd even noticed me. By the time I fumbled with the holster and pulled it out, soldier-boy had his gun pointed straight at my head, his feet locked in a shooter's stance. I'd have been the deadest wild-west gunslinger ever.

"Whoa. Jesus, I was only handing it over."

Justin dropped the gun a few inches but kept it pointed at me. "What the fuck, dude." He motioned with his hand, and I passed it over. Butt first and very, very, slowly.

"Sorry. I thought I was being efficient. We good?" I asked him.

He took the pistol and placed it in a drawer. "We're good. But don't ever make a sudden move like that. Dude, do you know how many Hajis wound up dead that way?" Something told me he had a precise number in mind, and I didn't want to know.

"Got it. No sudden moves. Can I go up?" I asked, lowering my hands.

As the elevator doors shut, I muttered, "Asshole."

"I heard that." His voice followed me to the tenth floor.

The ever-present Nurse Ball met me at the door. As I brushed past her, I couldn't help but look for signs of hosiery. I hated myself for even thinking about a woman who had nearly twenty years on me. She smelled great, though, and I'm pretty sure she heard me take a deep sniff as I walked by. Shaggy was asleep in there, but not dead. Today she smelled like strawberry and vanilla, and it made my stomach growl.

One corner of her crimson mouth turned up. "Something I can do for you?"

Busted. "No. No, I'm good. Mister Cromwell is in the office, I gather?"

She nodded. "You know the way." As I stepped by, she grabbed my arm and I noticed she cut her nails short and polished them a glossy vintage-corvette red. "He's having one of his good days. Try not to ruin it."

It's not like I went out of my way to upset people, I was just wildly successful despite myself.

The old man was out of bed and sitting at his desk in a sharp-looking sweater vest with all six of his hairs neatly combed over ear to ear. He even had what passed for a smile on his craggy face. Cromwell half-stood and waved me into the chair across from him.

My manners hadn't deserted me altogether. Mom McPherson would have been proud. "You're looking good... well... sir."

"Surprised to see the old man up? Me too, tell you the truth. With dialysis, you have good days and bad ones. So far, it's a good day. Hopefully, we can keep it that way. What have you got for me?"

I sat up straight, pulled out my notebook and took a deep breath. "I'm fairly sure Nasrallah has your item."

"Fairly?"

"He definitely took it. The question is where it is now. I think it's in his house."

Cromwell leaned back in his chair and made a steeple with his bony fingers. "How do you know he took it? My money was on Sanchez."

The ground solidified under my feet. I finally knew something he didn't. I put on my best professional voice. "Your item was stolen by two men, one of them a white guy and the other a tall African—maybe Nigerian."

"Sudanese."

"Huh?" The earth liquified again.

"He's from Sudan, a former army officer. Name's Abdul Badri, he handles security for Wafik. If it's Nasrallah, that is. Do you think he's the one who took my package? Doesn't sound like him, but all right. Does he still have it?"

There was the question I didn't want to answer. My hesitation didn't inspire confidence, so my client asked it again, "Does. He. Have. It?"

"My surveillance was interrupted..."

"You mean you nearly got caught."

"Nasrallah isn't the trusting kind. The fact that the family is gone, and it appears to be just him and Badri in the house, say they are keeping it close."

Cromwell's good mood was dissipating quickly, and one of his hairs shifted to hang in his face. He brushed it away. "But you didn't see it, so you don't know for certain."

"Not a hundred percent, no."

"And you didn't look, did you?"

I was close to losing my shit. My head throbbed and my eyeballs felt like they were being pushed out of my skull from the inside. "I told you, breaking and entering isn't on the menu. I'm not going to jail for something I don't even know what it is. Once we know for sure it's in there, I can figure out a plan. Maybe get them to move it and grab it then."

That brought the conversation to a screeching halt, and we both took a second to cool down. While he ran his hand over the liver spots on his scalp, I pretended to be fascinated by the shelf behind him. That germ of an idea reemerged, but I wasn't sure he'd go for it.

"What? Spit it out." He demanded.

I pointed to the second shelf. "You said that crying bowl..."

"Scrying. Scrying bowl. Christ, what about it?"

"Didn't you say it could find things? You said it worked, right?"

"You said you'd get the goddamned disk back for me. Isn't that why I'm paying you?" Tension hung in the air while his watery eyes studied me. I was stalling, not believing for a second that the bowl did what he claimed it did or he wouldn't need me.

He sensed my skepticism and slowly leaned forward with a creepy grin. "The power in that... don't laugh, damn you. It exists. But there are limits to its effectiveness, especially when searching for other magical terms. The results can be... unpredictable. Like looking in a mirror while looking in a mirror. Especially when the other object doesn't want to be found."

"Magic? Dude, seriously?" it probably wasn't wise to call the client, "dude," but it slipped out. I was still getting the hang of the whole professional thing.

He let out the same sigh I used to hear whenever grownups were disappointed in me. I knew it well and didn't like it. My face flushed, and my ass rose out of the chair to walk out. Cromwell slapped his hand on the desk blotter.

"Sit down. I'm not done with you. And there's something else we need to talk about."

This oughta be good. The old coot was serious. I counted to five, then sat back down to hear what he had to say. I never did the whole "slam the door and storm out," move very well, and needed to walk the line between obeying an order and doing the smart thing.

"There's the question of your... ability. I don't know how it will impact the other forces involved."

"What do you know about me?"

"Not nearly enough, that's for sure. But if you are half of what I think you are, even you don't know what you can do. That intrigues me. It's why I'm investing in you. God knows I didn't hire you for your brains."

"Hey, come on." It sounded whiny, but I hated being called stupid. Like calling fat kids fat. It's true, but still crappy.

"You're right. That was uncalled for. But one thing you've yet to learn is there are way stranger things in the world than you can even imagine. I've spent my life studying and collecting them. Odd things, Lupul. You don't even make the list."

Assuming Malcolm Cromwell really knew my secret—and the knot in my stomach told me he knew enough—it still didn't back up any of the other nonsense he was spewing. I figured I'd at least make the top ten.

"Show me then. Show me one of your freaking wonders. Make your magic bowl find that thing."

He was in a feisty mood. "Alright, you smartass. I will. Hand me down that bowl. Carefully."

I took a few steps to the bookshelf and pulled down the bowl, careful not to drop it. It was just an antique, badly painted salad bowl. It might have been porcelain, glossy and smooth as it was. The only wonder so far was how much my gullible client paid for it. I placed it on the green felt blotter in front of him.

"Blinds, please." I obliged quickly. He was going through with this, and my curiosity was building.

Following orders, I grabbed two bottles of water from beside his bed and handed them over. He shook his head.

"Open them, please. My hands..." Damned if I didn't feel sorry for the guy. I poured them into the bowl, filling it about three quarters. Then he motioned to a spot on his left.

"Stand over there. I'm not sure how you might affect this and it will be tricky enough as it is."

I took three steps back, but still close enough to have a view of the bowl and its contents. I wanted to see his technique. There was no way I'd be fooled by any cheap parlor tricks, having watched Gramma Mostoy work her customers over for years, and was hip to most of the hustles out there.

If my disbelief bothered him, Cromwell didn't show it. He turned the desk lamp off and bowed his head. He held a hand up to shush me before I said anything dumb. My molars ground the inside of my cheek so as not to break the creepy vibe he was going for.

Skeletal fingers caressed the rim of the bowl. For what felt like forever, the only sounds were his wheezing breath and the drumming in my temples. He stiffened his back the tiniest bit. I raised on tiptoe but saw nothing.

At first.

The faintest glimmer of light shone inside the bowl, a single brief flash like a firefly, then it disappeared. A moment later there was a second, then a third, flaring longer and brighter. Again, the water in the dish glowed, then faded, then shone brighter. All the while Cromwell's hands shook and his breath grew wheezier until I thought about running for Nurse Ball.

In the bowl's reflection, I could make out something that wasn't Cromwell's face or even his dimly lit office. By the light of a desk lamp somewhere else, the top of a desk in an office with familiar old wooden bookshelves appeared. It looked like, though it couldn't possibly be, Nasrallah's home office.

There was no guessing how he was doing this, and I couldn't pull my eyes away. Suddenly the water rippled, and the picture vanished. Cromwell shook his head and hissed, "Shit. Come on," and refocused. The rippling stopped and the light and the image, fuzzy like surveillance video but in full color, reappeared. It shifted ever so slightly left, then right, like a camera seeking something. On the edge of the desk was a metal object. I don't know which of us gasped louder.

"Is that..." A shake of the old man's head shut me down. We watched in silence as the image rotated in the bowl until I saw the dog-headed guy in the skirt. A dark shadow passed over the item, blocking the light. A long ebony finger nudged it and then pulled back as if it had touched a hot stove. Whoever it was bent lower over the disk to examine the object. We couldn't

73

hear anything, but it looked like whoever it was spoke to someone else. I wished the bowl came with volume control. The mystery man looked back and the disk and then around the room. For a split second, he stared right up at us, scrunching his eyes quizzically.

A black face, shiny with perspiration, stared out of the bowl. A ragged pink scar ran down each cheek, and deep black eyes squinted directly at me.

Without thinking, I took three long strides to get a better look. I put my head right over the bowl. "That's him. That's the guy who took your disk."

"No. Get back." I thought the old guy was being melodramatic, but two things happened at once. The first was the image changed. Quick strobe images of the faraway scene replaced the steady clear picture. The light flashed bright, then dark, clear, then hazy, then in focus once again. Before I could back up, something even stranger began. Steam rose from the room-temperature water in the scrying bowl.

From a million miles away, I heard Cromwell's voice shouting, "Move back. Get away..." but there was no chance of obeying. Curiosity glued me to the spot, staring as the steam thickened, then little bubbles popped to the surface of the water. The water in the bowl was boiling.

"What's happening? What the hell's going on?" Someone was screaming, probably me.

Cromwell's eyes widened. He stood up and shoved at my chest to move me away, but he was too late. As the water boiled madly, we heard a loud *crack*. A jagged black line bisected the bowl end to end, and it split open. The image disappeared as water spilled all over the desk, soaking everything. We stood on opposite sides of the desk, watching streams of water run everywhere. Neither of us spoke or moved.

"Fuck me." That was definitely me.

Nurse Ball threw the heavy doors open and charged in. "Is everything alright in here?" Cromwell and I turned to her, our mouths open, and nodded at the same time.

Every bit the professional, she grabbed a towel from beside the hospital bed in the corner and dabbed at the desk. "What happened?" She wheeled on me, her green eyes burning. "What the hell did you do?"

I tried to respond but only mustered a croaking sound. I had no freaking idea what I'd done, but beyond a doubt I was guilty of something.

She picked up the two useless halves of the bowl. "Oh, Mal... Mister Cromwell, your beautiful bowl." She held it out to him, but he ignored her. His eyes locked on me, and a huge grin pulled the wrinkles on his face back to his ears.

"Fuck me." This time it was him, but he didn't seem angry. Instead, he looked like a man who'd won the lottery.

What was I supposed to say? "I'm sorry. I'll pay for it..." If I worked for the rest of my life, it wouldn't replace that bowl, but it was all I could think to say.

Fortunately, he didn't hold me to it. Instead, he threw his head back, let out a whoop, and clapped his hands twice. "That was, truly, the most amazing thing I've ever seen."

The nurse ran her hand over his liver spots, checking for a fever, but he swatted her away. "Oh, stop fussing for Christ's sake. Well? Are you prepared to believe me now?"

My head bobbed up and down and he let out another whoop and slapped the desk. I pried my jaw off the floor and shut my mouth. Daylight seemed like a great idea and ran over to jerk the blinds open.

Sanity returned to the room along with the sun's rays. "Are we done, sir?"

The euphoria had worn off and his face drooped. Malcolm Cromwell looked tired and in need of a nap. Hell, he was twice my age, and I needed a nap. And a drink. Probably several.

His guardian fired tasers from her eyeballs as she said, "Mister Cromwell needs to rest now. I think you've done enough for one day, don't you?"

I watched, useless, as she guided him over to the bed where he plopped onto the mattress. Then he lifted his head. "The Anubis Disk, Johnny. I want it. You know where it is now."

"Yes sir, I'll get it for you." *Just as soon as I can figure out how to not wind up dead or incarcerated.*

Nurse Ball lifted his sweater vest over his head, the old man wriggling like a toddler avoiding bath time. "I said there's something else, it's important..."

"Sir, it can wait."

He slithered out of his vest and pointed to a soaking wet manila folder on his desk. "No, this is important. Look at that and tell me what you think."

With a shaking hand, I grabbed the papers, whatever the hell they were, and wiped them on my jacket. A hand like a vice clamp grabbed my arm. "You can read those outside. I'll see you out."

I shouted over my shoulder, "Honest, I'll get it for you."

His voice followed me out the door, "I need to know if that's you, Johnny, and if it's not, who is it?" Then the door hissed shut on its pneumatic hinges.

The nurse's voice contained pure frozen disdain. "What happened in there? And don't bullshit me."

"We were... I tried to... but... shit, he can explain it better than I can." That may have been the truest statement I ever made because I had no freaking clue how to answer her.

"I warned you to take it easy on him."

"On him? He's the one that... yeah. Okay. My bad." I hung my head like a disobedient kid awaiting punishment. The envelope slapped against my leg.

Whatever this new information was, I needed to read it somewhere else because I never needed anything as much as a cold lake breeze to clear my head. And to be the hell out of that madhouse. "I'll call later to see how he is. And about this." I smacked the brown paper across my palm. "I'll get him some answers. Take care of him, will you? He's the only client I have."

"Me too," she said.

Nurse Ball stood with her hands on her hips and studied me for a moment. The shadows of the blind slats angled across her face. The slight crow's feet deepened, but her eyes softened the teeniest bit. "Be very careful with him, Johnny." At first, it sounded like she was warning me about his frailty.

Then the replay echoed through my brain and it sounded more like a warning for my own benefit. An icy trickle ran from my neck to my tailbone.

It was time I got the hell out of Dodge.

CHAPTER 14

I sat alone in the Charger, banging on the steering wheel with both hands. Grateful for the chance to ask out loud what had been bouncing around my head of the last couple of minutes, I let it rip at full volume. "What the ever-loving actual fuck was that?"

There was no answer, but I felt better anyway.

I rolled the window down to let the cold air clear my head. It was two days to Halloween, which meant the sun was deceivingly bright. If you're on the sunny side of the street, you can feel a hint of warmth under the breeze. In the shade, it's just November bearing down on you. Chicagoans call that wind, "the Hawk." I let it sink its cold talons into me and closed my eyes for a blessed moment.

Finally convinced my head would not explode, I reached for the envelope on the seat beside me and opened it up. Nothing bit me or jumped out, trying to kill me. It was just two pieces of paper, printouts of online articles—one from the Daily Herald, the other from a local Berwyn news site. That was a suburb about 4 Metra stops from Downtown, and two miles or more from where I'd rescued Meaghan O'Rourke.

Second Animal Attack on Local Homeless

Both articles told the same story. Twice in the last three nights, a homeless person showed up at MacNeal Hospital with bad scratches, presumably from an animal. The first victim was a woman. Then last night a guy showed up half-naked and ranting. Neither said what happened, and Animal Control was on the lookout for a coyote or wild dog. They named none of the victims.

I need to know if it was you, Johnny. It wasn't.

If not, who was it? Way better question.

I read the articles a second, then a third time hoping something would pop out at me. Bad things happen to homeless people all the time, so that wasn't particularly notable. The part that worried me was the word, "ranting." That was code for "the guy tried to tell them and they thought he was crazy." I wondered what his story was.

Reports like these show up all over the country from time to time. When I traveled with the construction crew I'd come across them. Once in Yankton, South Dakota, and again in Kalispell, Montana. The Montana case actually turned out to be a rabid coyote, and they put it down.

It would be a cold day in hell before I went back to Yankton.

In a city this size it was unlikely I was the only Lycan but hadn't run into any and hoped to keep it that way. Despite all the nature documentaries about wolves being social pack animals, Lycans aren't wolves. We're just messed up humans who keep to ourselves as much as possible.

Cromwell, understandably, needed assurance he didn't have an out-of-control psychopath on the payroll. I had an alibi for last night, but not for the first attack. The only way to know for sure what was going on was to head out to the burbs and poke around. I pointed my trusty ride West.

If Chicago was a decent place to be a Lycan, it's an objectively terrible spot to live on the street. The short summers are hot and humid, while the endless winters can be literally murderous. The suburbs are worse.

In the big, scary, Windy City, people expect some degree of homelessness. There are social agencies and churches, and it gives the place character. As long as they don't hang out in front of the Art Institute or mess with tourists down on the Mag Mile, it's tolerated. The burbs, of course, were built for the express purpose of separating nice, middle class, formerly South Side, white people from the "them" of their choice. It would take some doing, especially in daylight, to find someone on the streets of Berwyn who could tell me what I needed to know.

I stopped at a bank and changed money so I had a roll of singles and fives. Talking money. Then it was a long, slow cruise down Ogden.

After scanning the sidewalks and alleys, I spotted something and whipped around the block to get a closer look. A shopping cart leaned against a busted chain-link fence. Somebody converted into a blanket fort. I parked and headed over.

"Hello?" Nobody answered. It was a good thing the waning moon cycle dulled my senses because I approached from downwind and the smell made bile burn my throat. I was still five yards away. Holding my breath, I took another step forward.

"Don't mess with my stuff," a voice shouted from a doorway. The speaker was taking shelter from the stiff wind. He was a black guy, matted hair sticking out from under a battered Sox hat. He pointed a gnarled finger at me.

I raised my hands and took a step back. With my most innocent smile, I said, "Good day, sir. Wonder if I might talk to you for a minute."

"Ain't moving that cart. This is public property." This wasn't the first time he'd had that conversation.

"Wouldn't ask you to. Just wondering if I can talk to you for a minute, okay? Name's Johnny. Johnny Lupul. What's your name, sir?"

He let out a wheezing laugh. "Oh, Lord. Nothing good comes from them calling you sir. I'm Sweet Lou. Least that's what people call me."

"Like Sweet Lou Whitaker?"

He scrunched his face. "Hell no. Not that Sox-killing Detroit motherfucker."

"A Sox fan. At least you're on the side of the angels."

"Damn right. Southside ride or die. They win last night?"

The White Sox hadn't played October baseball in about ten years, but who was I to ruin his day? "Don't think so. Travel day."

"Well, they didn't lose at least." You had to love the attitude.

The Hawk picked up, and the chill sliced right through my flannel jacket. "Lou, can I buy you a cup of coffee and ask you some questions?"

"Can't leave my stuff. Someone'll steal it. You a cop?"

"Hell no. Animal Control." I pulled out my wallet, flipped it open in a brazen bullshit move, then slipped it back in my pocket. "Can I get a cup, bring it back and we can talk?"

"That'd be nice, they don't' let me in there no more."

I motioned for him to stay put and trotted around the corner to the doughnut shop. There I grabbed two coffees, a handful of sugars and an apple fritter as an afterthought. It was the biggest bakery item they had, and it had a little fruit in it. Vitamins.

Sweet Lou took the coffee in both hands and put his face close to the lid, more for warmth than the aroma. "Thank you. Mighty kind." He offered me half his fritter.

"I'm good. Hey, do you know the guy who got attacked last night? Or the woman?"

"Ain't seen Alice since it happened. Think she lit out. Animal Control, huh? You gonna do something about the rats? They're some mean bastards."

"Nah. I want to talk about whatever attacked the other guy. What's his name?"

Lou stopped in mid-sip, his eyes narrowed through the steam. "You're not Animal Control."

I tried to look innocent. "What gave me away?"

"Cause the guy that messed Jerry up wasn't no animal."

"The papers said it was an animal attack, like a coyote or something."

He laughed. "Papers say the economy's good too—where's my damned job? They don't know shit. Some foreign dude tried to take Jerry's jacket. My boy fought him off, and the guy goes crazy, beating and scratching him. Damn near killed him."

Goddoubledammit. A Lycan wouldn't be able to make the change at this time of the cycle any more than I could and even trying would damn near kill him. But that kind of rage was possible, especially if he hadn't spent a lifetime learning to control it.

"You said this guy was foreign. Jerry tell you from where?" *Please let him be Chinese.*

"Ask him yourself."

"Where is he?"

Sweet Lou pointed to the pile of blankets and trash behind me. "In there."

From inside the makeshift tent came a wrenching cough, then two more, each longer and more agonizing than the other. I took a deep breath and walked over. "Jerry? You in there?"

A shaky voice came from under the sleeping bag roof. "Who are you?"

"I'm trying to find the guy who attacked you. Name's Johnny. Can I— come in?"

"It's okay, Jer. He's alright." Lou had left his windbreak and joined us. He bent to lift the corner of the blanket so I could get on my hands and knees to crawl inside.

Huddled in a ball was a small man whose eyes took up half his face, wrapped in a Power Puff Girls blanket and shivering, only partly from the cold. He let out a small whimper when I drew near. I inched forward, palms in the air.

"It's okay, man. I just want to talk to you for a minute about the guy who hurt you."

The mousey little guy shook his head. "Won't believe me."

"Sure I will. I believe all kinds of crazy stuff. Who did this to you?" Nothing.

"Was it a coyote?" He shook his head violently and turned away.

"It was a man, right? From somewhere else?" I turned to Sweet Lou for confirmation.

"S'okay, Jerry. Johnny's alright. Tell him." He didn't wait for his partner to speak, though. "Dude showed up a week or so ago. Polish or Russian or something like that. Jumped a pizza guy the other day, and we wouldn't let him hang cause we don't need the police hassling us. We ain't criminals."

Jerry nodded and finally found his tongue. "He h-h-h-hurt Alice too. Said he wanted my coat, but I wouldn't give it to him. I need it. It's cold, ya know?"

I knew. Hoping to hear that my gut had it wrong, I asked, "What's he look like? Tall? Short?"

Lou answered. "Not too tall but strong as a son of a bitch." Jerry nodded.

I already knew the next couple of answers but had to ask, anyway. "Tattoos?"

"Looked like prison ink. All kinds of crosses and shit."

My powers of denial were breaking down. "What about his hair?"

Jerry curled further into a ball, too freaked out by even thinking about it to be much use. Lou wasn't fazed. "Bald, but stubbly. Like he'd been shaving and stopped."

Max freaking Kozlov.

Jerry summoned up the strength to speak again. "Don't go after him, Mister. He's crazy." No kidding. If he survived my bite, he had to be going out of his mind with everything going on inside him. He was a vicious SOB to start with. Now he was stronger and crazy as a shithouse rat. *Nice work, Johnny.*

"Any idea where he is now?" The two men shook their heads, and I felt relieved. Maybe he took off. Nah, my luck didn't run that good.

There wasn't much more to learn from them, and my stomach couldn't handle much more of the dank funk under those blankets. I crawled backward into the alley, took a gulp of blessedly fresh air, and rose to my feet.

"What are you gonna do about this guy?" Sweet Lou hugged himself against the cold. His old winter coat had strips of electrical tape holding it together.

"I don't know yet, but... hey, it's good of you to take him in like that."

The old Sox fan shrugged. "What're you gonna do? Man needed help."

I reached into my pocket. "Do me a favor, make sure you guys get something to eat will you?" I pulled out the wad of singles and fives. It was only twenty-five bucks but looked like more, and the other man's eyes widened. I pressed it into his hand. "You're a good man, Sweet Lou."

"Don't know about that. Least I ain't a Cubs fan. Side of the angels, right?"

I laughed. "Right on. Take care, man"

I wandered back towards my car, taking deep breaths and trying not to lose my shit. I should have worried about Kozlov being out there somewhere but couldn't get the image of Jerry clutching that kid's blanket for warmth without even a decent coat to keep him warm. I wished I could do something more than throw money at him.

Unlocking the Charger, I kicked the white fender in frustration. Over the hood, I caught the red and white glow of a Target sign and got an idea. I had a credit card like a big boy.

Twenty minutes later, I was back at Lou's fortress with two winter coats and a six-pack of socks. Bill would crap his pants, using the company card for this, but at least I had the receipt. Maybe he could write it off. Call it a research fee or something. He did stuff like this all the time for his big-wig customers. It felt good to do something. Good enough that for one bright, shining moment I forgot there was a lunatic, sociopathic, newborn werewolf running around.

A fat sewer rat jumped out of a garbage can and scuttled away. He squeaked and bitched me out for a second, then scooted under the fence. I watched him for a moment, and that's when I saw the mangled, maggot-covered bodies of about half a dozen of his fellow rodents.

Most of their heads were missing.

Crap.

CHAPTER 15

"Wait. There are two of you?" Bill's voice squeaked a bit.

I wasn't sure how to answer him. "Yeah, kind of. I think it's the guy from the other night. The Russian."

"But you said..."

I leaned across the kitchen table, keeping my voice low so the old lady wouldn't hear. "I know what I said. I thought he was... dead, I mean. Turns out he isn't. And now he's out there and it's my fault."

"Does he know where you are?" I could tell from the wide eyes and tiny pupils he meant where *we* are.

Thinking about the trail of dead, headless vermin from here to Berwyn only made my conscience hurt worse, but I looked him in the eye and said, "Nah, there's no way he could know." I was usually a much better liar. I got away with it because Bill wanted to believe me.

It had been quite a day. I'd blown up my only client's prize possession, gotten a taste of something weird I never needed to see again, unleashed a shitstorm on a pair of innocent homeless guys, was no closer to getting that disk back from the Egyptian, and it was still only six o'clock. The good news was that sundown meant my stalker ought to be hanging around. That gave me a chance to fix at least one problem tonight.

Bill was so freaked out he never even blinked when I told him about the coats for Jerry and Sweet Lou. I took a last long sip of whatever Gypsy tea his gramma served and grinned at my buddy. "Want to help me catch the hoodie guy?"

His eyes lit up. "Yeah. What do I have to do?"

"Just walk from the car to my apartment without your stick. You can do that, right?"

"I guess. But why?"

It was a classic diversion. Whoever my stalker was liked to watch me come and go at night. The two of us would drive off. Bill would drop me a block or two away and come back pretending to be me. Red hoodie didn't seem to be any kind of professional, or even very good at the surveillance thing. It shouldn't take much to distract him, grab him, find out what his deal was, and scare the bejeezus out of the guy. Problem solved.

"I get to drive the Charger?"

"Not the important part of the plan, but yeah."

"But for the record, you're letting me drive the…"

"Christ, yeah. Grab your stuff and meet me downstairs in five."

A few minutes later we left through the basement door. Bill walked with his crutch and a plastic bag containing one of my flannel shirts and a spare cap.

"See him?" I asked, backing into the street.

My passenger looked around like a kid looking for a McDonald's on a road trip. The way his eyes bounced around it was no wonder I spotted the guy before Bill did.

Reflected in the rear-view mirror, someone stepped between two cars and watched us leave. In the amber glow of the streetlight, the sweatshirt looked purple, but it was our guy. "There he is. Six o'clock."

"Where?" Bill swiveled his head side to side.

"Behind you. Can't you tell time?"

"You don't have to be a dick about it. Jeez."

I'd planned to park on Pulaski, but it was a busy street, with a lot of innocent civilians, so I reconsidered. Instead, I made the left onto a side street before pulling to the curb. It was for the safety of the general public as much as for my car. Bill, like a lot of Chicagoans, didn't have a car, so he didn't drive much, and it wasn't pretty when he did.

"Okay. Put the flannel and the hat on and leave your stick in the car. All you have to do is park in the drive and walk into my apartment, so he thinks you're me. That should keep him busy." Bill eagerly changed into my red and black shirt, a size and a half too big for him, and then put the Blackhawks cap on backward like it was still two thousand and eight.

"What the hell are you doing? Turn that around. You're supposed to be me, not some douchey frat boy."

"Well, you are what you eat." He chuckled, knowing it always made me squirm.

"Oh, butch up." I twirled my finger, and he begrudgingly turned the cap the way God intended. Then he opened the door and, fingers maintaining contact with the hood, limped around to the driver's side. He was walking better, but he'd never be right.

I climbed out, trying not to look nervous as he slid behind the wheel and carefully adjusted the mirrors. "Give me a minute to get down that alley, and then..."

"John, I get it. Pull in, don't look around, walk straight to your apartment. You know I've got an MBA, right?"

"Sorry. You'll be great. It won't hurt too much, will it?" He shook his head, and I rapped on the hood of my car. "Okay, go get'em. I'll be there in a sec."

Trotting across the street, I heard the chirp of tires as he pulled out too fast behind me. Three seconds later a car honked, but it wasn't followed by a crunch, so I assumed both my friend and the car arrived in one piece. From down the breezeway behind a red brick four-flat, I saw a slim figure in a hoodie watching my driveway. *Got ya.*

Whoever it was, hugged themselves against the night air with their hands inside their sleeves, shifting weight from one foot to the other and never taking their eyes off our building. They looked more pathetic than scary, but a guy couldn't be too careful.

I pulled the Ruger from my belt, made sure the safety was on, and charged. I was about three long strides away when my target realized I was there and turned towards me. I reached out to put him in a headlock, pressing the gun to his head.

The hoodie slipped off, revealing a headful of spiky blond hair. A high-pitched voice shouted, "What the hell, man?"

I pulled my Ruger away and took two steps back. Then I offered a "what the hell" of my own. The sweat-shirted figure straightened, panting. Wide, bloodshot, blue eyes stared out from a pale face—sweating despite the cold. I knew that face.

Meaghan O'Rourke wiped her sleeve across her nose again and studied me. The wheels were grinding in her head, but she said nothing for the longest time. The kid stood there sniffling, twitching, and shuffling.

The gun went into my holster. "What are you doing here? Does Mr.... your dad know you're here?"

She let out a sour laugh. "No. Better that way." She stared at me, brow furrowed like she was trying to solve a vexing math problem. Finally, more to herself than me, she said, "You're not the guy."

"What guy?"

Her eyes focused as much as they were capable, and a shiver ran the length of her slim body. Meaghan started pacing back and forth. "The guy who came and got me." Her face scrunched up as she leaned closer, and I realized she probably should have been wearing glasses. "Hey, you used to work for my dad, right?"

"Yeah, for a bit. Out of high school, yeah." She must have been, like, ten years old then. I wondered what she thought her old man did for a living.

That bit of reality grounded her. She took a step back and looked around to be sure we were alone. "He's telling everyone he paid you to find me, and you brought me home and stuff." I avoided her eyes. "But that... thing. That wasn't you." It might have been a question, but she was talking more to herself than me, so I didn't answer.

"Shouldn't you be, I don't know, home or someplace?"

She sneered. "Someplace? Like rehab? Daddy told you, huh?" Venom dripped from her cracked thin lips and she uncoiled her spine to look taller, more defiant.

"You look like..." I was going to say shit. Or she was strung the hell out on something. She didn't give me a chance.

"Like I'm using again? Big surprise. Wonder why? I was doing great, you know. Clean three months. Then those Russian assholes grab me to piss off my old man, and then—whoever the hell it was—comes to get me. And nobody believes my story."

If she saw me wince, it didn't slow her down. "Not the cops. Sure as shit, not my father who just goes on and on about how much money it cost to get me back..."

There was no interrupting that rant.

"And then it turns out the big hero who saved the day is just some asshole loser who used to work for my father back in the day..."

"Hey!"

"So yeah, I'm using again. Big whoop. Maybe that's why I'm seeing monsters and stuff."

I was freezing, and she shook like Jello in a hurricane. "You look like you're cold. Maybe—"

"That's cause it's cold out, you fucking genius. You're good at this detective stuff, aren't you?"

The ungrateful little snot was right about the temperature at least. "Look, let's got to my place and get warm. We can talk about... whatever." I reached for her arm, but she yanked it away and took a step away.

"Are we going to talk about that, that thing? Because whatever that was, it wasn't you. And I need to know what it was or I will lose my freaking mind."

"Maybe you don't remember what you saw? You were in rough shape."

She grabbed her head, stomped her sneakers on the concrete, and shouted, "Don't treat me like I'm stupid. I'm not a little girl, and I wasn't hallucinating, and I'm not crazy. I just need to know what the hell happened to me before I lose my god-damned mind for good."

She might not have been crazy, but she was doing a good impression of it at the moment. A shadow moved in the window above us. Wherever this conversation was headed, I didn't need the entire world listening in. "Come on. Let's go to my place and I'll tell you what you need to know." *Or at least as good a story as I can make up on the fly.*

Meaghan bit her lip and glared up at me. "Don't fucking lie to me, okay?"

Instead of making a promise I couldn't keep, I just nodded and led us to my door. "Your father told you about me?" I thought client privilege went both ways, but I had a lot to learn, apparently.

"He's telling everyone about the kid who used to work for him, who's now some kind of badass. You don't look like much. Just saying."

There was no time to think about whether that was good news. "He's going to be worried about you. You should call him—let him know you're okay." She gave me a dismissive shrug, and it pissed me off. I spun her around and loomed over her in an attempt to look all grown up and responsible. "Hey, I talked to him when you got taken. You don't know. He's worried sick about you. And when you came home..."

"When I came home, he slapped me right back into rehab and wouldn't believe a word I said." Her eyes dared me to argue. If I wasn't there, I'm not sure I'd believe her either. I knew about parents not having your back.

Instead of arguing, I unlocked the door and brought her inside. Gramma had the heat cranked up to "sauna" but it felt great after being outside in just a shirt. Meaghan looked like she was thawing out. Unfortunately, so was her hoodie. It was more than a little fragrant.

"When did you leave... that place?" I asked.

"Two days ago, give or take."

The poor kid must have been out on the street all that time. "No offense, but you kind of look like it. Would you like a shower?" She met my Good Samaritan suggestion with a suspicious sneer. "Seriously. Just take a hot shower and we'll wash these for you. I'm not going to try anything. I know your old man, and he knows where I live." That at least earned me a sort-of laugh.

Maybe it was the heat, or wondering what to do now that she had me face to face. Maybe whatever was in her bloodstream was wearing off, but she suddenly looked exhausted. "Okay, yeah," she said.

I handed her a pair of sweatpants and a Led Zeppelin t-shirt.

"Zeppelin? Seriously. How old are you?"

There was a reason they call it classic rock, but this wasn't the time for a musical debate. "Don't be a bi—brat. Go clean up, you'll feel better."

As soon as the bathroom door clicked, I grabbed my phone and dialed a number I knew by heart.

A familiar Irish brogue said, "O'Rourke."

"Mister O'Rourke. It's me, Johnny Lupul."

The pause on the other end was longer than it should have been. "She's gone again."

"I know. That's why I'm calling. She's with me."

"You? What the Christ are you trying to pull?"

"Hey, hold on. I'm not pulling anything. I found her hanging around in front of my place. You're the one that lost her. I'm just letting you know she's safe." I would never have spoken to him like that if I was standing in front of him, but I wasn't. I let myself be salty. I was a grown-ass man, not his gofer anymore.

"You want more money, is that it?"

Asshole fathers were kind of my specialty, and I snapped at him. "Goddammit, this isn't about money. I just thought you'd want to know your daughter is safe is all. I'll keep an eye on her. No charge. Just thought you'd want to know."

"She's okay?"

"She's fine."

"Is she using again?"

"She's fine. I'll keep you posted. Just thought you should know."

"Yeah, okay." The line went dead. Two thank you's from this guy in the same lifetime was probably too much to ask for.

The door at the top of the stairs opened, and Gramma's voice barked down. "Kettle's on. Bring the girl when she's decent."

It was downright creepy how she always seemed to know when to put on the teakettle, but it was about the seventeenth least creepy thing that had happened today.

"Be right up."

CHAPTER 16

With wet hair, and in my t-shirt and sweatpants, Meaghan somehow looked even younger than her twenty-one years. She looked almost clear-eyed and a lot warmer than when she stepped into the shower.

"You don't have anything smaller?" she asked. Apparently, the inability to express gratitude was genetic with the O'Rourkes. Baby steps.

"Hungry?" I asked. She looked around for signs I'd prepared food down in my cave but I just pointed to the ceiling. "Upstairs. We've been summoned."

"No, I can't. Like this?"

"She's seen worse, and you really don't want to argue with her."

A grumpy female voice grumbled down the stairs. "Get your carcasses up here. Tastes lousy when it's cold."

"See?"

When we entered the upstairs kitchen, Bill sat at the table and Gramma was fussing over something on the stove that smelled of onions and Central Europe. She didn't say a word when we came in, just turned and gave me the once-over, then studied Meaghan for a long time.

"Meaghan, this is Bill. And Mrs. Mostoy." The girl nodded and looked down at the floor like she wanted it to open up and swallow her whole.

"Gramma'll do. Call me Gramma, honey."

I felt a stupid twinge of jealousy and looked over at Bill, who was outright miffed. Gramma wasn't a title most mortals were permitted to use. But her house, her rules. "Gramma, this is Meaghan O'Rourke. Her father is... a client of mine."

That information didn't interest the old lady because she turned back to the stove and stirred the onions and *pirogo*—Romanian pierogies—in a cast-iron skillet. When she was sure they were charred into submission, she slapped the wooden spoon in her hand and walked up to Meaghan, inspecting her like so much sausage at the butchers.

The girl couldn't look her in the eye. That earned her a "tsk, tsk," from the older woman. She then took Meaghan's chin and lifted it so she could look in those eyes. "What have you been taking?"

I expected her to lie, and I'm sure Meaghan thought about it but was straight enough to figure out that wasn't a good idea. "Oxy. Mostly."

Gramma nodded. "You need tea." She went to the cupboard above the stove where she kept half a dozen white tins of dried something that she called tea but tasted like the underside of a Chevy. As she reached up, Meaghan asked, "Do you have Earl Grey?"

"English piss-water. Trust me, I know what you need. A cup of this and some of my *pirogo*, and you'll be good as new. It'll put hair on your chest. Look what it did for this one." She pointed at me and laughed.

Out of the corner of my mouth I told the kid, "Don't argue. Better men have tried and never been heard from again."

She let out a teen-aged giggle and then said, "That'll be fine, thank you." So it was only me these people couldn't be polite to. Or maybe under all that attitude was a nice suburban Irish girl trying to get out.

Gramma took down a cannister next to the normal tea and spooned it into a pot, saying nothing. She had about half a dozen different blends going at any time, so I didn't think anything of it.

After some food and inconsequential conversation came the inquisition. Yes, Meaghan had known me since she was about ten. No, we hadn't kept in touch, although we met by accident about ten days ago. It impressed me. She might be shy and half-stoned, but the kid was an expert at the non-committal answers that kept adults off her back. No, her father didn't know where she was.

I opened my big yap to correct her. "Yeah, he kinda does." That earned me a look from both Meaghan and Gramma that peeled three layers of skin from my hide.

"Nobody likes a rat," Gramma growled.

I held my hands up in innocence. "It's okay, he knows you're safe is all. Told him I'd take care of you." *Whatever the hell that means, but let's burn one bridge at a time.*

Gramma resumed the inquiry. "What about your mom, she in the picture?"

Meaghan shrugged. "Sort of. She sits on her ass drinking wine and does whatever daddy says."

The old woman pursed her thin lips and squinted. "Isn't that what wives do? Support their husband?"

"Not if her husband is an asshole."

For a small girl, Meaghan packed away an awful lot of dumplings. I wondered if she'd eaten since leaving rehab. Junkie priorities.

Gramma slapped Bill on the arm. "Make yourself useful and clean the table, will you? Both of you. We girls have a few things to talk about." She took Meaghan's fingers, nails gnawed to the quick, in her hand and scanned the girl's face for a moment while my buddy and I hopped to our task. As long as that wooden spoon was within swinging distance, you obeyed.

Over the sound of running water, Bill tried talking to me, but I was occupied eavesdropping on the women. Being at my low-cycle lowest, it wasn't as easy as it should have been, and my friend wouldn't stop whining and whispering in my other ear.

"What do you mean you'll take care of her? What does that even mean? I don't want some junkie skank in my... our... house."

"Hey. I'll figure it out I had to say something, didn't I? And she's not a skank. She's just a kid."

He wrinkled his nose, and his eyes darted from me to the table and back. "You're not..."

"Jesus, no. She's what, ten years younger than me? And you know I haven't... don't... you know."

"It's way past time you examined that policy, but maybe don't start with this one. Still, cleaned up, she's kind of a cutie-patootey. Looks adorable in your shirt. Seriously, though, dude. Zeppelin?"

"When did everyone start hating on Led Zeppelin? At least it's not Iron Maiden. Look, maybe I'll take the spare room up here tonight and let her sleep down in my place."

The look he gave me withered my balls. "Dude, you're gonna let an addict you just met have your place all to herself?" When he put it that way, it didn't seem like such a good plan. "It's fine. If we have to, she can sleep here. For tonight. Gramma never sleeps anyway, she can keep watch. She seems to like the kid."

Judging from body language, whatever was under discussion at the table reached some kind of conclusion. Meaghan nodded compliantly and Gramma sat up straight and yelled over her shoulder, "Billy, get me my ball. The good one."

Really? The old girl's going to do a psychic reading on her? I'd watched her work over clients a hundred times. She was good, as were generations of Mostoy women before her but at the end of the day it was still a con and for the life of me I couldn't figure out why she'd bother with Meaghan. The kid not only had no money but wasn't in any shape to be psychologically manipulated. Usually, the old lady had more compassion than that.

I wanted to say something, but she didn't even look my way. Gramma just held up a wrinkled palm in the universal, "Shut your yap" gesture. I shut my yap. Bill scurried off to her room and brought back her crystal ball. It was no easy task carrying it while walking with a crutch. It was nearly the size of a bowling ball on a glossy black onyx base and heavy as hell. No doubt it impressed her rich customers.

"Not that one, dumbass. The good one. The *real* one."

"Sorry." He bit his bottom lip, pulled an awkward U-turn and came back a moment later with a different object. This was smaller, about softball-sized. The base was green wood, peeling and ancient. She never used this one with company.

Gramma's face softened as she took it from him. She placed the ball reverently on the table between her and Meaghan, giving it a quick polish with a napkin. Bill excused himself and clop-clopped off to his room, but not before dimming the kitchen lights. He knew the routine and was always embarrassed by his grandmother's act. I wasn't sure if it was the stereotype of the Gypsy fortuneteller her found offensive, or the outright fraud being committed. I found it fascinating, but then I had a higher threshold for larceny than Bill, the upstanding citizen.

I pulled a chair out to sit beside Meaghan, but Gramma gestured to a corner behind her. "Stand over there." Something in the way she said it reminded me of Cromwell's insisting I not get too close to the bowl, but this was different. Despite the bowl being legit, this crystal ball was definitely a fake. I moved where I was told, though.

I leaned against the sink, out of her eye line but where I could keep tabs on the proceedings. Meaghan was my client. Client-in-law. Something. I felt the need to protect her. Also, if Neil O'Rourke found out she'd been ripped off in any way—nothing good would come from that.

I was familiar with the routine. Fortune tellings, spiritual readings, whatever you want to call them were basically a hustle that anyone with an attention to detail and the ability to keep a straight face could pull off to some degree.

First came the instructions. Step one is to put the sucker at ease and eliminate distractions.

I could almost mouth the words as she smiled at Meaghan and said, "Okay, dear. Comfortable? Just take a nice deep breath. That's a girl. Put your hands wherever you'd like, but on the table is best. Like that. Perfect."

Then she'd start fishing for what the sucker wanted to know most. That way they were more likely to give away important information.

"So, now I want you to relax and think about what is most important to you. Your future, your love life, anything that's bothering you right now."

Meaghan nodded but said nothing. Silence pisses off a fortune teller to no end, but Gramma showed signs of nothing but uncharacteristic patience. There are other ways to the data she needs, and this old Gypsy was a genius at uncovering what she needed to know.

"You're seeking answers..."

Duh. Who wasn't? But again, Meaghan gave nothing away.

"You're worried about your future. You wonder what's in store for you."

I managed not to roll my eyes. She was on the streets with no money, a drug habit, and no home to go back to. Odds were good she had a few concerns. This time the girl bit her lip and nodded her head slightly. She leaned forward. I could see her getting sucked into the con and it made me angry, but I bit my tongue and let it play out.

There should have been more questions. "How's your love life? I see the letter J..." although if it were me, I'd use "O" for O'Rourke since she blamed her old man for most of her problems. Instead, Gramma just nodded and closed her eyes, waving her hands slowly over the glass sphere and not saying anything. It was a hell of a show, though not much of a soundtrack.

When it seemed the old fraud had fallen asleep, her eyes flew open and she let out a long, loud gasp. "I see blue skies. Your future will be bright."

And we were back to the regular program. Now came the conditions. No doubt she'd tell Meaghan she had to get clean for real and reconcile with her family. This was a lot of trouble to tell the kid something I'd said two hours ago. Maybe I should take up crystal balls. Of course, I said the same thing about Cromwell's scrying bowl. I kept my trap shut and stayed a spectator.

"Before then, there's a trial coming..."

Meaghan was buying the whole damned thing. She practically leaned across the table, her eyes darting from the ball to the old lady and back. Gramma's face changed. At first, the crow's feet deepened and darkened as she made a show of concentrating harder. Then as she leaned into the ball so their foreheads nearly touched, her wrinkly face became a mask of confusion.

Gramma's face morphed from befuddled to something I'd never seen on her in all these years. Fear. Almost panic. She was sweating, and her voice dropped to a whisper.

"There's a danger... I've never... Christ, that's..."

Meaghan's fear increased proportionately. "What is it? What do you see?"

"A black cloud... I've never seen anything so dark... and evil..."

That was too far. It was time to end the charade. "Come on, that's enough. You're scaring her."

Without tearing her eyes from the ball, she snapped, "She should be fucking scared. I've never felt anything like this."

The kid was shaking and near tears. "But you said blue skies. That my future was bright."

"If you get past this cloud, it is, child. But it's hazy. You might not make it through..."

Meaghan's voice went up an octave, and she nearly shrieked, "When? What is it?"

After what happened this morning, I knew better than to get close to them, so I stood by, useless. Gramma's head cocked to one side.

"Two, three weeks. If you make it past that..."

I'd heard enough. "What do you mean *if?* Knock it off. Stop it."

She either couldn't hear me or didn't want the interruption. She kept squinting into the depths of that damned glass ball. Her old hands shook.

Meaghan stood and slapped her hands on the table. "What is it? What's so fucking dangerous? What am I supposed to watch out for?"

"I don't know. It's out of your control, mostly. There's someone else..."

"Who?" Meaghan demanded. She was sweating and terrified. She kept looking uselessly into the glass, trying to see whatever had scared the crap out of Gramma.

The old woman, though, turned her head and looked directly at me with her eyes blazing and her breath coming ragged gasps. She raised an accusatory finger and said a single word in a deep growl.

"Him."

"What the hell did I do? What are you talking about, you crazy old bat?"

Gramma glared at me with a stranger's eyes for a moment longer, then shook herself like you do after bumping your head. She took Meaghan's hand, stroking the fingers slowly. "Shhhh, shhhh, honey."

We both peppered her with questions, but she motioned for us to shut the hell up for a minute so she could get her bearings.

At last, she seemed back to normal. "Okay, here's what I know. Meaghan, you have a trial coming. I don't know what it is exactly, but you need to be strong. Really, really strong. And you'll have help, but you need to keep it together. Can you do that?"

"I think so. But..."

Gramma's eyes had already turned my way. "And you... you're the cause." She saw the confusion on my mug. "You're not the evil, kid, but it is hanging all over you, like a fog, and it will be up to you to help this woman. If you're up to the task, her future is bright."

"And if I'm not?"

"Meaghan, you've had a rough night. You look like you could use some sleep. Take the spare room down the hall. I need to talk to Johnny for a bit."

The girl calmed down enough to take offense. "You can't just..."

"Bed. Now."

"But it's not even ten-thirty" she whined. She was probably just getting out of bed about now most night. Addicts are nocturnal creatures by nature.

"Believe me. With that much tea in you, you'll sleep like a rock."

Meaghan thought about arguing further, but yawned instead. She stomped off in search of the spare room, saving an extra dirty look for me. I followed, but a harsh voice stopped me dead in my tracks.

"You. Sit."

I sat.

CHAPTER 17

It felt like forever before she finally broke the silence. It took a lot of willpower not to slouch into my patented, world-famous, teenage punk in trouble pose. It wouldn't have mattered. It never worked on her, anyway. Eventually, the interrogation started.

"What the holy hell is going on with you?"

"What do you mean? I told you..."

"Knock it off. You can't bullshit a bullshitter, Johnny. Who is she, and what is she to you?"

"She's just a client's daughter..." Those raptor's eyes of hers pried the rest out of me. "She's Neil O'Rourke's kid."

"He's this big hot-shot client? I thought you quit working for that mick scumbag years ago."

"He's one of my clients. We—I—have a couple now." I told her a cleaned-up version of Meaghan's kidnapping by the Russians, and me helping get her out of there. I may have played up the fact that her old man paid me a lot of money, which earned me a nod of approval. I definitely forgot to mention my methods or Shaggy's assistance.

"Go on."

That led to a brief discussion about Cromwell, being on retainer, and recovering stolen property. "It's a lot of money, but it's all legal. I swear."

She shrugged. "Legal, I don't care so much. Is it dangerous?"

"A little," I admitted.

She studied me for a second, then bit her lip and shook her head. "Nope. That's not it. What aren't you telling me?"

Do you want that alphabetically or chronologically?

She pushed herself to her feet, wobbling a bit before steadying herself against the corner of the table. "I need a cup of tea. Want one?"

"No. Thank you."

She chuckled. "It's just tea, kiddo. You look like you could use some. I know I can."

This time she reached for the normal canister and pulled out a regular tea bag, so I relented. As she puttered, I put the time to good use preparing my defense.

The mug of steaming tea landed in front of me with a *plunk*. Gramma eased herself back into her chair and crossed her arms across her bird-like chest. "So? Give me the bad news."

"So, nothing. I've told you. I don't know what this black cloud thing is. Why don't you do your gypsy magic eight ball juju on me?" It had been a hellacious day and my whole body yearned for sleep.

"Do you think I haven't tried?" I blinked at her stupidly. "It doesn't work on you, Johnny. The Other World doesn't show you clearly. It's like—"

"A mirror, looking in a mirror, looking in a mirror?"

A flash of surprise and a twitch of fear crossed her face. After an awkward pause, she said, "Something like that. Yes. How do you know?"

"My other client, Mister Cromwell, tried demonstrating a crying bowl..."

She looked confused for a moment. "Oh. Scrying bowl. He had one? What happened?" She leaned across the table.

"It didn't go well." This conversation needed to end as soon as possible, but she was like a dog with a sock.

"And her?" She jerked her head towards the spare bedroom. "It's okay. She will sleep like a rock."

"I don't know. She just showed up."

"Nobody just shows up. Things happen as they're meant to happen. You and her, you're not... you could do worse."

Than a twenty-one-year-old junkie with major daddy issues? No thanks.

"Christ, no. I mean, she's ten years younger than me for starters."

She gave me an evil grin over her teacup. "Doesn't mean much. Some of my best times were with guys ten or fifteen..."

"Ewww, Gramma. Don't."

"You're no damn fun. But at some point, you'll eventually have to share your life with someone, kid. And I don't mean me and Bill. I mean a woman. Not for nothing, but that one's stronger than she looks."

"No. I can't. I can't ever be with anyone that way. You don't know…"

Those thin, brittle looking fingers tightened on mine. Her voice lost some of her edge. "Try me."

"I can't trust myself with… remember my senior year?"

"That's when your folks… you came to stay with us for a bit. All's I know is there was trouble with a girl"

Trouble. Understatement of the year. "Becky Robinson."

She was my prom date. The theme was "Full Moon Fever," which was more than a Tom Petty album. It was also, as fate would have it, the stage of the lunar cycle when I least needed my hormones in an uproar. She was way out of my league; smart and funny and dressed like a hot nerd. To me, she was an angel in that resale store dress with the slit.

"What happened, Johnny?" Gramma was using her fortune-teller voice on me, and I found myself wanting to spill my guts.

I hadn't ever told anyone but Bill. I didn't trust anyone else, and I wasn't exactly eloquent. The words kaleidoscoped in my brain before I could spit them out. "It was prom night, you know? We even got a motel room. For after."

Becky was radiant and smelled of dance-induced sweat, Charming Charlie perfume, and her desire. She wanted me. In my high-cycle haze, her pheromones filled my brain, and I wanted her, too. Just thinking about it, I wanted her even then. She made me feel whole, like there was nothing wrong with me despite school psychologists and messed-up parents.

But I wasn't alone in that room. Shaggy sensed her and wanted to come out and play.

I was only eighteen, and inexperienced both with girls and my condition. Being horny only made it worse. I swore to everyone I'd blacked out, but the ugly truth was I remembered every single, horrible minute of that night.

She was all over me. We'd decided this would be "the night," and she was at least as eager as me, which was saying something. There was a lot of bad-intentioned kissing and groping. Her mouth was hot and tasted like spearmint. I felt like Superman or something. She loved me, and if that's what it was, it went both ways. My senses were overloaded with her scent, her touch, the musical tone of her moaning when we kissed. It was clear she wanted me. The feeling was more than mutual.

I would gladly have sat there just remembering that first part and how excited and thrilled we were, but Gramma's voice drifted across the table. She snapped her fingers twice to get my attention. "So, what really happened that night?"

Shaggy happened.

There was no way to explain that to someone who didn't know first-hand. Maybe it was when Becky playfully bit my neck or the feel of her gel-tips digging into my back, but it became harder and harder to stay... me. Even now I can feel the flashes of heat. The scents intensified until suddenly I saw the world through Shaggy's eyes. It was like I was drowning. Each time I'd go away and then fight my way back. I didn't want to be anywhere but with her. But Shaggy was running the show.

I saw and heard it all. A button popped off her dress. A soft, "ow" as I bit too hard on a perfect, coral-colored nipple. Then, like from a thousand miles away, the cries of "Stop it." And, "Don't." Shaggy never completely burst out, but she saw him in my eyes, and the hand on her chest grew dark and hairy before I could control it.

I watched her face go from adoring to curiosity. Suddenly her eyes widened. Curiosity turned to betrayal. A second later it was horror.

That's when the screaming started.

"She wanted to stop, and I... I couldn't." *Shaggy couldn't. Same thing.*

"Becky was yelling. I tried to calm her, but the thing inside me wouldn't let me speak. I jumped off the bed, hoping that would get her to stop, you know? I didn't want to hurt her. I loved her, I guess. I tried to tell her."

The noises that came out of me only made it worse, and the look in her eyes ripped my guts out. I grappled with Shaggy for control. Harder than I ever had. When at last I could see through my own eyes, I wished I hadn't. By the time I was fully in charge, her dress was in tatters, and there was an ugly bruise on her arm. It could have been so much worse, had it gone farther. At least I hadn't...

Still, I wanted to curl up and die.

I kept puking my story up to Gramma. "Thank god, someone banged on the door and..."

Maybe it was the logical result of everything that happened that day, but the dam burst. I blubbered as I spoke, pulling my hand from hers to wipe my nose across my sleeve. Then I stared through streaming eyes out the kitchen window, wishing I could forget.

Instead, it all came back in a wave. The manager broke in. Cops showed up, the threat of charges and jail—turning eighteen wasn't such a blessing after all—and burning shame. The betrayal in her blue eyes was the worst of all.

"You stopped before something terrible—more terrible—happened," Gramma said, stroking my hand but unable to look at me. "You were just a kid."

No. I was something far worse. Fortunately, her prick lawyer father was more concerned with his reputation than her purity. When they found out, she'd used his credit card to pay for the room, the whole thing went away. At least officially. My parents kicked me out until my mom Eileen's pleading allowed me back in the house, but never all the way back in the McPherson's good graces.

She patted my hand. "What happened to the girl?"

"She's good. Last I heard, she became some kind of therapist. Probably from going through so much herself, you know? She's helping people in crisis." At least something good had come out of it.

Since then, dating wasn't really a thing for me. It's not like I hadn't been with anyone, I was at least *that* normal. But never in the weeks before and just after a full moon, and rarely with anyone I ever cared to see again. It was better than nothing. Sort of. It was better they just thought I was a dick, instead of something much, much darker and awful.

"There's a darkness in you, Johnny. I know that. Always have. But—" she took my chin in her fingers and turned me to face her. "I've never known anyone who fought that darkness as hard as you. You're a good man. Someone will learn that."

"No. I'm not." I wanted to be. So much that there were times I thought it better to disappear forever. Even die. Anything was better than stay whatever in hell's name I was.

"You are. But there's something else, too. Evil follows you. This black cloud of anger and hate and..." her eyes suddenly narrowed. "It's not you. There's another out there, isn't there? Like you?"

Nodding shook the tears loose from my eyes onto the table. "I think so."

She jerked her hand away, muttering something under her breath in Romani, and spit on the ground. "And you're responsible?"

There was no acceptable response. I let out a sob and dropped my head to the table. Briny tears scalded my eyes. "I didn't want to. You don't know."

She spat, pulled down her eyelid and swore again. "I do know. My people have known things like this for a long, long time. Most of them don't remember. Hell, they don't want to. Too busy being respectable. American. Like Bill's father and gorger mother."

She pulled her hand away and pointed her finger at my face. "They make fun of me because I keep the old ways. I know this is all—well, you don't believe it. But you're not as smart as you think you are, and it's finally catching up to you. I was prepared to keep your secret as long as it was just you involved. Because of Bill. But this other thing that's out there now... You've created something only you can deal with. I love you, kid, but you can't spread this darkness. It's evil. It has to stop with you."

I scrambled to reassure her. "It's okay, really. This guy—Kozlov. He doesn't know who I am or where... and I'm sure he doesn't know about Meaghan." I thought of frightened eyes poking out of a little girl's blanket, and the waking nightmare Jerry and the missing Alice were living through only a few miles away. This was all on me.

Her eyes locked mine in a tractor-beam and she whispered, "You're a good man, kiddo. But I can't help you with this. No one can. You need to handle it yourself. Like a man — undo whatever it is you've done. Because I will not let it, or you, be a threat to that girl. Or to Bill. Or me. Understand?"

Hell no. I don't understand at all.

But I nodded anyway.

CHAPTER 18

14 days past full. New moon.

The lowest day of the cycle wasn't prime meeting-with-a-client time, but I needed to talk to Cromwell about what I'd found in Berwyn and give him a valid reason for not retrieving the Anubis Disk yet.

Nurse Ball answered the door and didn't even bother to greet me. She just turned her back and waved me in. "This really isn't a good day for this," she said over her shoulder.

The way I felt, it wasn't a good day for anything except a fetal position and maybe a little day drinking, but that's why they call it work. "What's wrong?"

She stopped at the door to his office and dropped her voice. Her face was pale, and the sharp edges of her face looked fleshy, and her eyes were puffy like she hadn't slept. Her normally severe bun was sloppy, and dark locks of hair flew around her as she walked. She'd chosen a normal bra today, making her breasts look less like howitzer shells and more like normal boobs. I couldn't help thinking a bit of humanity, along with what I knew about her hosiery, made her seem somehow sexy. I was on my low-cycle. Sue me.

I shook off the thought like a dog in a bathtub. Maybe Gramma was right about my need to blow off some hormones before it got me into trouble.

"He's not been the same since the other day. And he's having a bad time with his treatments. I told him he shouldn't see you today, but he insisted." From the way she scrunched those eyebrows, it was clear she didn't lose these arguments often.

"He's the boss, right?"

"Something like that. But he's still my patient. Try not to blow anything up today, alright?"

In stark contrast to the other day, Cromwell was still in his bathrobe. He had a blanket wrapped tightly around him, and his bare feet with their gnarly toenails hung over the edge of the bed. He was in too much pain to fake pleasantries. We just nodded to each other while Florence Nightingale checked the settings on the dialysis machine.

It was clear he wanted to talk but didn't want his medical pit-bull overhearing. It was equally obvious she had no intention of leaving until she'd done her job. I watched in uncomfortable silence as she exposed his skinny arm. The loose skin was a mottled blue, green, and purple. There was a huge bump about an inch and a half long in the bend of his elbow.

She looked over her shoulder to me. "Are you squeamish at all? Afraid of needles? This isn't pretty."

"No, I'm good." Life would be a special kind of joke for a werewolf to be afraid of blood. Smells and loud noises got to me, even at my lowest ebb like today. The rest was easy. I watched her inject and then remove three plastic tubes from what she called the fistula and gently dab the spot with alcohol, then lay gauze there and fold his arm over it.

"Lay back now," she said gently. Hard to believe this was the same scary lady from the other room.

The old man waved her off. "I'm fine. Leave us." She almost bit her bottom lip off trying not to snap at him and settled for glaring at me instead. Nurse Ball briskly picked up the needles and dropped them in a plastic sharps case.

"I'm right outside if you need anything, sir." Her eyes added a warning to me that I understood but wasn't sure I could heed.

Once the door clicked shut, Cromwell motioned impatiently for me to get on with it. "Berwyn. Was that you?"

"No. I was at Nasrallah's place on Monday when the second attack happened. And the first..."

"Who was it then? Is there—another like you—out there?"

The answer was a long time coming. "I think so, yeah." The impatient grimace on his face meant he didn't need to ask the obvious question. "It's one of the guys who took Meaghan O'Rourke. I thought I'd killed him, but—"

The old man shivered under his blanket and looked for a moment like might puke, but after a tense second, he relaxed again. A long, jagged breath helped him regain his state of mind.

"Let me make sure I have this. You can pass your talent on to others. Like in the legends. That's worthy of additional study, don't you think?"

Was he crazy? No, it wasn't interesting. And it sure as hell wasn't anything I wanted to study closer. It had never happened to me before, and I prayed it wouldn't again. I wished I could forget the whole thing, except my mistake was out there somewhere hurting people and I didn't know how to find him.

I'd never had to explain this to another person before. "In most cases..."

"Such as yours, I gather..."

"Yeah, it's genetic. I was born this way. It's not something you have a choice in," not that Jim or Eileen McPherson ever wrapped their minds around the fact or cut me any slack. "But the others... most don't make it past the first bite. It's awful. Usually fatal." *Frigging South Dakota.* I tried not to let the images of all those bodies distract me.

"You have to be tough as hell to survive, and it makes you crazy in the process. I think Kozlov lived and escaped the hospital, but he's... I don't know. Insane, now. Can't control himself."

Cromwell grinned. "So, it's transferrable."

That wasn't the important part of my speech, but yeah, you crazy old bastard. I can pass it on. Like syphilis with teeth.

He made a quick grab for a teal-blue kidney dish beside him and slid it into his lap. He apologized with his eyes, and then gently retched into it. Nothing came out but a single long, sad strand of saliva. I jumped to help him, but he waved me away. After a few seconds, his eyes widened, and he dry-heaved again, this time loud enough to alert the sentry.

Nurse Ball marched in and elbowed me aside in her rush to check on him.

"What's happening?" I asked.

She ran a palm across his forehead and checked his wrist, then said, "His treatment was harder on him than normal."

Cromwell groaned. "I'm fine, you worry too much."

"You're not. And you are in no condition to deal with..." her head bobbed in my direction.

He wrapped his blanket around himself like a pouting toddler. "I said I'm fine, goddam you." Then he belched and his stomach spasmed again until he couldn't breathe.

She rubbed his back until the air refilled his lungs and he assumed some of his normal pissy attitude. "And my Anubis Disk? Are you any closer to getting it back?"

It was impressive how he could obsess about things and barf at the same time. "I'm sure it's still in Nasrallah's house. As I said, we either have to get me in there without breaking and entering or get him to bring it out and we'll take it from him then." A little strong-arming didn't offend my moral sensibilities like burglary did.

"Any ideas Mister hot-shot location and recovery expert?" Given the circumstances, his snarkiness was understandable.

"Actually, yes, but it will take a day or two to set up."

"Which he'll tell you about another time." The nurse pointed to the door. Neither the sick old man nor I were up to an argument. "Out."

I complied and waited until she closed the doors behind her and joined me in the main room. "I thought I told you not to upset him. What was that about?"

"Back off, lady. He's my client. If he wants you to know, he'll tell you." My head ached, my energy was zero, and I'd taken all the attitude from her I planned to.

She literally backed off a step and looked like she'd love to claw my eyes out. "He's my patient. And it's my job to keep him alive. For as long as I can, at least."

So, it was as bad as it looked. "Is he going to be okay? I know nothing about dialysis, but that means a kidney transplant, right? Don't rich people go to the front of the line for those?"

"Normally, but his condition is rare. An operation would probably kill him. That's why he's so obsessed with all this occult nonsense. Trying to cheat death, like that crap will make him immortal or something. You have something he wants, too. I just can't figure out what it is."

So what, it's transferrable. Surely he doesn't think if I turned him he'd ask nicely. No. Hell no. "I don't either. I'm just a hired hand."

A strange look passed over her, and her shoulders slumped. "I get it. You look like crap. When was the last time you slept?" A professionally cool hand rested on my forehead and she tilted my head down to meet her eyes. I shook her off. It was just a low-cycle funk.

"I'm fine. I'll be good in a week or two."

The cool skin of her palm felt good against my face. "Why is he so interested in you, Johnny?"

I removed her hand and stepped back. "I don't know. I swear. I just want to get him his stupid disk... thing back."

Nurse Ball crossed her arms and scanned me head to toe, tapping her foot. Then she cocked her head to one side. "Two weeks ago, you were amped up, ready to crawl out of your skin. I thought maybe you were tweaking. Now your ass is dragging, and you're telling me you'll be fine in a week. This happens all the time, doesn't it?"

Words weren't necessary. She placed two frigid fingertips to my throat and kept talking. "Two weeks ago was the seventeenth. The next full moon is in what, two weeks?"

Fifteen days, but who's counting? I could feel the pulse in her fingers as a counterpoint to my own. She glanced at her wristwatch.

"Your pulse is so slow, how are you even walking around?"

"I'm fine." I wanted to slap her hand away, but her gaze pinned me down like a hawk with a rabbit.

"I've seen this before. Physical activity impacted by lunar cycles."

"You have?"

"I was an emergency room nurse for twenty years. I've seen a lot of crazy things."

I tried not to look spooked and stepped away, suddenly intrigued by one of the paintings on the wall over her shoulder. "They say that's just a myth, that emergency rooms go crazy on the full moon. I read it in like National Geographic or something."

"The number of incidents doesn't change, which is what they measure. The level of crazy, though, it's harder to quantify but goes through the roof. Believe me." She mistook the panic in my eye for disbelief. "Relax. I'm not talking werewolves and shit. This is the real world, no matter what Cromwell tries to tell you. But hormone and adrenaline levels are measurable. I'll bet you bounce off the walls when the tide is high, don't you?"

I needed to end this conversation, and the urge to just run was strong. She was relentless. "They loaded you on Ritalin in high school, right? How'd that work?"

Like a freaking charm. That's why I'm so well-adjusted, you nosey bitch. "You're his nurse. Not mine. I'm just here to get that thingamajig and get paid."

"You're already on the payroll. He's a hard man to get fired from. I've tried."

She stepped over the coffee table where a squirt jar of hand sanitizer hid inside a fancy container. Taking two healthy pumps, she rubbed her hands together. "Can you do it? Get it back? Worrying isn't going to help him heal. Don't jerk him around."

"I'm not. Honestly. I can do it. I just need them to bring it out to me or I need to get inside that house, but I'm not a burglar. It needs to be done legally. Or at least close enough."

She chuckled. "Like a vampire? You need to get asked inside?" I wondered if she could see the hair on my arms jump to attention when she said that. The woman knew nothing about me or what I was, so it had to be just an expression. Even Cromwell was still only making educated—but frighteningly accurate—guesses.

I laughed her off. "Something like that, yeah. Hey, when he's feeling better, I could use his help with something. It's how to get into the Egyptian's place."

"Not if it's dangerous."

I assured her it was just a phone call, but coming from him it would have more impact than if I did it myself. Any danger was to me, but I wasn't her concern.

Her eyes rolled, and she crossed her arms across that chest of hers, tapping her ugly soft-soled white shoe. "What do you need?"

"Does he know anyone at Homeland Security?"

CHAPTER 19

12 days to the full moon- waxing crescent.

After a few days of calling around, it seemed Cromwell's best contact wasn't at Homeland, but the Centers for Disease Control, which explained why I stood in the middle of Bill's kitchen in a full-blown regulation hazmat suit. In true Chicago fashion, my buddy had a guy who had a guy who, in turn, knew a costume guy for one of the tv shows that filmed here. Two phone calls, a bottle of Glenlivet, and a drive to a warehouse on the Southside, and here I was walking an imaginary runway.

"Not bad. Can you breathe in that thing?" Bill asked.

I could, but visibility was iffy, and things would get awfully sticky— literally. Good thing it was November instead of August. Those damned suits were way heavier than they look on television.

In two days, we'd drop a dime on Nasrallah. If I played my cards right, I'd sneak in with all the other responders, just another scary-looking yellow blob trying to save the world from death and disease.

On the table sat a metal camera case covered in brand new hazmat decals. I'd put the disk in there once I found it and waltz out.

Cromwell, the devious old bastard, saved me from myself. The original plan, if you can call it that, was to call Homeland Security or Immigration. A rich Egyptian would make a lovely target for the anti-terrorist types, and I could rush in with the raiding team. But there would be way too many guns involved. Plus, getting caught impersonating an ICE agent would be a net negative for my personal liberty situation. A couple of calls set me up with a timetable, a close-enough-to-official CDC name badge, and the name of a lawyer—untraceable back to him—in case things went pear-shaped. Teamwork makes the dream work.

"You look like a giant Minion. Real heroic." Meaghan O'Rourke's bratty voice chimed in.

The blonde sat at the kitchen table across from Gramma for the second night in a row, a brand-new deck of tarot cards spread out between them.

"Pay attention, kid. Now, what card did I turn up?" Gramma asked.

Watching thought the foggy plastic face-shield, it was difficult to determine what was going on, but it looked like the old Gypsy was teaching the younger girl how to read fortunes.

Meaghan groaned. "Fine. The Fool. So what, that makes me an idiot?"

"I didn't say a word," Bill sniped from the other side of the kitchen. His distaste for the girl's presence was palpable, and his grandmother's mysterious affection for her didn't help his mood.

The old woman pointed a bony finger at her grandson. "You shut up. You..." she said to Meaghan, "pay attention. Depending on the mark, the Fool either means a traveler or someone who doesn't know they're in danger. See how he's carrying a pack and looks like he's about to step off a cliff? You say something like, 'you're going on a trip,' and if they are it blows their mind."

"What if they're not, though?"

Gramma's face lit up. "That's the good part. If they say they're not, then it means they're just naïve and ignorant of coming danger. You either know something they don't think you should, or you're warning them of danger ahead. Either way, they begin believing in you. Because they want to."

"Nice, teaching her to commit fraud," Bill was getting pissy like he always did when his grandmother did her Mysterious Gypsy act. He never even used the "G" word if he could help it. His family were Roma, and that's the only word he used.

"For your information, smart-ass, it's only fraud if you tell them something that you know to be untrue. You get them to fill in the blanks for you. Our family has done it for two hundred years, in case you've forgotten, and it's not as if cooking the books for fat bankers is any better come to Judgement Day. Oh, and it's not against the law to sell a little hope. There are worse things a girl alone on the streets can peddle."

"Like drugs?" Meaghan's post-adolescence snottiness flared up.

"Drugs. Or that bony ass of yours. It's your choice—no skin off my nose, girlie. Point is, every woman should have a way to make a friend or raise quick cash in a hurry if she needs it. Next card."

"You'd make more with drugs," Bill muttered. He avoided the dirty look they both gave him and motioned for me to twirl around for one last inspection. I declined, instead pulling the headgear off and wiping my forehead on my sleeve.

"I am guessing you have an actual plan here."

I fished my battered notebook out of my back pocket and flipped to the information I needed. "Thursday morning, we make a call at eight. It'll take about thirty minutes for them to show up with lights flashing, so I need to be there and ready to go an hour before."

"Are you? Ready, I mean."

As ready as I would be. Still, I'd cashed Cromwell's check, and this was the deal. Location without retrieval was kind of pointless.

"Why don't you put that in your phone?" Meaghan looked at my notebook as if she didn't know what they used such an antique for.

"I'll do it later," I lied. That damned phone was way too complicated, and at this point, I'd used it for four texts, a phone call, and to get the Sox score from Oakland because I went to bed before the game was over on the West Coast. It wasn't one of Bill's best investments, though I appreciated his efforts to drag me into the twenty-first century.

"You are so lame. Give it here." The kid held her out expectantly. I complied.

"This is a great phone," she said, as she scrolled and flicked and worked all kinds of black magic with her thumbs, which whirled like chopper blades around the keyboard. Her lip curled like burning paper. "Fuck sake, you don't even have your calendar hooked up. What's your email?"

I told her. More thumb-gymnastics followed. "Cool, you're using Me2." She pointed to the green icon Bill showed me earlier.

Bill perked up. "You know it? I figured he should be able to encrypt his texts."

"Yeah, some of the frat bro dealers are using it. Heavy-duty stuff. Can't break it without a court order and a world-class hacker."

That earned her a grudging, "huh" from my business manager. With a final scroll, Meaghan passed the phone back with a look like she was handing an innocent puppy to a kill shelter.

"Thanks," I said.

Meaghan wrinkled her nose. "You really don't know how to use a smartphone, do you? Are you using, like, any of the apps at all?" She sounded a little less bitchy and more like she cared. It would pass.

Bill snorted. "It's kind of sad, actually. A waste of good technology. Gramma uses more features than he does."

The old lady nodded. "It's how my clients get hold of me for readings. And dating, of course."

Meaghan pretended not to hear her. "But this is such a cool device. It's just a phone, not rocket science or something. God, how do you even wipe your own ass?" She seemed determined to pick a fight tonight, and I wasn't sure why. For two days now, I'd caught her looking at me when she thought I didn't notice. It was creepy as hell.

"He doesn't wipe. I've seen the laundry." Gramma cackled at her own joke, which inspired a round of "ewwwwws" and laughter. It was a sound I hadn't heard in days.

While Bill and Meaghan still circled each other like a cat and a chihuahua, I felt some tension leave my body. Sure, part of it was my lunar cycle being on a slight uptick and my nerves and senses returning to normal. But it was more than that.

Whatever this was, it didn't suck.

CHAPTER 20

11 Days to the full moon- waxing crescent.

When Bill announced about ten o'clock that he was heading out for a while, Gramma and I shared a surprised look but said nothing. This was the second time in a week he'd stepped out about the time he usually went to bed with no explanation. I had my suspicions, and I think she did too, but we long ago reached a tacit agreement never to discuss the subject of her grandson's private life. Not seriously.

Gramma said to Meaghan, "There are clean towels in the bathroom, kiddo." She'd all but moved the young girl into the spare room over her grandson's objections. Nobody asked my opinion.

"Thanks, but it's early yet. Maybe I'll go out for a bit."

"Nice try. You know the deal. If you don't go back to rehab, you can crash here, but it's my house, my rules. I'll make you a nice cup of tea." Whatever was in that brew, and I'd bet my balls and ten bucks it wasn't Lipton, seemed to detox the kid and keep her from climbing the walls at the same time. Then the lady of the house jerked her thumb at me. "Or I can have the stoolie here call your dad to pick you up."

"Jeez, Gramma." I know it was whiny, but I sure as hell didn't enjoy being the hall monitor. O'Rourke kept pestering me for updates, and I was keeping him at arm's length for now. Eventually Meaghan would have to deal with her father issues. Hopefully, before she couldn't. The accident that killed my folks ruined my own chance at a Hallmark moment, so maybe the board tilted a little too much towards her father's side. Regret's a bitch.

Gramma pulled the garbage out from under the sink and twisted it shut. "Here. The cards said you were going on a journey. Start by journeying your lazy ass out to the trash bins."

Meaghan attempted an eye-roll that might have worked in high school. Gramma's eyes turned to granite, and she held the bag out in front of her until the girl took it with a miffed, "Fine."

"And close it behind you. I'm not paying to heat the city of Chicago."

She shrugged on her ever-present red hoody and stomped out the kitchen door to the back deck, carefully closing the door behind her.

Meanwhile, Gramma put a newly filled kettle on the stove and lit the gas. I'd watched this routine a thousand times. Once the flame was set, she turned on the fan like she always did, although it wasn't actually connected to anything. It just blew the air—or if she had a bad cooking day, the smoke—around the kitchen, but it kept the building inspector off her ass.

"It's coming," she said, opening the tea cupboard and looking for Meaghan's special brew.

"What is?"

"It. The darkness. Whatever the hell it is you've dragged that girl into. It's close."

"Did the cards tell you that?"

"No, smartass. The guilty look on your face. He's still out there, isn't he?"

I bit my lower lip and studied the table in front of me. "Yeah, but he doesn't know who I am or where I am, so she's safe for now. Near as I can tell, he's twenty miles away in Berwyn. That's why you're keeping her here, isn't it?"

She pulled down mugs for all of us and put regular tea in mine and hers. "One of the reasons, sure. She also needs guidance. And company. This is no time to be alone, poor thing."

Since the moon was waxing, my senses were on the upswing. From outside I heard the lid being removed, then put back on the garbage can, and voices outside the building. Gramma couldn't hear it. She couldn't hear much at the best of times in the last few months.

"Are you ever going to tell me what happened that night?"

Hell no. The less she knew, the better.

"Too god-damn many secrets around here lately. And you think I'm a stupid old woman who doesn't get it."

"Oh, come on. I don't—"

"Yes, you do. Bill too. He thinks I don't know where his... what he is?" I tried concentrating, but the noise from outside kept distracted me. "Look, he's a good boy and I love him but I'm not holding my breath for great-grandchildren if you know what I mean. It makes him feel better to think I'm just a dotty old broad. I expect that from him. But you..."

I knew the conversation was important, but I couldn't stay focused. Something was happening outside, and it was driving me crazy trying to figure out what it was. There was a noise—a grunt maybe, like someone carrying, then setting something heavy down—and a single footstep on the bottom stair.

"You kids. You think you invented sex, but believe me. I've seen things that would curl your hair, bucko."

Now I had to deal with the noise and an unwanted visual. From outside came the sound of slow, heavy footsteps up the creaking back stairs.

"There was one guy. Everyone thought we were an item, but..."

That's not Meaghan. Or at least not just Meaghan.

"I pretended to be his girlfriend for a while, but we weren't fooling anybody..."

Crap.

That's when the back door flew open. Both Gramma and I jumped as Meaghan stumbled half a dozen steps and landed in a heap on the linoleum. The old lady ran to her with a "What the hell?"

I locked my eyes on the other figure. Framed in the door crouched a squat figure in a ratty old parka, stubbly dark hair on his scalp about the same as on his cheeks. Blood crusted a bright red patch of practically raw, infected-looking meat where his throat met the collarbone, held together by the remnants of hospital stitches. In his filthy hand was a wicked, and familiar, commando knife.

Maxim Kozlov stood in the doorway, panting heavily. As Meaghan and Gramma scuttled across the floor into the corner, I rose slowly to appear as non-threatening as I could. The Russian didn't move a muscle, just braced himself with his free hand in the doorway, wheezing and staring with black holes for eyes. They weren't just dark; they seemed to suck all other light into them. And they were focused on me.

"What the *fook* did you do to me?"

In the corner, Meaghan whimpered and buried her head in the older woman's shoulder. Gramma squatted, breathing deep and slow, her eyes darting everywhere at once like a hawk, saying nothing.

"I didn't..." it was a stupid thing to say, but I had to stall for time until an actual idea occurred to me.

"What did you do to me?" He screamed again, spit flying with every word. Drool coated the whiskers around his mouth and he was sweating despite the cold wind blowing in through the open door. His right wrist twitched, and he held that knife in a firm grip. The grasp he had on the doorjamb was even tighter since it was the only thing holding him up.

My brain scrambled to make sense of the scene. Just a few days into the new moon, I was barely out of my lowest cycle. He should be too. But while I was fully aware yet still sluggish, he seemed to be on high alert. Kozlov was living on a toxic combination of blood poisoning, insanity, and a need for revenge.

Placing my empty hands in front of me, palms out, I spoke as calmly as I could manage. "Look, Kozlov. I know what you're going through."

"What? What am I going through? You tell me." The crazy man tore at his jacket, baring one side of his body. It took a moment to decipher what I was looking at. I tried not to scream.

His arm, all tattoos, and indecipherable symbols in black ink rippled as if a dozen garter snakes wriggled under the surface of his skin. The flesh bulged and pulsed as whatever was within him squirmed to get out. The pain and horror in our eyes were matched by his own.

My flesh crawled and vomit boiled in my stomach. The Lycan force inside him should be dormant and unreachable. For me at this point, Shaggy may as well have been in a different body, which was too bad because I could really use his help right now. It would be another week before I could access his resources, at least without doing permanent damage. But that was because I'd spent most of my life keeping him under control. Not only didn't Kozlov have the experience to tamp down the new, murderous animal inside, he was also angry and crazy enough not to want to. I couldn't imagine what kind of monster he'd be when the full moon hit. He was terrifying enough as it was.

There was no way to fight him and win, so I began hostage negotiations. "Let the women go, man. This is between you and me. I can help you... I have the same thing inside me..."

From behind me, Meaghan shrieked. "What? What the hell is that?"

Gramma shushed her best she could, but whatever progress Meaghan was making in her sobriety just took a giant step backward. The girl whimpered and squirmed and tried to make herself as small as possible.

Two baby steps brought me to the middle of the room and in line with the door. Maybe I could bum-rush him, and I was reconsidering my "no guns in the house" rule. "I never meant to do this to you. I'm so sorry."

What was left of Max Kozlov—mottled skin, greasy hair, black stubbly beard, sneered and took three shaky steps forward. "Sorry. *Iisus Krysto*—I make you sorry."

The scream of the forgotten teakettle scared the crap out of all of us. Kozlov turned his attention to the geyser of steam and his blade towards Gramma, who stood and inched towards the stove.

"Move away, you old bitch. Both of you, over there." He swung his knife towards the table.

The old lady turned on him, her jaw tight and determined, but her voice shook like the frail old biddy she was not. "Look, young man, I don't know who you are or what you want with... him... but I'm an old lady, and I want my cup of tea."

Back in Mother Russia, Kozlov must have had a grandmother who loved him, because he froze for a moment, then nodded. "Sure. Da. But then over there."

"Thank you. Would you like some?"

"No, *spasiba*." Something inside him remembered its manners.

"Suit yourself." Gramma turned as if nothing was wrong and opened the cupboard beside the stove. She reached for a canister in the back. Not the regular tea. Not even whatever potion she'd been dosing Meaghan with. Her hand grabbed a white metal ten marked with an "x"—maybe it was a cross—in red nail polish. Moving like a helpless old lady, she placed it on the counter. Then she moved the kettle off the flame but didn't turn the burner off. The blue fire raged on full as she pried the tin open.

"If you're sure. You look like you could use some..." Then Gramma Mostoy's hand flashed out and grabbed a fist-full of the brown and grey powder from the tin. Rather than put it in the teapot, she threw it directly into the flames and shouted something in Romani.

Then she grabbed Meaghan, tackling her to the floor. "Stay down," she ordered.

A mushroom cloud of black smoke rose from the range top, filling the room and rising into the whirring fan which then spread the fog even further. Kozlov and I both stood with our mouths open, not sure what was happening.

We found out.

The other man was closer than I was, so he got the message a millisecond earlier. Kozlov twitched and rubbed at his eyes, then clutched his stomach and retched.

I couldn't see what happened after that because my own eyes burned like barbecue coals and my stomach did a barrel roll. I heard myself ask, "what the hell?" before the contents of my stomach appeared on the kitchen floor. I landed on my knees in a puddle of my own puke, with my head about to explode like a cheap balloon.

Kozlov was in equally bad shape. He swung his knife uselessly, then bent at the waist and leaned against the sink. "You old bitch, I'll—" His threat was interrupted by what little his gut contained spewing all over him.

Meaghan was curled in a ball on the floor, I was on my hands and knees and the Russian staggered around the kitchen cursing and waving that blade in blind, futile rage. The only person not panicking was Gramma. She stood statue-still, her lips pursed, hands on her hips, not at all surprised by the surrounding bedlam.

I was close to passing out, which wouldn't make me much use to anyone. I crawled forward, intending to wrestle the knife from Kozlov, who wasn't in any better shape than me. He was smarter, though, because he did the only thing that would help him at that moment. He stumbled for the door and made a break for it.

Amid a string of Russian curses, Kozlov grabbed for the door and a gust of frigid air blew into the kitchen, dispersing the evil fog. Not hesitating for a minute, he stumbled to the deck and down the stairs, coughing, puking and swearing the whole way down. Then he fled into the freedom of the alley.

Facedown on the floor, I watched as Gramma ran behind him, slammed the door and turned the deadbolt. She turned the stove off and threw open the window above the sink, then rushed over to check on Meaghan. Attempting to calm her, she rocked the girl back and forth "hush-hushing" her and humming a lullaby.

Me, she let lie on the floor until my vision cleared and my stomach stopped doing the cha-cha. "That wasn't tea, was it?" At least I still had my razor-sharp detective powers.

I could tell she didn't want to tell me, but I looked so pitiful her motherly instincts took over. "No. It was wolfsbane. Maybe a few other things."

I struggled to my hands and knees. "Wolfsbane? That shit really works?"

"Apparently." She stood over me and did that evil-eye-spit motion. "So, it's true."

Fighting vertigo, I staggered to my feet, then a chair. "How long have you known?"

"Years. I was suspicious when you were a kid. Later I knew."

"Why didn't you say something?"

"You saved my Billy. And you're a good man. I told you—I know how hard you fight that thing inside you."

"And you had that shit here all along? How come?"

Her eyes had that cold, dead look again. "Because sometimes you can't fight Darkness by yourself. I knew I'd need it someday. Just in case."

In case of something like tonight, or in case she needed to use it against me? I wasn't sure there was an acceptable answer.

Meaghan's eyes were wide and white as golf balls, her pupils mere pinpoints. "What are you?"

It was the second time she asked me that question. This time she deserved an answer. Gramma pointed to a chair and, although she wanted to stay as far away from me as she could, Meaghan obeyed and sat.

Where in God's name do I start?

"I've got this thing inside me," I said.

CHAPTER 21

Two bangs on my door woke me and sent me flying out of bed. I rolled onto the floor, grabbed my Ruger and took a shooter's stance before I knew who it was. It didn't sound like a pissed-off-Russian-werewolf kind of knock, but I wasn't about to get caught off guard a second time tonight.

The part of my brain that wasn't panicking remembered my weapons training from when I got my permit. "Fair warning. I have a licensed weapon."

"I know, dumbass. It's why I knocked first." Bill's voice came through the door a second before he did, his keys dangling from the knob. "Jesus, put that thing down."

He clomped over and sat in my good chair, easing into it and massaging the spot on his wrist where his crutch rubbed. While he got comfortable, I looked around for my jeans and got one leg situated before he started in on me.

"What the hell, dude. What happened up there tonight?"

I was still groggy. "What do you mean? What time is it?" I put the gun in a drawer and sat on the corner of the bed, facing him.

"It's like two-thirty. And you know what I mean. Gramma's still talking the junkie chick off the ceiling, there's smoke all over the kitchen, plus it smells like puke and oregano up there. What was that, anyway?"

"Wolfsbane. And saltpeter. Some other secret herbs and spices."

"Wolfsbane? That's a thing? Like not an old movie thing but a *real* thing?" He paused while his accountant's brain processed all the data. "She used it on you?"

"I was just collateral damage. That stuff's nasty as hell, by the way. Apparently, she's had it up there this whole time, just in case. For protection. Did you know?"

"From what—you? Wait. She knows?"

Oh, she knows a lot of stuff, buddy. But yeah. "I guess."

His brows met over the bridge of his nose as he puzzled it all out. "But if it wasn't for you…"

"Okay, it's like this." Twenty minutes later he had the complete picture: Kozlov, budding werewolf, revenge, Meaghan losing her shit, his Gramma's a badass Gypsy witch, blah blah blah. I left out the awful stuff, like if the Russian couldn't control his urges now, what a fricking nightmare he'd be in about two weeks. What Bill learned freaked him out enough as it was.

"So he followed what's her name…"

"Meaghan."

"Meaghan, the drug addict, skanky chick, whatever. This Kozlov guy found us through her, right? That's it. Tell Little Red Riding Hoodie she's out."

"Why me?"

"You're the one that found her and brought her home like some lost kitten. Send her back to her daddy. Or Rehab. I don't care, but she can't stay here. I don't want her in my house."

"Your grandmother might have something to say about that. She likes the kid."

"So do you."

"Nah. I just feel sorry for her. Seriously, she's not my style. Skinny blond, ten years younger than me. Hates Zeppelin. And that's without all her other issues, never mind mine. I don't need that kind of crazy in my life."

"Neither do I. And for sure my *puni daj* doesn't. She needs to leave so everything can get back to normal around here."

Except it wouldn't. Ever. My secret wasn't a secret anymore. Bill and Gramma knew. Now Meaghan and probably Cromwell. Kozlov, too, of course. Whatever normal life was, I'd seen the last of it.

"Will he come back?" Bill asked.

Maybe. Probably. Yeah, and he'll be pissed right off and even more dangerous with every day closer to the full moon. "I don't know."

Bill pretended to believe me. He stared into space for a minute, then gave a little cough. "Look, I know what you are, Johnny. Hell, you saved my life. But we can't have that stuff here. This freaking city is already no place for a gay cripple and a crazy old woman without inviting werewolves and junkies into our apartment. I let you live here for cheap because you're my friend and all. I really thought we'd be safer with you here. But this is getting out of control, don't you think?"

He wasn't wrong. "I'll deal with Kozlov. Somehow. Give me a few days to figure it out."

"And Meaghan? She has to go before something terrible happens. Please, man, because otherwise... I don't know..." He left the sentence—and the implied threat of possible eviction and homelessness—unsaid.

I grabbed two beers from my little refrigerator, popped the caps and handed one to him. Then I drained half of mine in one pull. "Where were you tonight, by the way?"

"I just needed to get out of the house for a bit. All those tarot lessons were getting on my nerves."

I grinned. "Bullshit. Who is he?" Bill turned tomato-red. "Aha. He's not another pretty frat boy, is he?"

He sipped his beer. "I met him a few weeks ago. He's nice. And he's out. Really out. Not married. Not 'bi-curious.' Just a nice normal gay guy."

I clinked his beer with mine. "Nice. How old is he? What's he do?"

"Jeez, dad. He's an intern at an advertising agency in the Loop. Goes to Columbia."

"He's twenty-two and still lives with his mother."

"Twenty-three, smartass. And how d'you know?"

"Seriously? You know what I do for a living, right? Okay, Watson, listen up." I stood and rocked on my heels with my hands behind my back.

"Fact one. He's an intern which means he's in college and still not working for enough money to live on. Yes?"

"Go on."

"Fact two. It's two-thirty in the morning and you're home. Alone. That means you either haven't closed the deal yet... tell me you've at least—"

"Yes, Jesus, yes. We have. Yes."

"But not tonight. Ergo..." I loved saying 'ergo,' because it made me sound smart and drove him up the wall, "... ergo you hung out until closing time but neither of you had anywhere to go. A roommate wouldn't care, but his mother would have a conniption. How'd I do?"

He bowed his head in defeat. "Prick. His mother's home and I couldn't bring him back here."

You and Gramma need to have a chat, pal. But that was a conversation for another day. "Let me get this thing handled for Cromwell on Thursday. Then I'll deal with Kozlov. Somehow."

My best friend sipped his beer and ran a hand through his hair. "Yeah. Okay. But Meaghan's out tomorrow."

"Fine. But you get to tell your grandmother," I said.

"Prick."

CHAPTER 22

9 days to the full moon- waxing crescent.

It took exactly thirty-four minutes from the time an anonymous phone call came into the Chicago office of the Centers for Disease Control until I heard the first sirens coming off the tollway.

The mysterious caller was Meaghan, who'd insisted on being useful. We'd coached her to use all the trigger words, like "biological weapon," and "airborne," and maybe most important, "Arab."

Although they didn't know it, Nasrallah's security team had provided me with the perfect spot to watch everything. After my last adventure on his property, his men had cleared all the brush and construction rubble a safe distance from the wall, but only as far as the vacant lot across the street. That meant there was a great hiding spot with a perfect view of the front gate. If my plan worked, they would park the emergency vehicles between me and the gate, rendering me invisible. Then I would blend in with the hazmat team and get into the house.

If it worked, I was in tall cotton. If it didn't, I'd be in jail and Bill wouldn't have to worry about evicting my hairy ass.

I had been tucked away in my little den since before dawn, already dressed in my yellow suit and huddled under a lean-to of plywood and two-by-sixes masked by dried branches and scrub brush. Except for the reek of mold which had me on the edge of a sneezing fit, it wasn't bad. The spot provided a good view as an armada of cop cars, ambulances, and semi-trucks doubling as mobile labs lined the quiet road on either side in front of the Egyptian's estate.

When everyone but the traffic cops were raising hell inside the gate, I emerged from my hole, slipped the headpiece on and grabbed my metal camera case. I stood and stretched, unseen by anyone. The giant trucks between me and the gate blocked everyone's view of the field, and they set the police watching traffic a quarter mile in either direction. Nobody paid attention to an empty field. I took a deep breath and trotted towards the action.

Run-waddling between trailer trucks, it wasn't easy to move quickly. Nobody really noticed me until I was nearly at the gate. Shockingly, Lady Luck had my back this morning. The gatekeepers were Lake County deputies, the usual suburban cop pairing of an old, bored supervisor and a young, overly eager rookie. Both put their hands to their guns with one hand while holding the other out like they'd practiced that move.

"Whoa, where do you think you're going?" The young one demanded as the other cop looked on.

I'd gone over this a million times in my head. The lie tripped right off my tongue. "Forgot the sample case in the truck and had to go back for it. If I don't get in there, it's my ass." I held the case- biohazard label first—as evidence. Between guilt, fear and trying to run in the suit, I had a healthy and convincing sweat going on. It added realism to the performance.

The rookie was playing the lead. The chance to show off to his training officer was irresistible. "You got ID?"

The semi-official-looking CDC badge hung from a lanyard around my neck and I held it high enough for him to see, but shaky enough he couldn't read it, so I bluffed. "Watson, Riley B. Lab tech, Chicago Region." He was trying to read the damned thing, so I poured it on thicker, "Please. Whatever they have in there needs to be contained or we're all in trouble."

The older cop asked, "They know what it is?"

"I'm not supposed to say, but they suspect anthrax. Won't know til we test it and we can't do that until I get this case to them." My real panic added a convincing note to my voice. All I knew about anthrax was it was bad, the only biological weapon I'd ever heard of, and drove the press and authorities into a tizzy so it was as good as any.

"Fucking ragheads. Knew it was gonna happen someday. Go on." Without another look, he waved me in over the objections of the younger, hopefully less blatantly racist, cop. I would owe Lady Luck a drink if this kept up.

I grunted my thanks and passed through the gate, waddling as fast as I could manage. Holding the case up in front of my face, I croaked out, "Incoming... Coming through..."

It hadn't honestly occurred to me how far the house was from the road. It took minutes that felt like hours to reach the front steps. Since I'd made it this far without getting shot, the officious woman in the CDC windbreaker the two Homeland Security poster children just waved me through. The good news was, I was inside the house. The bad news being that was as far as my plan went. I was now at the mercy of my own idea, which didn't bode well at all.

In the main room off the entryway, I saw the first part of my plan was going about as expected. Nasrallah was kneeling on the ground, hands clasped over his head, along with two terrified Latina housekeepers. Another big, white guy was face-down on the carpet, buried beneath two shouting, gun-waving Homeland Security goons. There was a lot of yelling, but at least no one had gotten themselves shot. I wondered if the guy on the bottom of that pile was the second guy who'd robbed Darrell.

Nasrallah was getting yelled at in Arabic by a guy in a yellow plastic suit. The government guy sounded scared. Nasrallah was calm as hell.

"I speak perfectly good English, officer. What is this all about? Please. I don't understand."

Had to give it to the guy, he was cool under pressure. Wafik Nasrallah would have made a great poker player except for one tell—his eyes kept flicking towards the stairs leading to the upper floor. The disk had to be up there.

My conscience pained me when I saw the two maids sobbing and clinging to each other. I hoped to God they had green cards. I wouldn't want to be the reason they got sent back to Guatemala or wherever. The white guy kept repeating the smartest thing he could think of: "I have a permit for that." It wouldn't help much in the long run, but it probably stopped him from taking a bullet judging from the looks of those Homeland Security chuckleheads.

Well as the plan was going, there was something wrong, and it took a minute to figure out what it was. *Where was Abdul Badri?*

The big African was nowhere to be found. It was too much to hope he'd taken a sick day. Odds were better he was still in the house, keeping an eye on the Anubis Disk. My bladder twitched a bit remembering the last time I'd seen him but there was no way of taking a bio-break in that suit so I suppressed the need and focused on the task at hand; find Cromwell's treasure and get the hell out with my hide intact.

Meaghan's call said to focus on the lab in the basement. I knew there was no lab; I assumed there was a basement. According to some HGTV show Bill made me watch, three-quarters of Chicago homes had one and it seemed a good bet. It also kept most of the team away from the upstairs. I slinked towards the stairs but wasn't exactly inconspicuous in my banana-colored ensemble. Nasrallah noticed me and frowned. He didn't want anyone going up there, and I don't think he worried about what they'd find in his boudoir.

At the top of the landing a long, expensive rug ran down the center of a wood-floored corridor. There were three doors on the left, two on the right, and then double doors leading to what was likely the Master Bedroom.

The first door on the left was open and two cops were ransacking what looked to be a young girl's pink sanctuary. Nasrallah must have been a weekend dad because there were no signs of a family when I staked out the place. Stuffed animals, or their white fluffy guts, lay in a pile on the floor as the cops did a thoroughly destructive job of looking for biotoxins. Cop logic—because if I was an evil genius with a little girl I loved, that's exactly where I'd store the good stuff.

The office, second door on the right, was wide open. They splintered the jamb where the deadbolt used to be. No one was in there at the moment. I took a quick step inside, hoping nobody saw.

Through the steamed-up plastic face shield, the room looked every bit the same as it had in Cromwell's scrying bowl. The dark bookshelves and window trim matched the huge desk that dominated the room. Since it was still mid-cycle for me my senses were decent but the plastic headgear made it almost impossible to see, hear, or smell anything except sweat on the inside of the vinyl window and my own panicky breathing.

Screw it. I removed the headgear and gulped in delicious oxygen. Now I clearly heard the chaos in the rest of the house. Things were getting more destructive as frustration turned into the righteous anger of bureaucrats who realized someone had duped them. There wasn't much time. My eyes conducted a frantic search for any sign of a metal disk.

The room was decorator-magazine picture-perfect. The only flaw was a small, faint square of dust marking where laptop docking station got snapped up by the Feds. On the desk was a metal mesh in-box with papers and receipts from an office supply store, and a coffee mug holding half a dozen expensive pens. Otherwise, the desktop was pristine. All but one drawer were open and bare of anything incriminating. The big drawer on the bottom was half open where they splintered the gorgeous dark hardwood.

It was too much to expect that the damned thing would just be sitting in the open where anyone could grab it, but that doesn't mean I didn't hope. Luck wouldn't be a lady if she was easy.

While not exactly my style, I tried to be methodical in the search. I began in the corner by the door, scanning and running gloved hands over the wall, then working my way to the corner by the big leather chair and lamp. I pressed my ear to the wall and focused, hoping something would tip me off to where the item—and probably Badri—were. Nothing. Not a damned thing out of place.

Everything was pristine and in order. The OCD cleanliness made Cromwell's penthouse look like a freshman's dorm room. *How do people live like this?*

My counter-clockwise journey around the office continued. When I got to the window, I stared out at the tree where poor Nestor nearly ate me two weeks before and thought about everything that happened since. No time to dwell on it.

Sliding across, I got to the lemony-waxed and polished bookshelves that took up the entire wall. Imposing volumes in multiple languages rose five full rows to the ceiling. They weren't just decorative, bookmarks and post-it notes showed someone actually read them. Impressive.

The hair on the back of my neck stood at attention like it always did when something was wrong, but I couldn't figure out what. There wasn't any way out of the house once it got raided, but the object of my search— not to mention one enormous, scary Sudanese guy—had vanished pretty much with no one noticing. Assuming that was impossible, there was some explanation I was missing. The room wasn't that big, so it's not like he was playing peekaboo behind the swiveling desk chair.

The room wasn't that big.

Closing my eyes, I envisioned the hallway. Three rooms long on one side, but only two on this one. Something was taking up an awful lot of space between these bookshelves and the master bedroom.

My gloved hand ran over the middle shelf while I pondered. Its surface was glassy-smooth. About four feet from the wall, I felt the thin line of a seam, then the smoothness continued. Before my brain registered; I retraced the path. There was a definite break in the shelf, small but noticeable. The same slim gap appeared in the other shelves at the exact spot.

Straining to block out the noise from the rest of the house, I put my head against the bookshelf and banged on the wood. Immediately, I heard a faint scuffling noise on the other side. Regardless of what the moon was up to, my ears seldom let me down. There was a space—probably a panic room—behind the bookshelf.

There had to be a trigger somewhere, but damned if I could find it. Just ripping books from the shelf until I found the right one seemed excessive. That's when I saw something on the underside of the desk. It looked like a miniature doorbell. I pushed it.

My ears picked up two things. The first was a soft, pneumatic *whoosh* as the shelf separated neatly and one side popped out, revealing the entrance to the panic room.

The second sound was less comforting. It was the *snick-snick* of a round entering a gun's chamber.

A rare piece of good judgment stopped me popping my head through the opening. "Badri, is that you?" I whispered, my face pressed into an ancient copy of Paradise Lost.

"Who are you?" The voice from inside was deep and heavily accented.

"I just want that... disk thing. The Egyptian one." Like there was a whole United Nations of supernatural oddities lying around and I needed to be specific.

"You can have the damned thing. Just get me out of here."

"Really?" Of all the responses I expected—defiance, possible martyrdom, calls for retribution—the one thing I was unprepared for was a sudden burst of common sense.

While he seemed a reasonable fellow, this was no time to get sloppy and lose my head. "I'm coming in. Don't shoot me or there'll be a whole SWAT team on your ass." There was no argument from inside, so I grabbed my metal case and slipped into the posh hiding spot. It was better furnished than my apartment.

The door clicked shut behind me, and I wondered just how screwed I was.

Abdul Badri appeared even taller in the confined space. His bald head wasn't so much shaved as polished to a high sheen, sweat glistening in the bluish LED light. In his left hand, he held something round and shiny. I assumed it was the object I was looking for, but my attention was laser-focused on his right, in which a gigantic pistol pointed at my most vulnerable body parts.

I had my own Ruger with me, but with my usual impeccable planning it was in my belt, which was zipped safely inside my hazmat suit.

Crap.

CHAPTER 23

"Just hand me the disk and I'll get us out of here." I flipped open the case, but Badri shook his head.

"No, I think I'll hold on to it until we are out of here. Then you can have it. And good riddance."

"Okay, fine." He had a point. And a gun. I let him hold it a while longer.

The gaunt Sudanese giant looked me up and down, pursing his lips like he was going to whistle. The question crawled across his face and settled behind his eyes. "Cromwell, right?"

I kept switching focus from the gun to the closed-circuit TV over his head, which showed fifteen-second flashes of different parts of the house and yard, to the disk in his hand. He was holding it casually, not at all concerned. Maybe it was harmless. Still, I'd feel better if someone locked it away in my case.

"Why do you do it?" he asked. "This is no work for honorable men." I shrugged. Talking was way better than shooting, and as long as he did one, he wasn't doing the other. He rambled on, but I was trying to tune in to what was going on outside, keeping one ear on the bookshelf door and one eye on the video monitor.

"Another crazy rich old man, stealing from each other, playing their little games. My employer outbids yours; he steals something from someone else, round and round. And for what? A bunch of superstitious bullshit. Temple treasures and holy relics. Fortunes, they spend. And most of them fake."

"That's a fake?" I asked. Given what happened with Cromwell's magic bowl, it seemed a fair question.

The big man sniffed. "What do you think? It's not even Dynasty period. *Nasrallah-said* knows that. They made it in the eighteenth century to scare off Napoleon. Blood sacrifices and such to bring Anubis, the god of the dead, back and free Egypt. Look at this nonsense."

His giant fingers spread out to show me the disk. I could make out a bunch of squiggles and shapes circling a central figure of a man in a skirt with the head of a Doberman Pinscher. "Half man, half-wild dog. Who believes this?"

"Crazy, right?" My need to pee was increasing, and I got an itchy feeling all the way up both furry arms looking at the thing.

"These crazy old men. They steal from each other, fighting over these trinkets and spending fortunes. Millions. And killing dogs. Did you know someone killed my dog? Why would a person do such a thing?"

I somehow looked more empathetic than guilty because he kept talking, picking up speed. "Forgive me. I'm not fond of confined spaces."

"No, you're good."

"I was a soldier once. An officer. Then I became head of security for a rich man and his family. Honorable work. A man's work. But now he has me robbing trucks like a common criminal. Pfff, I am finished with him. You should be too, my friend."

"Yeah, well, first we need to find a way out of here. Do you think you could put that away?"

"Oh, of course." He slid the Anubis Disk into his pocket.

"I meant the gun."

"No, sorry. I can't do that." At least he was pointing it away from my belly and to the side. I took the win.

The overhead monitor continued to show the proceedings below. At the base of the stairs, a dog-handler dropped to one knee to pet his German Shepherd. The damned thing kept looking up the stairs, but his tongue hung out like he hadn't a care in the world. Thank god I was still in a neutral stage and wrapped in yellow plastic.

Then the view switched to the yard where several Feds stood smoking. It looked like the tearing-everything-up part of the day was over.

The next shot was the office, or at least three-quarters of it. The door and desk were in view, the chair by the window was out of the shot but as long as we could see people come in and out, that was fine.

Badri and I both held our breath when a guy in an ICE jacket poked his head in, took a lazy look around and shouted over his shoulder to somebody in the hall. My ears heard him yell. "Clear," though I knew Badri wouldn't be able to make anything out through the thick fireproof walls.

In the family room downstairs, Nasrallah was on his feet and attempting to comfort one of the maids while giving the CDC folks the stink-eye. There was a lot of hand waving. I couldn't hear him, but I'd bet money the word "lawyer" was thrown around.

"What is your big plan for getting us out of here?" Badri whispered. Perspiration made his skin glow, but otherwise, he was calm. I could barely smell him, which meant he was under control. He was a professional soldier.

I, on the other hand, was sweating like a hooker in church. I loosened the snaps around my neck and leaned on the door. "We'll just wait. They're almost done. Unless they find something. Will they?"

"No, there is nothing here that would interest them. Not even this, since they do not understand what it is. You're right. We can wait them out." He slid to the floor, his back to the wall, and whistled softly through his teeth. Now that he had time, he studied me with that look a cop gives you when he's pretty sure he could find something on you if he tried hard enough.

"How long have you been working for the old man?" Badri's voice was level and calm now. That would not work to my advantage.

"A couple of weeks."

"Watch out for him," the man said, picking at his fingernails.

"That's what he said about you."

"Ha. He bloody well should," the soldier said. They apparently had a history. "But he won't have to worry about me after this. I'm done."

I had to admit. The day had me reconsidering my employment options. "What will you do?"

"I can find other security work. Honest work. And somewhere it doesn't snow. How do people live here?"

It helps if you can grow a fur coat.

As he rambled on, my eyes flicked up to the monitor. There were fewer people left in the house, and when we got a view of the front lawn, a line of people in blue jackets filed out to the road. Unfortunately, the two maids were in handcuffs and were being frog-marched towards the mobile labs and paddy wagons out front. No doubt Nasrallah would join them. Perfect.

"Looks like they're taking everyone in for questioning. We'll give them a few minutes once the place is empty and walk out of here like nothing happened. Then you can give me the disk and get on with your life. Hell, I'll even give you a ride into town."

He flashed me a smile. "That would be good. I drive Mister Nasrallah's car. I don't think he'd appreciate my taking it without permission."

We sat in silence for a while, looking at the video monitor, the ceiling, and pretty much anything but each other. I strained my ears to hear any signs of life in the house. My nostrils detected the scent of perspiration and a little fear. The big man was sweating now, despite the climate control. He offered an embarrassed chuckle, "I don't like small spaces very much. The sooner we get out, the better. What did you do before becoming a thief like me?"

"Construction." This was no time for sharing my resume, but he was asking to take his mind off his claustrophobia. The big man probably could have gotten my whole life's story if he really wanted it, I'm sure the Sudanese army taught interesting interrogation techniques.

The stream of officers crossing the lawn ceased and everything was quiet. I put my ear to the door and heard nothing but the hum of the electronic lock and the throb of the air conditioning. I relaxed and nodded to my roommate, picked up the fake hazmat case, hit the release button, and with a gentle whoosh, the door cracked open. Then I turned off the video cameras to the house and deleted the memory. No sense making the cop's job easier.

Badri brushed by me, eager to escape confinement. I was hot on his heels, hoping he didn't make a run for it, because what was I going to do if he did? My Ruger was still inside my suit, his was in his hand. He didn't run.

In fact, we'd barely taken three steps out of the panic room when he stopped dead in his tracks. I bumped into his back and bounced off of him as if I'd run into a tree trunk. I let out a "What the hell, man?" Then I saw what the hell it was.

A short, balding, Middle Eastern man sat in the leather chair by the window, right in the camera's blind spot. In Wafik Nasrallah's hand was a revolver—smaller than Badri's or even mine—but that was irrelevant because he pointed it directly at me. Accuracy beats firepower like rock beats scissors.

Badri didn't miss a beat. He moved to the side and then took a quick step back. I felt the barrel of his pistol against the small of my back.

Turning my head, the whites of his eyes were just slits. The friendly smile was long gone.

"Really, dude?" His face confirmed it. Really.

The man of the house got out of the chair with a little groan. "Do you still have it?"

Badri reached into his pocket and showed his boss the shiny bronze disk.

The Egyptian smiled. "Excellent work. And who are you?"

Before I could answer, Badri spoke up. "Centers for Disease Control. His name's Watson. Riley B." He spoke calmly for someone lying through his teeth. "I thought he'd be useful if we needed to negotiate an exit."

Added pressure against my spine told me the next line in this improv skit was mine. "Jeez, come on, man. Everyone's gone. Let me go. I don't even know what this is all about. I won't say anything. Promise. Quiet as the grave. Just let me go." If the role called for a slightly nervous coward who didn't know what the hell was going on, I was typecast.

Nasrallah was a harsh critic. "Actually, it would be better if you spoke, please. Who called the authorities on me?"

"It was anonymous."

A deep African voice cut off the le in mid-stream. "It was Cromwell."

The other man made a face like a five-year-old seeing Brussel sprouts. "Bastard. But we no longer need a hostage."

I let out a sigh of relief. "Great. I appreciate that. "

He sneered. "Make sure he's not found."

An enormous ebony hand gripped my shoulder and spun me towards the door. "Just walk." The ice in Badri's baritone offered no room for discussion. I walked.

With Badri steering me by the neck, I shuffled towards the door, trying not to trip over the booties of my hazmat suit. A small, illogical ember of hope still flickered inside me. He had me, true. But he also had the thingamajig, and we were about to walk out of the room together, just the pair of us. We could both be out of there and on our way. It was brilliant. We would pull it off. We were safe.

Nasrallah extended his free hand. The other kept the gun trained on my belly. "Abdul, give me the Anubis Disk, first. Please. We don't want to get blood on it."

And Lady Luck has left the building.

My future murderer—or my rescuer, it could go either way at this point—hesitated. Time stopped. I felt the gun barrel pull away from my back and my knees almost buckled with relief. Badri took a step away, which was good, and blocked my path to the door. Which was not.

"I will give you this foolish thing. And then I'll take my leave of you, Nasrallah-said."

For the first time, there was a nervousness in Nasrallah's smug voice. "Your leave?"

"I no longer work for you, sir. I will do this one last thing..." he nodded in my direction, "... and then I will leave." Great, I got the only hired goon in the world who insists on giving two week's notice before he quits.

"What do you mean? You can't just leave."

Badri grimaced. "I have said before, I am an honorable man. I am not a thief or an assassin. Especially for this madness of yours."

"You've killed far more dangerous men than this one, Abdul."

That stung. "Hey, come on—" Badri slapped the back of my head to shut me up.

Badri straightened up in a soldier's posture, and his voice carried authority. "No. I have killed, but this is murder. This I will not do."

His employer didn't appreciate the noble sentiment as much as I did. The two men glared at each other in silence for a long time. Too long. Long enough for me to think of something monumentally stupid to say.

"Let's just get out of here. Take the disk and let's go—"

If time had stopped a moment ago, it picked up speed now. Confusion, disappointment, and rage all flashed in Nasrallah's eyes. Badri stiffened beside me and lifted his weapon. I took a step to the side and crashed into the desk.

Two shots echoed in the small room, sounding even louder to my ears than they must have been. I slammed my eyes shut and ducked under the furniture. There was no more shooting, but from beneath the desk, I heard something heavy hit the floor.

Opening my eyes, I saw Badri's shoes exactly where they were before I ducked. He hadn't moved at all. I poked my head around the corner.

It was Nasrallah who'd hit the floor. Sure enough, his body lay on the carpet, a single bloody hole where his broad nose used to be.

"Dude, you shot him." I turned to Badri, who looked a hundred feet tall from that vantage point. He ignored my clever observation and stood, silently sneering at what was left of his employer.

In that stony black face, his eyes narrowed, and his breathing was shallow and rapid. His left shirt sleeve was turning crimson from just above the elbow to his wrist.

"You're shot. Jesus Christ, he shot you." Compared to his calm, I was getting frantic and jumped to my feet to take a closer look. I grabbed at his arm uselessly before he yanked it away.

"I'm fine."

"Fine? You're bleeding. Let me look." He held his arm out like I could look if I cared to, but he didn't care much either way. His huge hand still held the Egyptian metal in a white-knuckled grip. Rivulets of bright red trailed down his sleeve, puddling at the cuff.

This seemed a terrible time to be heroic. "Come on man, let's get out of here."

It took a moment for him to register what I said, but the fog cleared, and he nodded. Slipping his gun into his holster, he said, "Yes. Fine. Let's go."

I sprinted to the door and looked back. Badri hadn't moved. "Dude, come on."

The big man's head was cocked to the side. He stood staring at the hand holding the Anubis Disk while I tugged on his injured arm. "Badri, let's get the hell out of here."

He didn't budge. I pulled harder with the same result. Then I followed his gaze to what was happening in his hand but couldn't make sense of what I saw.

Blood flowed freely down his arm, past his wrist, and dripped onto the metal object. Badri made no sound except his heavy breathing, but I could hear—something. A hiss like water hitting a hot frypan, maybe. Trickles of red flowed into the etchings on the metal, but instead of pooling in the grooves, the blood evaporated as soon as it hit the metal.

No. That wasn't it at all. The liquid disappeared *into* the bronze. Badri and I watched, transfixed, as the disk soaked up the blood like a sponge with a sickening slurping sound. Then it began throbbing ever so slightly in Badri's hand.

My ears picked up the faint pulsing beat and the metal ever-so-slightly expanded and contracted, soaking up the thick red mess faster and faster. I don't know if the African could hear it or not, because he was catatonic, staring as the blood streamed faster and faster. His eyes widened, and he tried to scream, but only a small whine escaped his quivering lips.

I shouted at him, "Drop it. Let it go." Then I grabbed his wounded arm and shook it as hard as I could. If anything, he held tighter than before. I shook his arm again, but he wouldn't let go. Or couldn't. It was as if the disk welded itself to his skin.

I stared, gaping like a moron. There was no way of making sense of what I saw. It was all too weird for my pea brain to understand. The small-caliber bullet hole in Badri's arm began flapping wider like invisible fingers pulled it open, but nothing touched him. The blood ran faster now. The round metal was a sponge soaking up every drop of fluid in this body. The pulsing grew louder, the slurping sound made my guts churn. The trickle of blood became a stream, then a river.

Badri's dark face paled. Unable to speak, his eyes screamed for him, widening until I was sure they'd pop out of his head. His gun hand trembled violently until his weapon fell to the floor, but he didn't seem to notice. The empty hand spasmed and twitched, curling in on itself.

The dead hand turned ashy pale and dry, like a leaf left on the sidewalk. The chalky whiteness spread up his wrist and his arm as the pulsing of the metal and the soft hiss became an endless, sickening, slurping sound. That fucking evil object was sucking every drop of blood from his body and draining him dry.

The right side of his body, bloodless now, could no longer support his weight and he collapsed on his side. The soldier's tall, lean body twitched as he was slowly drained dry. Each part of him, once emptied of blood, stopped twitching and simply died.

I was too busy shouting to be any use. I wanted to rip the damned thing from his hand, but there was no way in hell to do that without touching it. *Fuck no.*

My stomach churned, my ears filled with the throbbing and liquid suction sound as Badri's life force left him and emptied into that horrible bronze monstrosity. For all the liquid it consumed, it never changed size. The bronze throbbed in his hand and demanded every drop it could get.

My nose caught the scent of urine. Badri—or what was left of him—suffered one final indignity. Then he crapped his pants. I almost joined him.

He lay there, stone dead. I stood gawking over him, trying not to upchuck. The flow of blood slowed to a stream, then a trickle again, until there was nothing left. The dry husk of what was once Abdul Badri lay on the ruined carpet. His body looked like it had been mummified or left in the desert for months, instead of standing, alive, in a nice normal suburban home only a few moments ago.

I covered my ears, trying to still the throbbing and hissing. When the blood-sucking stopped, the only sound in the room was my low whining. Stirred by the smell of blood and all that adrenaline, Shaggy stirred and that raised my panic level higher. Caught between fight and flight, I settled for hyperventilation, which wasn't helping one bit. It took several minutes for my brain to focus and think of the next step: getting the hell out.

Stepping slowly around the body, my hands reached for the wall to steady myself. I was still wearing gloves and somehow conjured up the brain cells to worry about fingerprints. All I wanted to do was get the hell out of there and leave this to whoever showed up. God help the poor bastard on cleanup duty.

Just don't get any blood on it. No shit.

The poor schmo who stumbled on the scene wouldn't have a clue what this thing was capable of. I couldn't just leave the Anubis Disk where it was. Two people were dead, and I was to blame. I didn't want the fucking thing but had to take it with me. That was the job, but there was no way I was touching it, gloves or not.

The hazmat case lay on the floor beside the bookcase. That would work if I could find a way to get the disk into it. Not taking any chances, I ducked back into the panic room to pick up my headgear to my fake biohazard suit. The suit wasn't real, but I could avoid contact with the relic. I didn't want to touch a thing. I didn't want to even breathe the same air and needed to find a pair of tongs or something to pick it up with. The best I could do was a stapler on Nasrallah's desk. Holding my breath, I slipped the open end over the metal and closed the stapler until it gripped enough to pull it from Badri's dead grip. Flakes of dusty skin came with it.

I lifted it gently and dropped it into my metal case, then slammed the lid hard and flicked the clasps down as fast as I could and leaned my weight on it. I held my breath, not sure what to expect next.

Nothing. Nothing happened next. Away from its food source, it was just an old, dead, useless dead disk of bronze.

I picked up the case and held it at arm's length as I speed-waddled out of the office, down the stairs and out the front door to the lawn. Anybody watching would have seen a bright yellow blob carrying a shiny box and mumbling, "Oh shit, oh shit, oh shit," past the gate and down the road to where the Charger sat waiting.

I opened the trunk, threw the cursed thing inside and slammed it. Then I tore the headpiece off and leaned over the hood, gasping for air and praying to a God I didn't believe in. I'd have been better off seeking the help of Anubis, but I didn't speak Egyptian.

CHAPTER 24

The neurons in my brain were popping like bubble wrap. Enough brain cells functioned to drive, but there was no way I could hold it together enough to get into the city alive, and the way my hands shook the tollway was out of the question.

I couldn't get the image of Badri's drained and shrunken corpse out of my mind. A better person than me would spare a thought for Nasrallah, too. My rational brain said this was Chicago. People got shot all the time—it was just another day at the office. What happened to the African was a different thing entirely. *I'd never seen anything like that. I don't think anyone has.*

How many times in the last couple of weeks had I said that? Exploding fortune-telling bowls, crystal balls that really worked, werewolf infections, and now blood-sucking doodads. I wanted my world to return to normal. And when you're a Lycan, that's a low bar.

Two years ago, I promised myself I'd never go through anything like Yankton again. *Wrong again, Johnny.* I'd take that South Dakota shitshow over today's madness every time.

A buzzing from my glove compartment pulled my head out of my butt and back to the real world—if that's what this was. Cromwell was calling. By the time my shaking hands held the burner phone, it had gone to voicemail. There was no point listening to the message. I just hit redial and, in a buzz and a half, the old man himself answered.

"Johnny, nice of you to pick up. Do you have it?"

"Yes, I have it. Nasrallah's dead. Badri too." I was definitely not using my indoor voice.

"But you have it."

"Christ on a crutch. Yes, I have the damned thing. Did you hear me? Badri killed the Egyptian and that... thing killed Badri. It sucked the blood—sucked him dry."

The old bastard paused for a moment. Then in a soft voice, he said, "I told you not to get blood on it. Are you alright?"

"Yeah. I'm fine. It's locked up for now—"

"But it worked. It actually drank his blood? I heard the stories, but it's not supposed to do anything without the whole ceremony. That's amazing—I want to hear all about it. Bring it to the apartment right now."

"You really don't want that thing in your house."

"I really do. Fine, I can see you're in no condition to be sensible, anyway. I'll send someone trustworthy to pick it up from your house."

The sooner the better. You might think about an armored car. "Uh, sure. Okay. My place is—"

"I know where it is. We'll talk tomorrow. Here, first thing." Then he clicked off.

Somehow my trusty Charger got me home without killing myself or anyone because my mind was not on traffic. Someone stood in the upstairs window watching me pull into the drive and sit there for a few minutes pounding on the steering wheel and screaming myself hoarse.

I got out of the car and looked up. Meaghan witnessed the whole performance and had to be wondering just what the hell was wrong with me. I considered bringing the case inside with me and then thought better of it. If bringing an addict into the house was enough to get my ass evicted, Bill would draw a hard line at blood-sucking metal. Since I didn't want to end up living in an alley with Jerry and Sweet Lou, it made more sense to keep the damned thing in the trunk until somebody came to get it.

My apartment was dark and quiet, and I stood for a few seconds in my own, normal, not-weird-at-all room with nothing trying to kill me. Deep breathing stilled the thumping in my brain and chest. Then the pounding got louder and more insistent, and I realized it wasn't my circulatory system, it was the door at the top of the stairs.

"Johnny. Johnny, are you okay?" Meaghan pounded on the door and I realized that for the first time in ages, someone had locked it.

She sounded needy, and I couldn't deal with her drama at that moment. I barked at her, "Yeah. I'm fine."

"Let me in. I need to talk to you."

Maybe she did, but I sure as hell didn't need to speak to her—or anyone. "Go away." I could hear her through the door, and she wasn't going anywhere. "Give me a minute. I'll talk to you in a bit."

She banged and kicked at the door until I let out a very Shaggy-like growl and ran up the stairs, threw the deadbolt and wrenched it open. Without waiting for her, I stomped back downstairs and nearly got bowled over when she hugged me hard from behind.

"Are you okay? I was so worried."

"I'm fine."

She locked her arms around my waist and pressed her head to my back.

"What are you doing? I'm fine. I just need some space. Can we talk about this later?" I tried squirming out of her grasp, but she held me tighter than Badri held that—the memory gave me the strength to break free of her, leaving her grabbing at nothing but air.

Meaghan's eyes were red embers, like she'd been crying all night. "You're not okay. Something bad happened. I know it did."

"I can't talk about it, and you don't want to know." The kicked-puppy look on her face made my gut spasm, but I had no time for her. "I'm fine, I just need some time—"

"You have to talk to me. You do. And don't be an asshole."

Under the circumstances, I think I was entitled but felt the need to defend myself. "I'm not being a—I'm not. And it's none of your god-damned business, anyway."

"Yes, it is."

"No, it's not. Now get out of here. Leave. I mean it."

She drew a big snot-filled breath and wiped her eyes with her sleeve, then stiffened her spine and crossed her arms, defiant, and looked me dead in the eye. "Someone died today, didn't they?"

"It wasn't me."

"Don't be a dick. I need to know."

I needed air, and she was sucking all the oxygen from the room. I paced back and forth, avoiding her gaze. "You don't want to know. Even if you do, you're better off not knowing. Believe me."

She stamped her foot. "Don't fucking patronize me. I know. Someone died." Then her voice dropped to a whisper. "Maybe two people."

She had my attention. "How could you know that?"

Meaghan reached inside her hoodie pocket and pulled out a new deck of tarot cards. She held them like they were rattlesnakes instead of cardboard. "These. These told me, okay?"

I backed away, almost stumbling over the corner of my bed. She stood with watery eyes full of misery and panic, waiting for me to say something. Anything. I had a million questions, but nothing to say.

"I saw it. Clear. Two deaths. And I thought one of them was you, and..." The distance between us disappeared as she flung herself at me and wrapped her skinny arms around my waist and burrowed her face into my shirt. She barely reached my pecs, but damn near crushed the air from my lungs as she squeezed me, sobbing wildly.

I stroked her hair and let the kid cry herself out. "I'm fine. I'm okay," was the best I could come up with. It didn't matter. Her tiny body shook against mine with wracking sobs, eventually slowing until a final sniff left us both silent.

"I thought—I thought that..." Whatever she thought was forgotten when she reached up to my mouth in a desperate, awkward attempt at a kiss.

I nearly reciprocated out of instinct before my brain kicked into gear and I stepped back, pushing her away with more force than intended. "Whoa. No."

She backed halfway across the room, her eyes full of pain. She began weeping again, and the only thing I could think of was to offer another sympathetic hug. I wrapped my arms around her and stroked her hair. She looked up and smiled. Then my good intentions imploded because she dove in for another kiss, which I evaded by turning my cheek.

"What the hell? Come on, cut it out." I held her at arm's length while I sought a distraction. "How did you know, really?"

"I told you. The cards. I was reading them this afternoon—I'm getting really good. Gramma said so—and then I. I don't know. Just saw it."

"Those aren't real, they're just a con. You're smarter than that."

Meaghan pushed away and paced back and forth. "No. they're not. The cards... They talk to me. Sometimes too much. It's creepy as hell. But it was so clear. You were in danger. Then two deaths. Plain as day. Did it happen?" Her eyes wouldn't accept less than the truth.

A nod was the best I could do. Meaghan stood, expecting an explanation I had no intention of giving her. "You're better off not knowing. In case the cops come around—you know?"

That was a reason Neil O'Rourke's little girl could get behind. She sat on the edge of my bed, and before I could think about it, grabbed my hand and pulled me down beside her. She leaned her blond head on my shoulder. "I was so worried. What if something happened to you?"

"You'd be fine. You're a tough kid." I couldn't resist a chaste kiss on the top of her head. She smelled like drug store shampoo and vanilla with just a hint of something else. Something I vaguely remembered but knew was a very, very, bad thing. Her pheromones filled my nose and then my brain, and in my over-stimulated condition I responded. My groin started tingling, and I fervently wished the feeling away. She must have sensed it, too, because she turned her head toward me and closed her eyes expectantly.

"No. It' not like that, kiddo. It can't be."

"Why not? I'm not a kid." Except she was. At least too much of a child for me. And a client's daughter. A rapidly deflating part of me expressed disappointment, but I stayed strong.

Desperate to change the topic, I asked, "You said the cards talk to you. Like *talk*, talk?"

"Exactly. Like they're whispering in my ear. This was so loud. Like they're screaming, almost."

"What did Gramma say?"

"She says I'm a natural. And the longer I'm clean, the stronger I'll be able to receive the messages." Her lips trembled while her whole body shook. "I don't think I can take them any stronger. I need—something. To distract me. Please?"

The look she gave me almost shattered my noble intentions, but before I had to decide, the white glare of headlights pulling into the driveway lit up my apartment. An engine revved, then shut down outside.

Cromwell's messenger.

It gave me the excuse I needed. "We'll talk about this tomorrow. I need to take care of some business."

Delicate fingers played with the button on my shirt, and it was all I could do not to slap them away. "Promise?"

"Yeah. Promise. Now get. I have to handle this, and the less you know the better."

She wanted to fight me, but a single no-nonsense knock on my door changed her mind. "Tomorrow. No bullshit."

I gave her something that sounded like a yes and pushed her towards the stairs. A second, more insistent, knock followed. "Coming. Just a second."

As soon as the door closed upstairs, I grabbed my Ruger and held it in one hand, stood behind the door and opened it with the other.

"Are you going to let me in, Johnny, or leave me freezing my ass off out here?"

Of all the people Cromwell could send after that evil thing, the last person I expected was Nurse Ball.

CHAPTER 25

Cromwell's nurse-slash-pit bull brushed me aside with one arm and blew in with the November wind. "Damn, it's cold out there." She stopped dead and looked around my subterranean lair. "Really?"

I slammed the door and flicked the deadbolt as quickly as possible, lest something even scarier followed her in. "What are you doing here?"

Nurse Ball pulled her blue and orange Bears wool cap off and shook her head. Black hair hung to her shoulders, the first time I'd seen it down, and it looked... good. There wasn't a touch of grey, and I wondered if she had help there. *Shouldn't someone her age be going grey?* Then she unzipped her ski jacket. Wearing a red cable-knit sweater over black leggings and black boots, she looked as unlike the imposing nurse from my nightmares as she could and still be the same person. In fact, she looked damn good. Then I shook off that thought.

"I came to pick up the—Mr. Cromwell's package. Where is it?"

"Why you?" Before she could answer, a better question came to mind. "How did you know where I lived?"

She pulled her phone from a coat pocket and waved it at me. "You have Mr. Cromwell's phone on you, right? The stupid look on my face was answer enough. "If you don't want the boss to know where you are, turn off your damned phone. You're not very good at this, are you?"

As much as her smugness annoyed me, I couldn't wish what was in my trunk on her. Or anyone. "It's too dangerous. I'll bring it to him myself. In the morning." She opened her mouth to say something but didn't get the chance. "I'm serious as dick cancer. You don't want to touch that thing. Two people are already dead because of it."

"Dead? Christ, Johnny. What did you do?"

"No. Jeez, no. I didn't kill them. One shot the other, and then that thing in there—shit, I don't know... Ate the other guy?" My voice was an octave and a half too high and I knew how crazy it sounded but was past caring. Nurse Ball might be a badass, but even she was no match for the Anubis Disk.

The more my voice screeched, the calmer she became. Classic psych nurse training. "Okay, slow down. Tell me what happened. And breathe." She shrugged her jacket off, threw it on the bed and faced me. Those green eyes locked on mine. "You called the CDC..."

Once I'd pulled the cork from the bottle, I rattled on until I was a sweaty, wild-eyed ball of adrenaline. "... and then I got the hell out of there." Maybe because the nurse wasn't delicate like Meaghan. Maybe because if I didn't vent, my head would explode off my shoulders, but I spared her nothing. My arms flailed and my voice cracked while she got every freak, gory detail and took them like a champ. On the other hand, I'd worked myself into a lather and my senses had jumped to Defcon One. My heartbeat thrummed in my ears, and I smelled the reek of my own fear.

Nothing she heard shook her Arctic demeanor. I might as well have given her the weather report.

"Are you okay? You're not hurt?"

Pacing like a bear in a cage and running my fingers through my sweaty hair, I nodded and avoided her gaze. "Yeah. Yeah, I'm fine. But—" Then my mouth made some kind of *gaaaaaah* noise that expressed my frustration better than real words.

"Look at me," she said. I didn't, so she said it again, making it clear compliance was in my best interest. Nurse Ball closed the distance between us, and cool fingers pressed against my forehead. Then a thumb pulled down a bottom eyelid and examined me. She didn't say a damned thing.

Even though my heart rate returned to normal, I still sensed everything around me. The little "hmm" noise as she looked into my eyes, the soft "smack" as her dry lips parted. A car drove by our place far too quickly for such a crowded street. A creaking floorboard upstairs suggested Meaghan had her ear pressed to the door.

My nose worked overtime, too. She smelled like cinnamon gum, faint but expensive jasmine perfume, and herbal shampoo. Ginger, maybe. When she placed two fingertips to my throat to check my pulse, I had to back away so my system didn't overload.

"You're not running a fever," she said. What she meant was, I wasn't delirious. "Oh, for Christ's sake, stand still. What are you, five?" This time she took my wrist, checked my pulse, and cupped my face in long, French-tipped fingers and continued breathing deep and slow. She did exactly what I'd done to Meaghan a while ago, and it worked. The sweating stopped, and my eyes sunk back into their sockets.

"I'm good. Thanks." I pulled away from her.

"That's quite an endocrine system you have there. I'll bet your adrenaline and testosterone levels are spiking like mad. Been a long time since I've seen that."

"You haven't seen this."

"Actually, I have. I told you—in the ER, but never this long before a full moon. I've known guys like you. You will be a real handful in about eight or ten days. Am I right?" She studied me like a bug under a microscope. I just clenched my jaw and kept my trap shut.

Her voice changed, and she became all business. "Did you leave anything behind at the house that could lead to you or Mister Cromwell? Touch anything? Leave DNA, fingerprints?"

The ice queen was back in command and I felt more grounded. Life was as it should be again. "No, I wore a hazmat suit and gloves the whole time. The house was empty when I left, and I shut down the cameras."

"Good. You got anything to drink in this place? You look like you could use one. God knows I can."

It seemed a strange prescription, but who was I to argue with a professional? God knows I felt the need for a little somethin'-somethin'. That occasional need was exactly the reason there was rarely anything stronger than beer in the fridge. I'd tried the self-medication thing. There was nothing wrong with getting rip-roaring drunk during the weeks when Shaggy was safely hibernating. But the last thing anyone wanted was my not being in complete charge when he was restless. My alter-ego needed to be kept on a short leash.

"Beer?"

"Long as it's not light."

"Hardcore, huh?" I fetched my last two beers, popped them with a church-key, and handed one to her. "Uh, want a glass?"

She toasted me with her bottle and took an unladylike slug, "As you said, I'm hardcore." We stood in awkward silence, sipping and looking everywhere but at each other. Finally, I sat on the bed and gestured to my lounger. She shrugged and sank into it, only grimacing a little as she probably wondered what she might catch. About four sips in, she broke the silence.

"How have you kept it together? Everyone—like you, I mean—was a wreck. Most of them were in jail or on the way. You seem like a good guy."

"I don't know about that." People kept telling me that. Didn't make it true.

"Yeah, you are. I mean you're a mess, but it's a miracle you're not a complete train wreck."

"Thanks?"

She leaned forward, resting her elbows on her knees. "You keep everything that goes on inside you through... I don't know what to call it. Brute force, maybe. It's impressive. Really."

There was no good answer to that. I did it because the alternative was unthinkable. It's not like I had a lot of role models, but I'd seen what happened when Lycans lost control. I couldn't name a single old werewolf. That wasn't a coincidence.

"You're obviously single."

Ouch. "What gave me away?"

An arched eyebrow and a wave at my lodgings were all the response needed. "How do you blow off all that steam?"

"Yoga. A lot of stretching." I could have added deer poaching and almost eating Russian gangsters, but we were having a good time.

"Yoga? You don't seem the type."

I'd heard that often enough not to take it to heart. "Really? You should see my downward dog."

"Why, Mister Lupul. Are you offering?" It was only through masterful muscle control that I didn't pass beer through my nose. If she noticed, Nurse Ball didn't make a big thing, just laughed at her own comment. *Who knew Frau Blucher had jokes?*

In the ensuing silence, I heard the ticking of my old wind-up alarm clock and a TV upstairs. Meaghan must have grown tired of eavesdropping. There was no other sound in the room except the rustle of leggings rubbing together as the nurse crossed her legs at the knee, leaned back in the chair and drained her beer.

Her eyes took me in again, but this time there was a hint of bemusement on her unpainted lips. Other than telling her to get the hell out, I couldn't think of what to do or say, so I reached for her empty bottle and placed them both on the counter beside the cracked porcelain sink.

She rose out of the recliner. "I doubt most women can handle your... moods. Must get lonely."

I shrugged. It was best not to dwell on it, but recent events had me more aware of my isolation than normal. She continued picking at the sore spot.

"You're a nice guy. Probably makes it harder on you because you care about other people. That's a rare trait in a man, regardless of his glandular situation."

Glandular situation? Now, there's a polite way to put it.

"It's too bad. You're a good-looking guy. A bit furry—but some women like that. Most of them couldn't handle someone like you on your best day."

"And you could?" It came out nastier than I'd planned, but this was not a conversation I needed to have with a near stranger who could— mathematically—be my mother.

She ignored the dig and took a step closer, reached out and brushed sweaty hairs off my forehead and out of my eyes. "You probably don't give them a chance. You protect them, don't you?" Those jade eyes left heat signatures on my face.

"Protect them from what?"

"You."

Like the girl tonight. Like so many others since Becky. Because I wasn't a complete bastard, despite what bubbled out of me from time to time. The woman stood close enough to me that the cinnamon and jasmine wafted through, along with a new scent. I'd detected it earlier on Meaghan, but that was soft, faint, almost tentative. A deep sniff confirmed what I feared—the aroma was stronger, more insistent. More assured. Nurse Ball wanted me. Or at least thought she did.

Do you want some of this, lady? My better angels shot down the idea immediately. I'd have never even considered such a ridiculous notion if it weren't for the stress hormones zinging through my veins, and what Meaghan had stirred up. I didn't blame her for that; she was just a kid. But Nurse Ball—I wasn't sure if I was angry, confused, or something entirely different.

"Don't." It sounded either noble or whiney, I couldn't tell.

"How long has it been since you let off some steam?" The dirty look I shot her raised both her eyebrows. "That long? I could help with that, you know."

I felt a stir between my legs and my cheeks caught fire. "You don't want to do that," I said.

"Why not?" She stepped closer, filling my nose with all of those scents. The sound of her low, deep respiration threw fuel on the coals.

I tried to side-step, but merely banged into her. Those breasts, housed in a soft bra and sweater instead of the usual shell casings, pressed against me. The throbbing in my crotch was almost audible. I pulled my hips back so she couldn't tell. "Miss Ball."

"Francine," she corrected. Her chuckle was like warm caramel. A confident hand ran down my shirt to my jeans. Her lips parted. "I'm not scared of you."

"You fucking should be."

"I'm not. I'm not a little cheerleader who doesn't yet know what she needs. Some of us like a little—adventure—from time to time. You don't know what it would take to frighten me."

Deep inside, Shaggy stirred, and I felt a flash of panic. Contradicting urges collided in my skull.

Do you think you want this, lady? You really don't.

Except maybe she did. Before I could determine which it was, my mouth was on hers, tasting beer and saliva and need. My hand gripped her waist, fingers digging into the skin above her leggings. My mouth almost swallowed her face and she let out a little "mmphh." I jumped back like I'd touched an electric fence.

"I'm so sorry—"

"Shut up." Then her mouth captured mine again, and that cool, assured hand gripped me through my pants. "Trust me, I'm a nurse."

It took everything I had to pull my mouth away. "You don't know…"

"Isn't that half the fun? Not knowing?"

"What if I can't control myself?"

"That's the other half." She squeezed again, and we both moaned. Perspiration and the tiniest dash of fear only made her smell more irresistible. A soft, pink, pointed tongue ran across my bottom lip.

"I trust you."

Nobody had ever said anything hotter to me in my life.

The dam burst. Hands reached for what was closest. Teeth clumsily collided. Buttons flew across the room. My rough hands ran over the soft flesh of her stomach beneath her sweater. Her breasts were soft and sagged a little, but the hardened nubs under my thumbs drove me crazy. Greedy lips followed fingertips. It had been too long, I couldn't even do the math. A familiar tingle started at my tailbone, then finger-walked up my spine.

Gravity took over as we tumbled onto the bed. Both of us reveled in groans and gasps and couldn't tell whose was whose. Fingernails and teeth raked my chest and shoulders. The bolts of pain reached to where Shaggy stirred, restless. The effort to keep him under control created blazing streaks of tension that ricocheted from my fingernails to the balls of my feet to my brain to the part of me that was so hard I was afraid it would burst.

I didn't care if she heard me sniffing like an animal; I inhaled her skin. The heady mixture of sweat and jasmine was jumbled up with something else. There was a strong hint of fear—less than she'd have smelled on me, likely—but there was something else, too. It wasn't the terror of someone afraid for their life.

This was wild and uncontrolled. It was the rush you get riding a bicycle too fast down a hill, or jumping off a high diving board. Fear was the wrong word. What I smelled was more like *thrill*. Her unfamiliar scent overrode my common sense. She had no need for protection, and I didn't want to provide it.

I closed my eyes one last time to make sure Shaggy was in check, then allowed my body to relax and engage in some of that thrill myself. It was intoxicating and clarifying all at once. I surrendered to it—clutching—grabbing, licking, nibbling. Growling. We both growled.

Which of us was the aggressor changed from one second to the next. Slick, sweaty skin slid against the other body. The friction of my hairy legs against smooth thighs threatened to ignite a flame, and I didn't care if it did. My knee pushed hers farther apart.

"Do it."

I shouldn't. This isn't right. But it feels...

I obliged her, keeping just enough control that we both gave out the perfect groan and thrust again just to hear it. Then once more, slower. Then faster. The music changed tempo and volume, and I almost forgot to worry about losing control.

On outstretched arms, I looked down at her face. She was no longer in control either, but didn't care any more than me. Her wide eyes smiled into mine. She nodded, which was all I needed. The odors and sounds threatened to burst out of my brain in the most amazing way. I recognized another new sensation. I was having fun.

She was on top. Then me. Snatches of words filled the room, most of them obscene or garbled as our mutual thrusting reached a fever pitch.

Nurse Ball—Francine—returned my grin with a smile free of shame or guilt. Then she took one of my hands in hers and slowly, deliberately placed it on her throat. Before I could think, I squeezed, just enough that fear for her shot up my spine and I eased off. Shaggy nearly burst free, and I panicked, thinking I'd gone too far. Francine let out a frustrated growl, then put my hand back and said, "Yes, goddammit. Please."

Gritting my teeth, I let out a deep roar as I felt the soft flesh under my hand. She made an animal noise and thrust up to meet me. Her eyes flew open and challenged me.

If you say so.

Francine tensed, then let out a shrieking laugh. I didn't lose control so much as abandon it. My hips pumped once. Twice. Maybe three times.

We both howled and mashed our mouths together until I was unaware of anything except a blinding explosion of heat and color. There was a scream that didn't come from me. Francine twitched and wriggled beneath me, and I collapsed on top of her, panting for breath.

For several seconds the room, the woman, and everything else disappeared. Then I heard a soft voice from under me say, "... let me breathe." I tried rising up on my arms but had to settle for rolling to my left until our slippery torsos were both exposed to the night air.

I turned to look at the mysterious woman in my bed. Francine lay with her arms over her head, nipples red and swollen. Dark streaks of ruined mascara circled her eyes. She turned towards me and in a little-girl voice, said: "told you I wasn't a-scared of you."

Then she honest-to-God giggled and buried her face in my hairy, matted chest without the least embarrassment.

Too soon, Francine turned back into Nurse Ball. The thick red sweater covered the marks I left on her breasts and stomach. The leggings slid up, hiding bruises just below her knee.

I had to ask. "Are you going to tell Cromwell about this?"

She gave me an indulgent smile. "No, are you? This was a simple pickup and delivery. The rest was off the clock."

"He'll know, though, won't he?"

She shoved her hair back under the Bears cap. "Probably. One way or another." She took a long look around as if to make sure she'd left nothing incriminating behind. "Get dressed and let's get that thing out of your trunk."

I sat bolt upright, my head clear. "No way. I'm serious."

"I'm not..."

"Afraid. Yeah, I know. But I'm scared spitless. I'll bring it to him first thing in the morning. At the apartment or anywhere he says. But you're not taking it."

When the scolding school-marm look didn't work on me, she grabbed my bicep. "Seriously, that's why he pays me the big bucks. And they underrate nurses when it comes to danger. Why do you think we all sleep with cops and firemen? Hell, even Florence Nightingale died of syphilis."

"Really?"

She gave me a "Johnny-don't-be-a-moron," laugh. "No, but that's what they told us in nursing school so we'd behave."

"How'd that work?"

Nurse Ball, who wasn't Francine anymore, ignored my little comment and dug in her purse for her keys. " For real? You're leaving it out there overnight?"

"Anybody tries to break into my car gets what's coming to them. But yeah. I'm sure as shit not bringing it into the house."

She headed for the door, and I leaped out of bed to open it for her. She put a hand on my cheek as I leaned in to kiss her. She politely avoided my lips and planted hers on my cheek. "You're a good guy. See you tomorrow morning. Don't be late."

I watched her get into her car and drive away. Then a blast of the Hawk brought it to my attention that I was naked for the neighbors to see, and I shut the door.

A squeaking board upstairs reminded me someone was home. Meaghan. I wondered how much of that she heard but couldn't think about it. I went back and collapsed on my bed.

CHAPTER 26

8 days to the full moon—past half.

I jerked upright in bed, and my first thought was: *check the car.* My second thought occurred when I was halfway to the door: *put on pants.* I slipped a pair of sweats over my nakedness and ran out in bare feet to where the Charger sat, unmolested, in the driveway.

It took three tries to get the key in the trunk lock and pop it open. The metal case lay where it was the night before, innocently lodged between the spare tire and my aluminum softball bat. Just to make sure, I flipped the catches on the case and used my thumb to crack it open just enough to glimpse the Anubis Disk. In the cold dawn's light, it was just a boring piece of shiny metal sitting on a bed of black felt. Nothing evil, no sign it had bled a man dry in front of my eyes. I let out a sigh of relief that came out in a big frosty cloud.

The sunrise was so beautiful, and the air bit the inside of my nose so pleasantly, that I could almost believe yesterday never happened. Then I saw the long, red scratches down my arms and it all came back to me in a rush—especially last night. I hurried inside on tiptoe so the neighbors wouldn't see me wearing only my sweatpants and sporting a morning boner.

I closed the door behind me and was doing a little warm-up dance when my smartphone pinged. Praying it wasn't Cromwell, I flipped it over to read just one word.

Breakfast

If Bill was inviting me up for breakfast, it meant he wanted to talk. Given the tone of our last conversation, I wondered if this was a peace offering or another excuse to chew me out. I thought for a second, turned the water on in the shower and let the moaning in the old pipes fill the building before replying:

In the shower, be right up.

I examined myself in the rust-dotted mirror while waiting for the water to heat up. The face peering back at me looked like it had survived a minor fender-bender. Besides the scratches on my arms, neck, and back, there were bruises on my biceps, a swollen lower lip and what looked like—not that I'd ever had one before—a hickey the size of Lake Michigan on my suddenly hairless nipple. Definitely a sweatshirt kind of day.

Not knowing what to expect, I took a moment to gather my thoughts at the top of the stairs before throwing the door open and saying: "Morning. God, that smells good." It did. Bacon, coffee, and pancakes is one of the great combinations of all time no matter how delicate your olfactory senses are.

Bill sat at the dining room table in front of a stack of pancakes. Some of them looked undercooked and pale, while others were nearly black. "Morning. Sleep well?"

I waited for the follow-up joke that didn't come.

"Yeah, good. You?"

The screaming smoke detector interrupted us. Meaghan stood cursing and oblivious to my presence, or pretending to be. She used a spatula to flip over a black disk had once been a pancake. I poured a cup of coffee and bit my tongue.

"How'd it go yesterday? With Cromwell's... thing?"

"Good. I'm taking it to him this morning."

"You okay?" He was waving a syrupy fork at the red lines on my cheek.

"Yeah. It got a little hairy for a while, but it's all good. I'm fine. Job's done."

Bill stabbed one of the less charred pancakes and tossed it onto my plate, paused, then added one of the raw ones to even things out. "Think Cromwell will be happy?"

Meaghan slowly entered, carefully balancing a plate of carbonized flapjacks. She added them to the shrinking pile and sat down without looking at me or saying a word. She just flapped her napkin with more force than necessary and stabbed two pancakes in one thrust, dragging them onto her plate. I'd gladly take the silent treatment for now, at least until we were alone.

Bill and I continued to gab about yesterday, me providing as few details as necessary. We talked about how I would need to pay his costume guy for some damage and other semi-normal things. Maybe nobody would say anything about last night's other adventure.

A raspy voice and the shush-shush of slippers on linoleum came at me from behind. "What the hell did you do to that girl last night? I didn't know whether to applaud or dial nine-one-one."

I dropped my head and groaned. Bill tried to hold it together, but his stifled snicker became a full-blown snort. Meaghan made a small choking noise, threw her napkin on the table, and ran from the room.

Crap.

I pushed my chair back to go after her, but the old lady put her hand on my shoulder and pushed me back into the chair. "Time for that later. We need to talk about something more important. Do you know where that Russian bastard is?"

Damn. For about thirty seconds I'd managed not to think about Maxim Kozlov.

"I know where he was last seen. I'm heading up there as soon as I deliver the package to Cromwell." I looked to my friend for help. He sat with his cheek full of half-chewed pancake like a giant chipmunk. He seemed fine with his grandmother leading the discussion.

Gramma's voice dropped to a whisper, and she kept one eye on the kitchen to make sure Meaghan didn't walk in. "Good. That cloud is getting darker and nearer. It's all I can do to look. And that poor lamb is freaking out. You need to get this over with."

"I said I'm on it. I don't like it any more than you do. Let me get the doo-dad to Cromwell and then this is priority one."

Except I didn't know how. I for sure would need to be at full strength, and the moon wouldn't be full for another week. If I could just keep eyes on the Russian until then, I could take him on. Maybe. Somehow.

Bill managed to choke down his food. "It's just that we worry about you. And with that—thing—out there, we're all on edge." After another gulp of coffee, he added, "Is this what it's going to be like all the time?"

"It's a dangerous job. But it hasn't been a problem until now, has it?"

He put his fork down and leaned across the table, trying to keep the stress out of his voice. "I know, but it's not just you, is it? I've got your back, but there's my grandmother to think about." Between the two of them, I'd trust Gramma over him in a firefight, but his point was valid.

Gramma piled on. "And Meaghan. That poor kid spent last night just flipping the cards over and over, making sure you were okay."

Like that was my fault. "You're the one that taught her. Suddenly it's my fault she's hooked on it? And she believes in that crap, too. You do know she's an addict, right? Obsession is kind of what they do."

Gramma's voice dropped and her woody fingernails dug into my arm. "Watch your tone. That girl has a gift like I've never seen. She's the real deal. Don't look at me like that, you little shit, it's true. Problem is she's so damaged. Just one big, raw nerve and she hasn't learned to protect herself yet. Not like I have. It's a royal bitch for me, so I can't imagine what she's going through."

"I... we, can't take much more of this." My friend couldn't meet my eyes. *Et tu, Billus?*

"I said I'm on it." The table went silent. My appetite disappeared and the sticky syrup clung to my mouth with a nasty after-taste. Or maybe that was the pancakes.

Gramma stared at me over her coffee cup. "So, who was she?"

"No one." *No one I plan to discuss with you, ya crazy old bat.*

"Humph. Didn't sound like no one. I haven't heard noises like that in a long time. Hell, I haven't made that sound in forty years. I remember one time..."

Bill covered his ears. "For the love of God, I'm eating."

I rubbed my temples, trying to concentrate on banishing that image and clear my head. The first order of business was to unload the blood-thirsty time bomb in the driveway. Then there was Kozlov, although what I'd do once I found him was a mystery.

Maybe then things would get back to normal. I needed normal more than I needed sleep, food, or Ozzy Osbourne, and I needed all those things in abundance.

From the kitchen came the crash of a glass hitting the floor and someone shouting, "shit, shit, shit."

And then I'd have to deal with Meaghan.

One nightmare at a time.

CHAPTER 27

I waltzed through the front door of Malcolm Cromwell's building with a metal case in my hand and a song in my heart. Justin did a double-take when he saw the three-circle biohazard stickers.

"Whoa. What the hell's that?"

I was in a perky mood. "This little old thing?" I asked, waving it in front of the meathead. "It's Cromwell's missing package."

His surprise was stronger than his bullshit attitude. "No shit? Dude, how'd you find it?"

My voice grew flat and serious, mocking him. "If I told you, I'd have to kill you. I don't discuss my clients."

"Asshole." He took my Ruger and placed it in a drawer. As I passed by he added, "Have a good one." Well, that was progress of a sort.

I still hadn't figured out what to say to Miss Ball—Francine, when I saw her. As usual, she decided for both of us.

"Mister Lupul. Good to see you again." She was all white starch and crimson lipstick with no sign of welcome or even recognition. Her uniform was buttoned to the top, and she wore a white long-sleeved shirt under it, covering her to the wrists. It was cold out, even for early November, so I'd be the only one wondering why she was so bundled up.

She spoke loudly enough for Cromwell to hear at the other end of the apartment. "He's been waiting for you."

Before I said something lame, she spun on those squishy white shoes and took ten steps towards the inner sanctum. Without breaking stride or looking back, her fingers hooked the hem of her nurse's uniform and lifted it in the back just enough for me to see the top of her sheer white thigh-high stockings. Then the curtain fell, and she was the old Nurse Ball again.

"Mister Cromwell, he's here." The old guy nearly broke a hip jumping out of his desk chair to greet me.

"Is that it? Let me see."

I set the case on the desk, then put both hands on top and leaned towards him. The nearing moon was shortening my temper. "I'm fine, thanks. Which is more than I can say for Nasrallah and Badri."

His tortoise-shell glasses magnified his watery pale eyes and made him look like an actual tortoise. "A shame. But they knew the risks."

"I didn't."

"But you got it, and here you are. Well done. Using the CDC as a distraction was a rather clever move—even if that was my twist on your original idea. You've got real potential. Oh, stop pouting, you knew this was dangerous when you took the job. It can't be any riskier than when you worked for O'Rourke."

"Which I quit, don't forget. I don't mind playing the odds. Like you say, it's the job. But I need to know what I'm up against so I can be ready. It could have been me instead of Badri back there."

His brow furrowed. "I thought you said they were both dead."

"Badri shot the Egyptian. That... thing... killed Badri."

The old man licked his dried, cracked lips. "And there's no way to trace it back to you? I can't be involved in any way."

"You're good." *And once again, I'm fine. A little shook up, but thanks for your concern. Prick.*

Dark-spotted hands caressed the case and then clicked it open and lifted the lid. To be sure, the disk didn't look like much—just a few square inches of shiny metal with hieroglyphics scratched into it. If I was underwhelmed, Old Man Cromwell looked like Christmas came early.

"How did it... how did the African die?" He looked like he ought to be wrapped up in a blankie waiting for a bed-time story. His eagerness seemed in bad taste, but proper decorum wasn't my area of expertise. And it was his dime.

"He was bleeding from where Nasrallah shot him—"

"Wait, Wafik shot him? Why?"

I looked for some sign of guilt or something in his creepy pale eyes. "Because he was tired of being a thief and wanted to something more... honorable. His words. We were almost out with the disk, but Nasrallah caught us. Badri shot back and killed his boss. Don't worry, ballistics will prove it. But he was bleeding pretty badly from the arm." I shut my eyes against the slo-mo replay my brain began showing on a loop.

Cromwell couldn't take his eyes off the thing as I continued, "The second the blood hit that thing, it—it just drank it. I don't know how else to put it. It started slurping it up and he couldn't let go… it just kept going until there was nothing left."

"Marvelous." Not the word I'd have used, but then I was sane. "I want to see how it works," he said.

"No way. "

"Johnny, I have gone to considerable trouble and expense to procure the Anubis Disk. I want to see what it can do with my own eyes. What's the point of owning powerful things if you can't experience their power?"

"What's it supposed to do, anyway? Why would someone create something like this?"

"The story goes that fanatical Egyptians created it to prevent Napoleon's invasion. If you offer a blood sacrifice and chant the words written on the disk—these here—it would summon Anubis, the God of the Dead. But you have to do both parts of the ceremony. Apparently, it will accept the blood without the rest of the ritual. I never knew."

Cool story, but it still made no sense to me. "How is this going to help you with—that?" I waved at his sexy bed and dialysis machine combination.

Cromwell's eyes looked huge through those thick lenses as he stared at me. "I'm facing Death. Don't much care for it, as you can imagine. Anything that can cross back and forth across that divide might help keep me alive for a little longer. Even if it doesn't, it is still kind of fascinating, don't you think? Kills the boredom."

It wasn't really a question, so I kept quiet as he answered himself. "And if it doesn't work, well, I have it and no one else does. How do young people say it? Scoreboard?"

If he was that desperate to see a guy with an animal's head, I could pop in about a week from now for free, but my boss was already undoing the button on his wrist. He pulled the cuff up his arm to where the fistula stuck out of his elbow. The blue and purple mottled skin looked like it hurt. "Miss Ball won't like this one bit," he muttered.

Neither did I, but then he wasn't scared of me. Since I couldn't just tackle the old coot and tie him down, the next best solution was to make sure he didn't get himself killed in the process. Against my better judgment, I said, "be careful." That was one of those phrases you said when you had nothing else to offer. By the time you had to say, "be careful" or "calm down," it was usually way too late.

Cromwell jiggled and tugged on the plastic stent until a single large crimson drop appeared on his skin. I took his wrist and held it about three feet over the disk. "Don't get any closer. And whatever you do, don't touch it. Once Badri's blood made contact, he couldn't shake it off."

My client licked his lips again and gave the loose skin on his upper arm a squeeze. The drop swelled until gravity took over and it fell, landing dead center in the disk. It covered old Jackal-face. I squeezed my eyes shut and waited.

"Is something supposed to happen?" he asked. I opened one eye. The blood still lay on the disk, running into the crevices around the symbols but otherwise inert and harmless. We almost cracked our skulls together, leaning over to look closer.

"I don't know. It started just as soon as—" Whatever I was going to say got cut off by the soft sizzling hiss of water on a hot griddle. Then, as Cromwell's eyes widened, there was a soft "slurp," and the blood vanished, leaving no trace.

"Jesus Murphy," he whispered.

Cromwell grabbed his right arm and squeezed again. Without thinking, my hand slapped his away. He shot me a look that might have frozen me in my tracks, but he was only the second scariest thing in the room. "That's enough. You've seen it."

For a second, he looked like he would try again, anyway. "Don't make me call your nurse."

With a disappointed sigh, Cromwell lowered the lid, hit the catches and straightened up. I heard his vertebrae crack and pop with the effort, and his breathing grew a bit shallower. My nose picked up the scent of hand sanitizer and good old-fashioned fear, so I relaxed. He would obey common sense, for the moment at least.

I took his elbow and helped him into the chair. He grunted his thanks and then gave me a grin. "Good job. You did well. Passed the first assignment with flying colors."

"Thanks." A pilot friend of mine once said that success was determined by where you set the bar. Any landing you walk away from was successful. If you can use the plane again, it was perfect. This mission had been—barely—successful. But if the client was happy, I guess I was too.

"I told you there was more where that came from." He turned his giant computer monitor towards me and ran his fingers over the keyboard. Some kind of complicated chart appeared. "These are all items I'm looking to add to my collection. A shopping list, if you like. This could keep you busy for a long time at nine thousand a month, give or take. Plus expenses."

I wasn't an expert at reading spreadsheets, but it showed cities—London, Budapest, and Las Vegas were the first three—and a bunch of codes that likely told him what they were and what kind of creepy super-powers they possessed. There were also a series of numbers that were so big it took me a minute to realize those were prices.

Damn.

My mouth flapped several times before words came out. "I'm not stealing these things." Badri's words about honor still echoed in my head.

"Not asking you to. I am attempting to buy each of these items once they're located. At a fair price. Some of them I'll just need you to collect them and escort them home. Others might take some... convincing. You're familiar with that kind of work. O'Rourke speaks highly of your skills in that department."

There were a few times I'd had to lay hands on someone in the natural course of collection work. Usually, they were dirtbags, so I didn't feel too bad. When my cycle was high, and I needed to blow off some energy, it felt pretty good. Too good, after a while. I began looking forward to those assignments. Much as I enjoyed punching people when I was in the mood, I hated knowing I'd hurt them. So, I quit before I did something irreparable. But there wasn't any arguing with someone who could put the fear of God into the scariest guy I ever knew. Besides, my resume wasn't that impressive if I had to go job hunting. And there was the small matter of a hundred grand a year.

I was so busy justifying my work to myself I didn't realize Cromwell was still talking until he said, "All of this depends on your being discreet and staying off the radar. What's going on with your other project. The other one... like you?"

"I'm working on it. Should take about a week."

"Seriously, I would hate to see our partnership suffer because of unwanted attention." He let the threat hang in the air. "If you need help, within reason, don't be shy."

I enjoyed having an apartment and collecting the old man's money. Both of those things would disappear if I didn't do something about Max Kozlov pretty damned quickly.

The way he couldn't keep his fingers from stroking the case was making me nervous. Maybe it was better to remove the temptation. "Would you like me to put that somewhere for you?"

"Yes, I suppose so." He reached under his desk and the bookshelf behind him hissed open a crack. It was the same kind of panic room Nasrallah had, just a little smaller and more luxurious. Maybe all freaky rich guys shared a contractor. "Put it back there, if you would. I'll find somewhere more permanent later."

I picked up the case, took it into the room and set it against the wall. Then I stepped back and watched it close, feeling a lot better once there was a foot of concrete and a bookshelf between myself and the Anubis Disk. Hopefully, for good.

He sat at his desk, playing with an ivory letter opener, his mind already working on the next problem like I wasn't there. The object looked innocent enough, but I couldn't help wondering if they had used it in human sacrifices or something. I wouldn't be surprised. The whole damn world was strange and creepy now. After thirty years I was learning things weren't at all what I thought they were, and it didn't sit well. I'd have been happier not knowing. This old codger was trying to corner the market on weird.

"Mister Cromwell? Why do you do it? Mess with these things, I mean. They're dangerous, not to mention crazy. You have everything you need. Why not just take it easy and enjoy life?"

He turned the blade over in his hands. "When I was your age, I thought I had it all figured out. The world worked on a very simple set of principles. First of which was, if you had enough money, things would work out the way you wanted. As I got older, though, I learned that there are things—forces—at work in the world that few people know about. Knowing and controlling them is real power. Life, death, whatever is in between. That's more powerful than mere money."

"I always knew rich people were nuts."

He let out a loud "bah" of a laugh. "Maybe. I prefer to think that people like myself—and Wafik Nasrallah, peace be upon him—have the luxury of not worrying where our next meal is coming from and so have the freedom to indulge our higher curiosity. Truth be told, it's not the money that drives us so much as fear. The closer we get to the grave, the more we seek the power to prevent the inevitable."

"But that thing. What does that have to do with keeping you alive?"

"They created The Anubis Disk to bring back the God of the Dead and help drive Napoleon out of Egypt. Can it bring the dead back? You might say no, but the blood sacrifice part of the story seems real enough. Who can say for sure? My scrying bowl was certainly real enough, although this makes up for that loss."

I pointed to the ivory knife. "And that? What does that do?"

He seemed surprised. "Opens letters. Some things I collect just because they're beautiful. Look at the carving on this ivory. Balinese. Perfect. Other things I invest in because of their long-term interest. That disk, some of the more arcane pieces, you."

"I'm not something you can just buy."

"Really? Look, I hate to be harsh but I'm old and I'm sick and I'm too tired for bullshit. You would rather be just about anywhere else, yet here you are. It's not because of my charm. But the check cleared. And the first of the month another check will come, and you'll come running when I have another job for you. Grow up. It's an investment I'm happy to make. Partly it's because you have a set of talents I find valuable. Then there's the greater mystery of Johnny Lupul, isn't there?"

I hated the thought of being a lab rat. Even a well-paid one. But here I was, no sense arguing. "Anything else I can do for you, sir?"

If he got my sarcasm, he ignored it. "No, have a good day. I'll call when I need something else."

Seconds later, Francine—still in full Nurse Ball mode—was perp-walking me across the living room towards the door. Out of the corner of her mouth, she whispered, "Whatever that thing is, he's happy with you. You did a good job."

"Just one of the many services we offer, ma'am."

"Speaking of which, last night was interesting. Any chance of repeating the experiment? We still have a few days until... you know."

"That's not a good idea."

"You didn't enjoy yourself?" She ran a finger down a scratch she'd put there the night before.

"It's not that. The closer we get to, well, the top of my cycle, the less control I have. The more dangerous it is."

She smiled. "I'm willing to take that chance."

Her answer went straight from my crotch to my brain before I smothered it. "I'm not."

"You're really worried about me, aren't you? That's sweet."

When did the world decide I should be the grownup? Nobody warned me it would suck this much.

"I'm really not. And this isn't some kind of game. I can't control myself when my... glands act up like that. A week before and a few days after. It's not safe. For either of us."

"If you say so. But I'm game when you are. You might want to put a little disinfectant on that scratch." Cromwell probably had surveillance cameras all over the place, so I did my best to behave professionally, like we hadn't tried to sexually eviscerate each other only twelve hours before.

She gave my elbow a subtle squeeze. Loudly she said, "Thank you for coming, Mister Lupul. See you soon."

Then her voice dropped, and she whispered, "You're sure it has nothing to do with the little blonde I saw watching at the upstairs window last night?"

Double crap.

CHAPTER 28

The upside of not having much experience with women is I seldom had to deal with what my late dad, Jim McPherson, laughingly called, "girl trouble." I simply did not understand how to deal with them. Unlike during my glory days on the construction crew, just packing up and leaving town in the morning wasn't an option now.

Meaghan was a good kid going through some terrible shit, I didn't want to hurt her. That said, there was zero romantic interest on my part. Nurse Ball—my brain still couldn't wrap itself around calling her Francine—was a different matter altogether. She had twenty years and a metric crap-ton of crazy on me, but *damn.*

And they were both distractions from the task at hand; Kozlov.

I didn't know where he was or the foggiest clue what to do if I found him. When I found him. Failure wasn't an option. I always hated that expression, because it was always an option, just the one you least wanted. It was also the most likely.

I was looking for one crazy, violent, Russian needle in a haystack of nine and a half million people. There were two places he'd been for sure. One was Berwyn, where he'd terrorized Jerry and Sweet Lou. the other was the back alley of our apartment. Since pretty much everyone I cared about in the world was there, it seemed best to secure the home front first.

Back at the apartment, I did a quick reconnaissance. Out front it smelled like November, all moldy leaves and potential rain. The Jack-o'-lanterns on the neighbor's porch were already being nibbled by squirrels, so there was the funk of half-rotten pumpkins in the air but nothing more sinister. It was just another day on the North Side.

The wrought-iron gate complained when I pushed it open to check out the breezeway between buildings. The kid next door's soccer ball was laying there again, so I gave it a gentle toss over the low chain-link fence. That would save the poor little guy from having to knock on the door and face Gramma, who kept threating to keep it each time. The old girl was more or less harmless, but she put the fear of God into me, so she must have seemed like the Wicked Witch of the West to an eight-year-old.

Thinking of Gramma, and then the unsuspecting people next door, not to mention Jerry and Lou only added to my sense of failure. It was my job to keep them safe from my mistake, and so far, I'd done a crummy job of it.

The postage-stamp of browning dandelions and crabgrass we called a backyard could use one last mowing. Bill assigned yard work as part of the rent, and I was delinquent. Thanks to Neil O'Rourke though, I was paid up through the end of the year so he let me slide. One of the annoying things about Chicago this time of year was if you thought Mother Nature had gone dormant and left the yard alone, the damned thing continued to grow. If you gave it a late mowing, it would snow the next day. If it was nice in the morning, I'd take my chances and tackle it then.

Scoping out the alley, I noticed that everything was neat and orderly as it ever was. There were bags of garbage in the cans, but the lids were on. The trash bin with the claw marks sat unmolested, last week's marks faded to simple ragged lines of discolored plastic. A trio of rats scrambled over them, trying to find access. They sniffed me about the time I smelled them and scuttled off, unhappy but with their heads attached. Kozlov hadn't been back.

My guts lurched to think how out of his mind the poor bastard must have been to do something like that while still in his human form. Shaggy at his shaggiest avoided the nastier forms of vermin. It was more fun to chase deer, rabbits, and the occasional bad guy. Then again, I'd had years coping with what lurked inside me. He had three weeks. I felt a twinge of sympathy despite myself.

A flash of red drew my eye upwards. Meaghan was on the back deck with her hands buried in her hoodie pouch, staring off towards the north. She looked down for just a second, saw me watching, and found something way more interesting to look at in a different direction.

Given the choice, I'd have rather faced Kozlov, but it was time to deal with whatever the hell was going on between us. I stood directly below her and looked up.

"But soft, what light through yonder window breaks?"

Meaghan looked at me like I had three heads. "Huh?"

"The balcony scene? Shakespeare?"

"Oh, yeah. Haha."

Good start, Johnny. "Can we talk?"

She looked over her shoulder. Someone—probably Gramma—was in the kitchen, so Meaghan came down to meet me. Her head hung low, and she was biting the hell out of her chapped bottom lip. She stopped three or four steps from the bottom so we stood eye to eye. "What?"

It was way too cold to be outside without a proper jacket, and the kid shivered like an angry chihuahua, waiting for me to say something. I tried but had no idea where to start.

"Look about last night," was as far as I got, then ran out of ideas.

After letting me wiggle a while, she let me off the hook. "It's fine. I was an idiot. I just thought..."

"You're not an idiot. You've been through a lot. And you need someone to talk to. I get it, I do. But I... it's not like that."

"Hey, I get it. I'm a mess. Who wants to deal with all this?" She held her arms out for me to take it all in.

She wasn't wrong. Waifish blondes weren't my type to start with. Add in the ten-year difference, a major drug habit, unresolvable daddy issues, and stir. And that was just her half of the dysfunction cocktail.

"You're a good kid. I'm just trying to help."

"I'm not a fucking kid," she said, exactly like an angry kid. "And I don't need your help."

"Really?" I plopped my ass on the bottom stair. She hesitated, then joined me.

"So why are you helping me, then?" Her eyes flashed. "Is my father paying you?"

"I wish." That part slipped out by accident and I scrambled for a way out. "You were cold. And what kind of dick would just leave you out on the street? And then, you know, the old girl took a shine to you."

"She's nice. Weird as fuck, but nice."

"So, are we, you know, good?"

"I s'pose. I'm just not used to—most guys expect something." It didn't take much imagination to picture someone taking advantage of her in any number of ways, and my neck hair bristled at the idea.

"I'm not most guys."

She leaned her head on me, lifted my arm and put it over her shoulders. I jumped up. "I thought we just said…"

"Jeez, relax, hairball. I'm just fucking freezing. We can't all grow our own fur coat. Can we go in now?"

I stood up to wipe the dust from my pants. The stairs needed a good sweeping. Tomorrow was definitely chore day.

Having negotiated peace on one front, I was free to obsess about Kozlov. It would take a minor miracle to find him before anyone got hurt, and I was all out of magic.

But maybe Meaghan wasn't.

"Hey, Meags. Last night you said you saw… you know. How did you do that?"

"I told you, I was bored, so I started doing a reading on you."

"You were worried about me?" That was kind of sweet.

"I was really bored. There's only so much tea and reality TV I can stand. How does she watch that crap? Anyway, I'm looking at the cards, and suddenly I get this image of two dead people. I thought one of them might be you. Freaked me the fuck out."

If you'd asked me two weeks ago, I'd have said the old Gypsy was *BS-ing* when she read her cards or did her hoodoo with that ball. But now anything seemed possible. I grabbed Meaghan's little ice cube of a hand and pulled her up the stairs behind me.

"What's the hurry?"

Ignoring her protest, I dragged her onto the deck and threw open the kitchen door.

"Shut the door. I'm not paying to heat half of Chicago." Gramma Mostoy barked and turned to look at us. Her face damn near fell off at the sight of Meaghan and I holding hands. She gave me the *"what-the-hell-have-you-done-now"* look, but there wasn't time to explain. I disengaged, ran to the kitchen table and began removing dishes and unopened bills.

"Meaghan's about to do a reading for me."

"I am?" the girl asked.

"She is? What kind of reading?"

"She's about to find Kozlov for me."

Meaghan grinned. "Cool."

Gramma wasn't smiling. "No way. It's too god-damn dangerous. She's not ready. I'll do it."

"No." Meaghan slapped the table. "You said I had the gift, let me use it. He needs my help." I feared for her life since nobody had won an argument with the old girl since the first Bush administration.

Instead of snapping Meaghan like a twig, Gramma rolled her eyes and pointed to the table. "Fine, but I'm sitting right here. And she'll need tea." The kid made the universal yuck face, but there was no arguing with *puni daj* when she was in battle mode and nobody had ever won two fights out of three.

I was still half-frozen from being outside. "Yeah, I could use a cup."

"Her tea you don't want. There's a Coke in the fridge, drink that and stay out of the way. You'll just mess things up. No offense."

There was a flurry of chair scraping and light lowering. I grabbed a pack of tarot cards from the shelf, but Gramma ordered Meaghan to fetch her own deck. Something about bonding. Who was I to argue?

After downing her tea—or whatever the hell that stuff was—Meaghan nodded that she was ready. Gramma took her hands and wrapped them in her own. "Okay, honey. Are you sure you want to do this?" Meaghan gave her a steely, determined look.

She sat across from the girl. "Fine. You're looking for that black cloud. The king of swords is your subject, so put it in the middle of the spread."

Meaghan shuffled through the deck until she found the card and placed it face up towards her. I didn't know if that represented me or Kozlov. Then Gramma put one hand over the card and beckoned me over with the other.

"Okay. Have him give them a shuffle." She shot me a look over her shoulder. "And then you step the hell back when you're done. She doesn't need you gumming up the works."

I was never a card shark, so my hands shook and half a dozen cards flew out of the deck. Red-faced, I picked them up and started over. Gramma's eyes judged me the whole time, while Meaghan stared down at the table, eyes squeezed shut in concentration.

After about five shuffles, she reached out, and I placed the deck in her hands.

Gramma shooed me to the far side of the room. "And stay there. Don't speak until spoken to."

She put a wrinkled hand on Meaghan's shoulder. In a far softer voice than she'd used on me said, "Okay. When you're trying to find the answer to a single question, which spread do you use?"

The kid's voice cracked. "An ellipse?"

"Are you asking me or telling me?"

"It's an elli... wait. I know this." She stared at the deck for a second, her jaw clenched and her eyes welled up a little. I thought our experiment was over before it even started. Then she sniffed and nodded her head once, her mind made up. "The Merkaba. I need to focus the energy on a single point."

For the first time that night, the old girl smiled. "Atta girl. Clear your head. Take your time. And you—" she pointed at me. "Keep your big mouth shut. Just let her do her thing. And for the record, this is a really, really, bad idea."

She wouldn't get an argument from me, but it was the closest thing to a plan we had. I shut my trap and watched as Meaghan laid one card face down below the king and looked to Gramma for approval. The old lady just gave her stone-faced silence. Stoically, she laid the third card to the left of the king, and the fourth went above it. A frown crossed her face, and she moved it to the other side. This time she got a grunt of approval.

When she was convinced the first three cards were in the right spot, she quickly placed the fifth card above the third, the sixth above the fourth, and the seventh at the top. She stopped and stared at it, panting like she'd just run a marathon.

Gramma's voice changed, becoming soft and low like she was crooning to a baby. "Okay, begin. Start with Experience." Meaghan's hand moved and hovered over the second card, then flipped it over. "Good. Now influence... Opportunity... Potential... Progression..."

With each word, another card turned face-up in the same order she'd placed them until only one remained. "Now, Manifestation. Only when you're ready."

Meaghan flipped the last card over so hard it nearly folded in half.

I leaned forward, expecting some kind of revelation. There had to be some physical reaction. A lightning strike, something. Absolutely nothing happened. Meaghan sat and stared at the table. The old lady stared at her, and I stood like a hairy scarecrow, too afraid to speak until spoken to. Other than the faint hum as a car drove by outside, and a fly beating itself senseless against the kitchen window, there was only silence.

Just as my head was about to burst, Meaghan pointed a finger at the fifth card, then at the seventh and back again. Her lips formed words nobody heard. Back and forth, she moved from one to the other, and the mumbling continued. She shook her head and did it again.

In a faint voice, she said, "This doesn't make sense."

Gramma harrumphed and skewered me with her gaze. "I told you this was a bad idea. Kid's not ready for something like this."

Meaghan's hand shot out and grabbed her skinny arm tightly. "I didn't say I didn't get anything. I said it doesn't make sense. Shush."

Used to doing the shushing, Gramma sat back and left Meaghan to it. The girl sweated and mumbled, then wiped her forehead and leaned back with a heavy sigh.

I couldn't help myself. "What?"

"Quiet, idiot." Gramma barked.

Meaghan touched her on the arm. "No, it's okay. I just—wow. I didn't see Kozlov, but I saw someone who knows. I think."

The old woman's face scrunched up. "What do you mean you think?"

"It's crazy. Makes no sense. When I asked where he was, I got this big black bunch of nothing. Like you when you try to read him." She meant me. "But then I found someone who knows."

"Who?" I asked.

"That's the crazy part. All I heard was 'two men and a child's blanket.' Over and over."

Gramma tried consoling her. "That's okay, sweetheart. It was a lot to ask. Don't feel bad."

I didn't share her gloominess. "Brilliant."

"Huh?" they asked in unison.

I bounded over, took Meaghan's face in my hands and kissed her on the top of her head. Then, without thinking, did the same to Gramma, dodging the slap that followed. "Two men, you said. And a kid's blanket?"

"Yeah. So?"

"So, I know who can find him." I flung the door open and ran downstairs to fetch my car keys.

CHAPTER 29

5 days until the full moon- waxing gibbous.

That late in the fall, the moon rises over Chicago while the sun's still going down. As I drove south, then west, it hung big and bright in sky. I could easily make out the craters. It was perfectly round except in the top right corner where it looked like someone had shaved about twenty percent of it off. In just five days that sucker would be full.

Even now, I felt my blood buzzing in my veins. The energy was building, but easily contained. My body was looking to run, or fight, or, well, Miss Ball had taken care of that other temporary desire. This was my favorite part of the cycle, but then I knew what to expect. *How's Kozlov feeling tonight?* It had to be awful enduring these crazy energy surges in his blood, but with no idea of what lay ahead.

Reaching Berwyn, I zig-zagged down alleys looking for the Powerpuff Girls print that would lead me to Jerry and Sweet Lou—two men and a child's blanket. There was nothing in the lane behind the doughnut shop where I'd found them the first time, nor in the next three. My imagination concocted all kinds of horrible scenarios and wondered if I was too late— that Kozlov found them before I could and what that might mean. Then I spied a green sleeping bag flapping in the wind. Bingo.

I pulled into a parking lot half a block down and the Charger's engine gave a little hiccough after shutting off. The choking sound made me cringe because I'd have to make some hard decisions soon. Should I get it fixed or just put it down like a sick Schnauzer and get something else? Not a Lexus, though. Bill could kiss my fuzzy ass.

My adopted mom, Eileen McPherson, taught me at least one lesson that stuck: never show up at someone's house empty-handed, especially when your hosts aren't expecting you. *It's just not done, you see.* It was especially true when their house is a shopping cart liberated from the corner supermarket. I popped in and bought three packages of beef jerky, a box of power bars, and a treat for Lou. Two big apple fritters.

I crossed the street into the alley where two figures stood beside the combination shopping cart and tent. One was Sweet Lou—the Sox cap a dead giveaway. The other person was a big white guy in a sky-blue windbreaker whose arms windmilled around in a way that meant he had his panties in a bunch about something. That was never, ever good news.

From the far end of the alley, my ears picked up the white guy's voice, "I've told you guys to get the hell out of here. I'm calling the cops."

The superior, bullying, *whatchagonnadoaboutit* tone in his voice made my blood boil, but Lou handled it like a champ. "Now, sir. There's no need to do that. We just need someplace to keep our stuff. We don't want no trouble."

His calm demeanor didn't seem to matter much. The other guy's voice grew more aggressive. "And that cart came from our store, didn't it, ya fricking thief? Do you know what that costs us every year?"

When my cycle is nearing the peak, the part of me that wants to just punch someone in the face is harder to keep under control. Shaggy, of course, encourages such behavior. Back on the construction crew, it led to occasional Friday night melees, and when I wasn't punching bikers, I could take out my rampant energy on the two by fours. The part of my personality that keeps me out of jail usually holds the reins fairly tight. But it had been a bitch of a week. And this guy's face was especially punch-able.

"Is there a problem, Lou?" It was a rhetorical question, but it did what I wanted it to do, get the attention of the jerk with the jacket.

Windbreaker Guy had a Ditka mustache, a wide clip-on tie, and a name tag. Guys with their names immortalized in plastic are the worst. Ted—if his nametag was to be believed—faced me.

"Yeah, there's a problem. It's just not yours. Back off." He pointed his finger at my face. Classic rookie mistake.

"Excuse me?" I asked. This would get good as long as I didn't completely lose my shit. I'd feel a lot better after I decked someone, and Ted would do nicely. My rational side knew I needed a good reason, preferably self-defense, to avoid getting arrested, though.

"Him and his running buddy have been bothering our customers. I'm asking him politely to take it somewhere else. And give back our cart."

"All right sir, we'll move it along..." Lou was still playing it calm, but then it wasn't the first time he'd had this conversation and knew the drill.

I sighed loud enough for Ted to hear me and placed the grocery bags at my feet. "Come on, man. Just let him be. Why don't you go back to the Quickie Mart and stop picking on people can't defend themselves?" My knuckles made a satisfying *crack* as I flexed them into fists and released them. Then I did it again, just to hear the sound.

"Whattaya, going to fight me, you whack job?" I was giving it serious consideration and took a step forward in the hope old Ted would oblige me. Unfortunately, he knew the magic words.

"Big man. Go ahead, I'll call the cops. I'll sue your ass if you lay a hand on me." The asshole looked like he'd do it, too. If he wouldn't fight me, there was always Plan B. It wasn't nearly as much fun but got the job done. I opened my flannel jacket just long enough that the Assistant Manager in Charge of Whatever got a good look at my Ruger.

He took two giant steps back and held up his hands. "Whoa, whoa, whoa. Let's not get crazy here. I don't know what your deal is—"

"My deal is I don't like bullies picking on my friends. Go on, get out of here." I did that thing tough guys do where they pretend to lunge at the other person just to watch him freak out. Ted did his part and took off running, the tie flapping in the wind. It didn't feel as good as decking him would have, but at least he was out of the way.

Lou was less pleased than I was. "You know he'll call the cops on us, right?"

I blinked stupidly. "Probably. So?"

"So, now we have to find somewhere else, and fast. Cops've been busting our balls for a couple of weeks trying to move us out. Where we supposed to go?"

Even with the cold wind, my cheeks burned. There were usually unintended consequences when I did stuff like this, and I hadn't taken Lou and Jerry into account. I held the groceries out as a peace offering. Lou took them with a tip of his cap.

"Thank you kindly."

"No problem. We'll think of something. Where's Jerry?"

He pointed to a shed at the end of the alley. "Back there somewhere. He saw that guy coming and took off. His nerves still aren't too good."

"But he's feeling better?"

"I guess." Lou leaned in, dropped his voice and tapped his temple. "Boy's still not right if you know what I mean. What brings you around here, Mister Animal Control?"

"I'm still looking for that Russian guy. You have any idea where he is?"

"He's still around somewhere. A drunk got rolled the other night. Got beat up kind of bad. I think it was your nut job. He didn't put anyone in the hospital this time, so Five-O isn't working up a sweat." Then he put the groceries in the cart, turned his back and began pushing his house away.

"Wait, Lou. I'm sorry, man. My bad, I didn't mean to get you guys in trouble. But I have to know. Do you know where he is, exactly?"

"Come on, I'll show you."

Since I was the one that got them evicted, the least I could do was help him move. I stepped in and took the car by the plastic handle. "Here, let me." The shopping buggy only had three good wheels, so it took some work to get the rhythm. Up ahead, Jerry poked his head from around the building and gave a little wave, although I don't think he recognized me.

"They cleared out the park by the river a month or so ago, probably safe to head back that way." The black man played tour guide for about five blocks, telling me who got killed where and what shopkeeper sometimes put leftovers out for the homeless. Jerry fell in alongside but didn't say a word.

The reek from the cart's contents and the bodies of the two men assaulted my nose. My stomach churned in protest. At one point I pretended to tie my shoe just so I could turn away and gulp fresh air. Holding it as long as I could, I went back to pushing.

Three blocks further on, we reached a busy intersection. Kitty-corner was an old twelve-room motel that was miraculously still in business. The paint job hadn't been refreshed in a decade or more, and the sign with the giant arrow had half the bulbs burnt out. The board read:

Rooms 2 l t Day Week Month
Direct Dial P ones
Free H O

My tour guide pointed. "He's been staying here. Or was, last I heard. The only place left around still takes cash."

Okay, you found him, Mister Detective. Now what?

"Great, thanks. Stay here a minute. I'll be right back."

When he saw where I was headed Jerry grabbed my arm and let out a frightened whimper. Lou patted his friend's shoulder and took his wrist and pulled him off me. "It's okay, Jerry. He'll be back. Promise."

I jogged across the road to get a better look at Kozlov's hideaway. It looked no more inviting on closer inspection, and I tried to imagine the Yelp reviews.

The front unit doubled as an office. An older black lady was watching one of the Judge shows—Judy, Roy Brown, whoever—on a small TV. She was so wrapped up in it she never saw the big hairy white guy peep in two of the units then skulk around back.

Soon as I turned the corner, the acrid smell of urine in the parking lot damn near knocked me to my knees. Through watery eyes, it looked pretty much as expected. The door of room nine had unpainted wood where the brass unit number should be. In unit eleven, an old man blew smoke and Old School hip hop out the window. It was way too cold to have the windows open, but maybe he wanted to make sure he got his damage deposit back.

In the far corner of the litter-covered asphalt, the dumpster sat behind a wooden barrier. Around it were three bursting trash bags that someone didn't have the strength or motivation to lift into the bin, three needles, a mostly empty bottle of Fireball, and half a dozen dead rats. Two of them still had their heads attached.

Kozlov was here. Or had been recently. But it would be five nights before I'd be in shape to take him on. I would need all the Shaggy-help I could get, and even then, there were no guarantees. Was he here now? I needed to know, but there was no way I was hanging out here for five days.

I finished my orbit of the building without catching hepatitis on the way and saw my two friends across the street. Jerry gave me a jaunty wave, and I waved back. That gave me an idea. Not a particularly good one, but it would help smooth over some of those unintended consequences.

I knocked on the office door.

Five minutes later, I had learned a lot from Dolores, the clerk. Kozlov was in unit twelve on the end, there was something creepy about him but he kept to himself, the telephones in the rooms worked and could be charged to the room although nobody used them anymore, and her daughter Monica needed to leave her no-good boyfriend LeShaun but wouldn't listen to her mother. Not exactly a reluctant witness, that one.

When I got back across the street, I reached into my pocket and pulled out the key to room four. "It's paid up for two weeks, but I need you guys to do something for me."

"What?" Lou eyed me suspiciously as Jerry grabbed the plastic keyring from my hand.

"Kozlov is in the room on the end. I need you to call me twice a day and tell me if he checks out, or anything weird happens. Don't talk to him, don't let him know you're watching. I'm coming back in five nights and I'll deal with him myself. Can you do that for me?"

"Deal with him?" Lou asked.

"I owe him one."

"Us too. Two weeks, you said?"

I looked at the two of them and their three-wheeled motor home. "Til the sixteenth. Figured you could use a bed and a shower."

He grinned at me. "Maybe even catch a Sox game on the TV." Someday I would have to have a serious talk with my new friend. Lou leaned in like he was letting me in on a secret. "Jerry could use a shower. He's getting a little ripe."

"Take care of him for me, will you?"

"Will do," he said, offering me a salute.

I had eyes on Kozlov now and felt better. That gave me five days to come up with an idea of how to deal with him. A hundred and twenty precious hours to figure out how to take down a werewolf without getting myself killed in the process.

CHAPTER 30

I stood in the kitchen surrounded by three people, all shouting some version of "what happened?" until I couldn't take it anymore.

I had worried Bill, Gramma, and Meaghan sick; I got that, but in my current sensitive state all the shrieking and crowding was too much and I snapped. "Jeez. Give me a second, will you? Honest to Christ." I know I sounded like an asshole, but it would only get worse over the next few days.

The Mostoys were used to my ways, moodiness they called it, and Bill and Gramma backed away. Meaghan still hovered too damned close. I glared at her so hard it should have left bruises, but she wouldn't back off.

"You don't have to be a dick about it, I just want to know what happened."

How could I explain the situation, so they understood? Sure, I'd found Kozlov and had eyes on him. Other than that, I hadn't done a damned thing about it. And, okay, he was hunkered down, and I'd know if he left. What I couldn't predict was what the blazes to do about it. The facts were all jumbled in my brain. Sorting them into a coherent story was taking a lot of effort and that took oxygen, which was in short supply at that moment. "Is anyone else hot in here?" I threw open the window, getting hit by a blast of November air that felt like a gift from heaven.

After some calming deep breaths, I felt better. "Okay, let me take another crack at this. I know where Kozlov is."

"How d'you find him?" Bill asked.

"Meaghan told me who might know. Two, uh, friends of mine. They knew where he was. They're watching him now and they'll let me know if anything changes."

Gramma's frown tried to dampen Meaghan's proud grin. "Beginner's luck. And you're sure he's not coming back?"

I'm not even sure of my own damned name at this point. "Absolutely. He's fifteen miles away. They'll keep a good eye on him. It's only for, like, five days."

Meaghan bit at a fingernail. "What happens in five days?" Then the light dawned. "Oh."

"Yeah. I'm not going to do anything until I'm, uh, prepared. Then I'll deal with him."

Bill used his accountant's voice. "And when you say deal with him…"

Seriously, bruh, you're gonna make me say it?

He didn't. "And if you can't? Deal with him?"

"Then you'll get to rent out the downstairs anyway, won't you?"

Gramma glared at her grandson. "What do you mean rent out the downstairs?"

"Nothing, Gramma," we said at the same time.

My head pounded, and my stomach growled like a dog at a cat show. That sent the old girl into action. "I'll make us something to eat." As she scoured the fridge and banged pots together until I thought my skull would crack, Bill and I pulled up chairs at the kitchen table. Meaghan plopped her butt in a chair, and I waited for Bill to say something bitchy, but he ignored her.

Instead, he asked, "What's your plan?"

If I had one, I'd have gladly shared it. I knew *what* I had to do, just had no inkling of *how*. The frustration wasn't doing anything for my mood. "I don't frigging know. Yet. Sorry, I'm still working on it."

"You know where he is, why not just go after him there?" Meaghan's teeth were working on yet another nail, and Gramma threatened to slap it from her mouth.

"It's a little motel, with too many people around. It has to be where nobody else can get hurt. I need something isolated, somewhere we can be alone." What I meant was no witnesses.

"What's around there?" Bill asked.

"I don't know, okay? It's not like I'm an expert on the greater Berwyn metropolitan area."

Meaghan had reached her thumb and was gnawing away. "There are always plenty of empty places in a town like that. We used to find all kinds of spots to... you know, get high. Just use Google Earth or something."

"Huh?"

She held out her hand. "You are so lame. Give me your phone. This isn't that hard." I obeyed, feeling like a four-year-old. My supposed best friend laughed. "This is easier on a laptop but—just a second." Her fingers tapped and swiped and did some kind of voodoo, then she turned the screen towards me. It was an aerial view of the western burbs.

"Where is he hiding?" The kid enjoyed playing teacher. Or maybe just busting my balls. Either way, she was having a grand old time.

After two wrong guesses and some zooming in and out, I found the motel. "Here. See, it's a busy intersection."

"Okay, let's pull out." She extended two fingers to expand the view. Two thick blue-green lines dissected the screen, one going North-South, and the other across the bottom of the screen, West to East. "What are those?"

I was trying to make sense of it all, but Bill chimed in. "That's the Des Plaines River, so the other one must be the Sanitary Canal. I think. Look, it's all industrial. Lots of empty buildings. Zoom in on this." He pointed to a block of squares near the water.

Meaghan did her magic finger thing. "Ugh, just a sec. This is so much harder on a phone."

"You don't have a laptop?" Bill asked her.

Meaghan glared at him. "He's not the only one who can't be trusted with nice things, okay? Here. See this?" The street view revealed a block of four industrial buildings. Impenetrable chain link fencing surrounded three of them. The fourth just looked sad, with a broken iron gate and half a dozen broken windows.

I scowled at the screen. "That one looks empty. That might do the trick, it's only two miles-ish from the motel. I'll check it out tomorrow. Hey, this is great, Meags. What would I do without you?"

She slapped the phone into my palm and walked away. Bill shook his head at my denseness. Then he held a finger to his lips and head-bobbled at the stairs.

I nodded. "Grab some beers, will you?"

"You don't have any downstairs?"

"Drank the last of them the other night, with... I'm out."

He handed me a pair of bottles and we headed downstairs. My apartment was dark and cool, just the way I liked it when my metabolism heats up.

I popped the beers and poured his into a stein. We clinked glasses and sipped in the silence good friends indulge in.

After a few silent seconds, he said, "you really don't have a plan, do you, Sherlock?"

I shook my head.

"You have a gun, right?"

"Dude, I can't just shoot him."

"You've killed people before." He knew damned good and well I had. He was there. But it wasn't with a gun. "Or do you need, like silver bullets or something?"

I couldn't help but laugh. "That silver bullet stuff is bullshit. I mean, when someone is—turned like that—their system is so much stronger than normal, so it takes more to bring them, us, down. Back in the day lead musket shot wouldn't do it, so you had to use something harder. Nowadays they have armor-piercing everything. He can die just like anyone else."

"Then you can too. That's why you should shoot him. So he doesn't hurt you first." My friend was tearing up, and it was always hard to carry on a conversation when he got like this.

"It's not that I don't want him gone, but that's just—I don't know— premeditated murder or something. The cops'll get involved and it'll be a mess. Whatever I do, it needs to solve the problem but not land my ass in jail."

"At least you'd be alive. I can't lose you, man." Bill threw his arms around my neck and stayed just shy of bursting into tears." I can't. You're my best friend."

Even at my most even-leveled, feelings weren't my strong suit. I patted his shoulder twice. "I know. I love you too," I said to the wall over his shoulder.

While he pulled himself together, I tried to puzzle it all out. If the warehouse worked out, I had the *where*. It had to be the full moon, so *when* was a given. But *how*? I needed to end the threat of Kozlov without going to prison or getting myself torn to bits.

My buddy wasn't wrong, I'd killed before, but this felt different. The guy who'd attacked him that night had it coming. And at least with Badri, I'd done nothing myself except watch him die. That should have made me feel better. Should have doesn't mean it did. That brought on an instant replay of the disk sucking the life from him and how horrible and helpless I felt. A shiver ran up my back. It was all I could do not to howl out my frustration. At least I'd seen it happen. What would the cops make of the corpse? The only saving grace was they'd never know it was me.

"Okay," Bill said, wiping his eyes, "what are you going to do?"

"First, I need to scope out that warehouse and see if it will work. Then I need to talk to Cromwell about something."

"Another case already?"

"Not exactly."

This was something way, way crazier.

CHAPTER 31

Night of the full moon.

The full moon would be up in two hours and I was as prepared as I would ever be, which was no great comfort. It wasn't ready enough. There was no protocol for taking on a psychopathic Lycan who, literally, didn't know his own strength. And no do-overs. The universe was only giving me one shot at this.

Driving to the old factory near the canal with a bloodstream full of pre-werewolf hormones and the prospect of a grisly death awaiting me was no fun. I tried focusing on the road, but my eyes kept drifting to the seat beside me. There was my Ruger, a duct-taped bag of God-only-knew-what Gramma had given me, and a metal case with a biohazard logo that I had hoped never to see again. This would not be a great time to get pulled over.

The warehouse would be my last stop. I'd had a little time to prepare for my big date with Kozlov.

The madness started early. It took a while just to get out of the house. When Shaggy is pounding on my brain to get out, I'm not exactly the picture of patience and grace and was in no mood for an emotional sendoff, but Gramma and Meaghan didn't get that memo. They ambushed me before I could sneak out of my basement and assaulted me with well-meaning, but not practical, advice.

"Take care of yourself, kiddo."

What a fine idea. Thank you for your sage advice, oh wise woman. The old girl meant well, and I regretted being a smartass, so I settled for thanking her and trying to brush past them out the door. It would not be that easy.

Meaghan had been up half the night, flipping those damned cards to find some way that I didn't end up as roadkill. "You shouldn't be alone. You need someone there who has your back." Then she threw her arms around me and clung like a suckerfish on a dirty aquarium. It took both Gramma and me to peel her off.

It was a sweet sentiment. But as much as I appreciated the idea of not being alone, I would be. Had to be. This was my mess, and nobody else could clean it up. God alone knew how this would end, but the last thing this production needed was witnesses. Or collateral damage.

"Here, this might help." The old lady held out a gallon baggie full of ground leaves and powder, packed so full it was like a pot dealer's wet dream. "It's wolfsbane and some other things." Even through the thick plastic, the stench assaulted my nose and my stomach threatened to boil over.

"Thanks, but..." I couldn't finish the sentence. Whatever this concoction was, it would probably kill me before Kozlov ever caught a whiff.

"Hold on." Meaghan snatched it from her hand and ran up the stairs. She returned five minutes later with the first bag tucked inside a second, or maybe even a third, then wrapped in duct tape and smeared with the old lady's arthritis gel.

"Here. This should be better. Weed dealers do it to throw off drug-sniffing dogs. Does it help?"

It did. The thick funk of eucalyptus and mint nearly knocked me on my ass, but it beat the hell out of the wolfsbane. "Thanks." The smell also brought tears to my eyes, which Meaghan misinterpreted. She threw her skinny arms around me again, kissing me hard. Before she or Shaggy could get the wrong idea, I shoved her away.

"I gotta go." It sounded way more macho in my head.

My first stop was Cromwell's apartment. Since it was a Sunday, there was some new bonehead at the door. At least I didn't have to deal with Justin. To my relief, Nurse Ball had the day off. A middle-aged Asian housekeeper answered the door and scowled at me, then ushered me in. Whether it was a language barrier or mild loathing, she didn't speak, just led me to the old man's office and shut the door behind me.

It took an hour of bargaining, horse-trading, and a modicum of whining, but I left with the Anubis Disk. The price Cromwell demanded in return sent the creepy-crawlies up my spine, but if I beat Kozlov, it would be worth it. If

I lost, it wouldn't matter much to me, and the old man would get what he wanted. Best not to dwell on either outcome.

Last stop before the OK Corral was the motel. I parked a block away, just in case the Russian saw the Charger and got it in his head to settle all disputes right there in the parking lot. He'd have his chance soon enough, but safely away from prying eyes. I couldn't stand the thought of innocent people getting hurt. Plus, getting disemboweled on YouTube would really suck. My gun went into my holster, Gramma's baggie got zipped into my gym bag, the hazmat case went under the passenger seat. Like I knew what I was doing, but of course I didn't.

Lou threw open the door to Unit Four before I was three steps away. "Where you been, man? Your guy is acting nuttier than squirrel poop. Got everybody all rattled. The maids are just throwing towels at the door and running."

"It'll all be over soon enough." That didn't comfort either of us. "He still there?"

Lou grabbed my arm and pulled me into the dank, over-heated room, slamming the door behind me. I braced myself for the smell, but all I detected were cleaning products and dust bunnies. There were clothes draped over every available surface. The boys clearly took advantage of hot running water to rinse out their clothes after Christ knows how long. I wondered what would happen to them in a week when they had to leave these luxurious accommodations. That led to an ugly suspicion I wouldn't be around to find out.

Knock it off. Stay positive.

I'm positive I won't be around to find out. Better?

"Where's Jerry?"

Sweet Lou hung his head. "Boy's lost his damn mind. Just stands out there by the dumpster, staring at Kozlov's door. He'll come in when he gets cold enough, I s'pose. So, boss, what's our plan?"

It was the first time I'd ever stated my strategy out loud and hoped it sounded more logical to him than it did to my own ears. "About six o'clock, I want you to deliver this to Kozlov. Just slip it under his door and run like hell."

I handed him a folded piece of paper. In Meaghan's handwriting were big, clear letters:

Let's end this.
Meet me here at 730
Lupul

Then it had the address and a crude map to the warehouse a little over a mile and a half away. A normal person could walk it in twenty minutes. With his metabolism at full roar, I'd be shocked if he didn't just fly there.

"Then at exactly eight-fifteen, I want you to use this." I handed him the burner phone. "Tell whoever answers where I am and to come pick it up."

"Pick what up?"

"They'll know."

It would only be one of two options, but since Lou wouldn't be there, it wasn't his concern. Forty-five minutes was more than enough to do what needed doing. Despite what you see in the movies, fights are usually over in less than two minutes. It doesn't take long to die, and there are seldom any good speeches.

Lou squinted at the phone and used both hands to flip it open. "Never used one of these before."

"There's only one number on it. Just hit redial." I showed him the big button. It took a couple of tries, Now I sympathized with Meaghan dealing with my techno-illiteracy.

"I'll be damned. Okay, where do you want us?"

"What do you mean? I want you here." *I want you safe and warm. I'd stay with you if I could.*

"You really doing this alone? A man's gotta do what a man's gotta do, huh?"

"Something like that."

He sniffed. "You know that's some bullshit, right? We want to help."

The earnest look he gave me almost got me to cave, but my problems weren't his. The two of them, especially poor Jerry, had suffered enough for my mistake. Let them be warm and safe for a few days—it still wouldn't make up for what I'd unleashed on them. Not to mention the missing Alice wherever she was. And Gramma, Meaghan, and Bill. Jesus, what a mess.

"You've already done more than I should've asked. Thanks, man." I stuck out my hand, and Lou solemnly shook it.

"Take care of yourself, Mister Animal Control."

Animal control. In a sick way, I guess I was.

On my way back to the car, I circled around the back to check on Jerry. Sure enough, in the amber glow of aging streetlights, the skinny homeless man stood beside the dumpster's wooden enclosure, slapping his arms around himself for warmth and stomping his feet. It was nipple-exploding cold out, and Jerry's breath came out like he was vaping, but his glazed eyes stayed locked on Kozlov's unit.

When he caught me out of the corner of his eye, he offered a smile and lifted his hand. Jerry looked like he was about to yell something, so I put my fingers to my lips, urging him to keep quiet. Kozlov hadn't bothered him since the original attack, there was no need to bring him to the Russian's attention this close to the end.

Once back in the car I cranked the heat, turned Physical Graffiti up high on the stereo and headed for the warehouse on the canal. Two hours and this would all be over.

One way or the other.

CHAPTER 32

Mike Tyson once said that everyone had a fight plan until they get punched in the nose. Replace punched with "ripped apart by razor-sharp claws and teeth," and that's pretty much where I was. Something was bound to go wrong—probably horribly, irreparably wrong—but a plan would limit the number of possible catastrophes.

Over the last few days, I'd visited the building multiple times. The old warehouse wasn't perfect, but it would sure do. There was the lackadaisical security—twice a day and once in the early evening someone would roll by in a marked car and pretend to look the place over. Usually, they parked across the street for however long it took to scarf down a coffee, then left.

The old logistics depot had multiple entry points, not including the chicken-wire reinforced windows. There had to be a dozen ways Kozlov could escape, assuming he showed at all. But I had one spot that would work to keep him contained. The old loading dock at the back had double doors leading from the main plant, then the dock itself, a wide-open patch of smooth concrete. To prevent vandals, the owners had bolted the loading bay doors shut. The fire marshal would be pissed, but the insurance company would dig it. If I could somehow, someway, stop Kozlov leaving the way he came in, it was a perfect trap. Unless you take into account the fact that I was the bait and would be in there with him. Details.

"Two men enter, one man leaves," sounds a lot more entertaining when you're home with the popcorn.

The echoing, empty space was pitch black, but that didn't bother me. My eyes, ears, and nose all worked overtime. If Kozlov's inner rage monster was anything like mine, the room may as well have floodlights.

I dropped my gym bag and the case in the far corner and took inventory.

In my holster was my pistol, which was fine until I changed, at which point it would be worse than useless. It's a little tricky to pull a trigger with fingers the size of Snickers bars and seven-inch fingernails. It would be so much easier to just plug the bastard as soon as he showed up but, I didn't know if, a) I was capable, b) It might bring the cops before I dealt with him, and c) If I shot him and didn't kill him the first time, I'd just piss him off. I would only get one shot.

Next was Gramma's bag of werewolf repellant. This was the Gypsy version of a hydrogen bomb; mutually assured destruction. The old girl meant well, but unless I could figure out how to use it without fumigating myself, it wouldn't be much use. It stayed on the floor for the time being.

That left the only thing I had besides the clothes on my back. The Anubis Disk didn't look the same with its finely etched edges rimmed in grey, dry plumbers caulk and a three-foot round loop of ribbon attached to it like the world's ugliest Olympic Medal. It was straight out of the "seemed like a good idea when I thought of it" department. The only way to get it in contact with Kozlov without touching it myself would be to hang it around his neck or arm. If he had even the slightest scratch, the bloody thing would do the job I couldn't bring myself to do. *If. A lot of ifs.*

The Russian was unlikely to cooperate, and I'd be working with Shaggy-hands. The bigger the loop, the better my odds. I leaned it against the case with the ribbon spread as wide as it would go.

This cockamamie scheme would only work if I didn't go full Lycan. I needed enough of Johnny in control to pull this off. Odds were good Kozlov would surrender completely to his monster side, so he'd be working on pure instinct, rage, and bloodlust.

Goody goody gumdrops.

The moon was pulling me inside out. The urge to change had the hair on my arms standing on end and my extremities tingling. I had the advantage of knowing what would to my body. Kozlov had some unpleasant surprises coming. It was the only edge I had and couldn't let it go to waste.

First things first. Desperately hoping no security guard got proactive and found me naked in a freezing, empty building, I stripped to my underwear. The more warmed up and stretched out I was, the faster and less painful the transition would be. The change can take as little as thirty seconds, but the screaming and pain can go on a while. Kozlov wouldn't be as prepared as I would, and every millisecond could mean the difference between life and death.

While stretching out, I listened as hard as I could but heard nothing but the wind blowing and a metal sign banging against a wall somewhere in the dark. Taking a deep, cleansing breath, I bent from the waist, stretching my arms as far in front of me as they'd go. Next, I pointed in the other direction and felt the sinews in my shoulders strain. The burn was welcome, and I went through a slow but strenuous yoga routine. By the time I was in an eight-angle pose, I was as close to calm as humanly possible and knew the change would be as efficient as it could be.

Which was still a bitch.

It was freaking cold, and I regretted that when the time came my boxers would have to go as well. One of the six thousand things movies get wrong about Lycans is that image on every poster where the monster wears the rags of a shirt and pants torn from the knee down. As you twitch and swell, your muscles not only change size, but location. You might tear through clothing, but not without restricting circulation, a lot of pain, and significant chafing. And forget trying to bust out of blue jeans. Better to just remove them entirely and hope nobody sees you.

And that you remember where you put your clothes. There's a whole other story.

With my body and mind prepared, I went over the plan yet again. The part that eluded me was how to stop Kozlov from leaving the room through the only door once he was inside. The big sliding panels were too heavy for one person, even with Shaggy-strength, to shut them without working electricity. I needed something to block the door that I knew would stop him.

Anything that wouldn't keep me in wouldn't slow him down much. My eyes desperately scanned the room over and over. It was empty except for the contents of my bag and three hundred square feet of bare concrete. Seeing the bag of wolfsbane again, I got a monumentally stupid, borderline-suicidal idea.

I brought the bag to the corner of the room nearest the door. Then set it on the floor where I could get at it in a hurry.

My heart damn near screeched to a halt when I heard the faraway crunch of tires on gravel. No way Kozlov had a car. That had to be a security patrol or a cop. I hoped they did their usual half-assed drive by. For sure, I didn't want them popping in for a visit. If they found me here, I was guilty of naked trespassing, if that was even a thing. The blood froze in my veins until I heard them pull away, then it thawed and began pumping through me.

It wasn't long after that I heard the rattle of chain link fencing and the broken door scraped open.

Showtime.

I shucked off my underwear along with my last shred of dignity and moved to the wall beside the double doors.

"Kozlov, that you?" If it wasn't, I was truly screwed. The question bounced off the walls.

"Where are you?" His question bounced back to me.

"Marco—" I shouted. There was no response. "You're supposed to say Polo. They don't play that game in Russia?"

He must have figured out where the sound was coming from, because there was a grunt and the slapping of rubber soles against the floor got louder and nearer. Good. When he changed, his footwear would hobble him. A small ember of hope glowed within me.

"Lupul you asshole, where are you?"

I cupped my hands and yelled as loud as I could, knowing the echo would drive him that extra, little bit buggier. "Straight ahead, Max. Come and get it."

The footsteps and grunts drew closer, preceded by the foul funk of sweat, BO and rage. I slipped against the wall and quietly skulked to a corner near the door where I picked up the bag of wolfsbane. It took immense concentration to allow just a single long claw to emerge from my hand without giving Shaggy full control, but I managed to get a sharp enough nail to poke a hole in the duct-taped package. Then I took as deep a breath as I dared.

Everything happened at once. Kozlov stormed into the room at a full run. He skidded to a halt pretty much in the center of the room. He wheeled around, eyes and nostrils flaring.

With my lungs as full as I could make them, I dashed across the doorway, tearing the package of wolfsbane open and leaving a three-inch pile of weeds, twigs and grey dust across the opening. Then I dropped the bag and ran to the left wall where I could breathe again.

The Russian got a whiff of the noxious stuff and took several long steps back until he backed into the far-left corner of the room. It did nothing for his mood. He rubbed a sleeve over his eyes and shouted, "What the fuck is... are you naked?"

I looked down. "Oops. My bad."

"You're crazy." I didn't argue with him, but it was definitely the pot calling the kettle black. He had on the same clothes he'd worn in Grammas kitchen, and they were much the worse for time. His hair had grown out except for a bare friar's patch on the very top. No wonder he shaved his head. The goon was going bald. The ten-year-old in me wondered if his wolf-self would have bare patches in his hide. The thought made me snigger, but the moment passed when I looked at him again. His eyes were wide as silver dollars, and his breath came out in staccato bursts. The guy was in a crap-ton of pain. Kozlov kept shaking his head, probably to fight off the demons building to the eruption point in his skull.

Even in the pitch black, there was no mistaking the hatred on his face. "What did you do to me?"

"I'm sorry, Max. You won't believe me, but I didn't know this would happen."

"What would happen? What is this?" He held out his arms. Long coarse hair was already sprouting despite his efforts to keep it under control... The skin rippled and undulated wildly. His tattooed hands flexed into balls, then opened over and over.

"You want to know what it is? Take a good look, dude."

I changed.

If you surrender, the transformation happens fast. Try to fight the feeling, it can be long and agonizing. Since I was relaxed and focused, it took less than a minute. My hands and legs burned as the muscles stretched like bungee cords. Because it happened so fast, it hurt like hell and I slammed my eyes shut, swallowing a scream.

When I opened them, the world came to me through Shaggy's eyes. Blinking twice, whatever I looked at was outlined in grays and greens, but everything in the room was visible despite the darkness. Inside the lines everything was sharp and in high definition, outside was slightly out of focus. I locked my attention onto Kozlov—frozen in place by confusion and horror.

Hoping to catch him before he could complete the change, I leapt at the bastard. What lived inside of him, though, caught my scent and knew what to do better than his human side. In the time it took for three leaping steps, he morphed. It happened so quickly it could only mean the human side had abandoned all control and the animal was in charge.

I hit Kozlov square in the chest and we rolled across the concrete, then leaped to our feet, ready for another attack. The beast within him assumed total control. Before his head or face fully formed, I felt a claw slash my arm and knock me to the ground to my left. The asshole was strong as hell and working on autopilot.

In my whole life, I only ever fought one Lycan as strong as me and barely lived to tell the tale. It made sense that since the old *blatnoi* was tougher and crazier than me in human form, he'd also have the advantage now. My Johnny-brain was never my strongest asset, but it was the only advantage I had. There was very little of Max Kozlov left in my opponent.

As expected, I heard the cloth tear as the werewolf exploded out of his clothes, at least where the seams didn't hold. He slashed at himself, trying to get free from the restrictions. That gave me a razor-thin opening. I pounced again, teeth first. It was sheer glorious freedom to feel his hairy flesh in my mouth and tear at it. There was no need to hold back. Blood filled my senses and the Shaggy part of me roared in triumph, nearly overwhelming the little control I maintained.

There was blood. And so much pain. The rush went supernova in my head.

The Kozlov-thing shrieked and rolled away from me, then launched his own attack. This wasn't my first rodeo, and I dodged his incoming body, sending him skidding empty-handed across the cement floor. That close to the door, he picked up the scent of the wolfsbane. Howling and shaking his head, he roared his displeasure. The good news was my plan worked; it would stop him from escaping. The bad news, no surprise, was it trapped me in there with him.

In a low crouch, I waited for him to come at me again. He dropped to all fours, eyes locked on me and roaring a challenge. I roared back, reveling in Shaggy's rage, but not his insistence on charging first. Scattered thoughts overlapped each other, and it was hard to focus.

There's something we need to do.

I couldn't remember what that was. I was too busy tamping down Shaggy's fury and bloodlust. There was a plan, but I couldn't access it through the haze.

What the hell was I supposed to do?

Shaggy demanded dominance, and I had to shove him to the background for a moment to clear my head. He wasn't happy and pushed back so hard I nearly succumbed.

Meantime, Kozlov paced to his left, then his right, keeping his back to the door and the putrid, toxic wolfsbane barrier. I studied his movements, examining how his muscles flexed and waited for the telltale tension signaling an imminent attack. With me running the show instead of Shaggy, I knew I'd be slower than I needed to be.

Scanning the room for some clue as to my next step, a glint of metal caught my eye.

Something... the disk. Get it around his neck.

Shaggy was pushing for an all-out attack, and my control became more tenuous by the second. There was no easy way to reach the Anubis Disk. I needed to sidestep and shuffle, gradually making my way to where it lay, all the time keeping my eyes on Kozlov. To turn my back on him invited attack and certain death. I inched along, maintaining alpha-wolf eye contact.

Kozlov followed. I could see in his face how delighted he was at the prospect of backing me into the corner.

Good. Let him come.

Blood dripped from the gash in my arm and the pain throbbed up and down my body. Shaggy's impulse to fight and kill was detracting from my focus.

The disk. I'm supposed to... do something. Right. I just wasn't sure what. The Shaggy backed off enough for me to remember. With a triumphant growl, I reached for the Anubis Disk, then stopped cold.

Don't touch.

A shiver of fear run up my spine as the sane part of me poked its head up. Bleeding as I was, the fucking thing would claim me instead, and this would all be for nothing. I hooked a claw under the ribbon and lifted gently, careful that it didn't swing back and touch me by mistake.

Both claws—hands, whatever—held the ribbon open in a huge loop. It left me exposed to attack, but if I moved fast enough, I could loop it over Kozlov's neck and dodge. I faced my enemy and howled a challenge.

Come here, you hairy Russian dick.

Whatever it sounded like in real life, Kozlov obliged, screaming back and using those powerful back legs to launch himself at me, black eyes flashing chaos and death. Everything in me wanted to greet him claw for claw, tooth for tooth. It's what Shaggy wanted, for sure.

Shaggy shut up. I got this.

Screw fight or flight. I needed to be perfectly still until the other monster's head entered the circle. One bounce, two, and then he left the ground and came at me, claws swinging wildly. His head was perfectly aligned with the loop. I felt a rush of victory. This was going to work.

It didn't work.

One of those flailing claws caught the ribbon, tearing it from my grasp. The damned thing skittered across the smooth concrete floor towards the door. Before I could worry about that, his body crashed into mine, slamming me against the wall. Jaws snapped shut inches from my face. The reek of his hot breath and spit covered my furry face. I slashed back and shoved against his body with all my strength. He jumped back and crouched low, preparing another run at me.

The disk. Where is it?

Shaggy didn't care. He led the charge and the rewarding feeling of flesh under claws supercharged me.

Kozlov kicked out and sent me somersaulting over him. That's when I saw the disk, laying in the open about ten feet from the door. Maybe I could get to it if I was willing to risk the wolfsbane kicking my ass. I was. Shaggy wasn't.

Okay, we'll do it the old-fashioned way.

Shaggy could have the fucker. I made myself as big and scary as could be, preparing for another assault. Just as I was about to release control for good, I caught a whiff of something on the air.

Two somethings.

Kozlov smelled them too because he lifted his head and turned towards the open door where two figures stood in the opening, statue-still from fear. Shaggy inhaled their terror, and the thrill ran the length of my body.

A familiar voice whispered, "Holy Mother of God." It was Sweet Lou. He and Jerry had followed Kozlov despite my warnings.

The other werewolf picked up the scent and roared a challenge to the two men. The only reaction was a small whimper and the odor of urine. Poor Jerry.

My last thought as Johnny was that at least they were on the other side of the chemical barrier and were safe, at least for now. Then the cosmos exploded into shrapnel of light, smells and sounds as Shaggy took over for good.

I threw myself at the other Lycan and hoped for the best.

CHAPTER 33

The Kozlov-thing sensed them too. He lifted his head to emit a warning howl that shook the walls. Scenting Lou and Jerry's fear only drove him deeper into madness, and I'm sure he was planning what he'd do to the two of them once he disposed of me.

I was past caring. Without the disk, this was Shaggy's fight now. Kill, be killed, it was all out of my control. The world was a swirling kaleidoscope of sensations—flashes of light, snatches of odors, the deep blue-red of blood and the electric tingling rush of terror. Everything spun around. My body couldn't orient itself, and I was badly off balance. We grappled and rolled, one second rewarded with the feel of flesh in my teeth, then punished by agonizing surges through my entire being. Kozlov and I tumbled, ran, flew, fell. The scent of our mingled blood pushed me higher.

When the world stopped spinning, there was enough of me there to realize I was on my back, staring up into the crazed, gore-covered, slobbering face of whatever had control of Max Kozlov. This couldn't be worse.

Come on, Shaggy. Do something.

There was nothing to be done. I lay with my throat exposed. Time slowed, and I waited for the end. In wolves, if an alpha had its opponent on the ground and obviously defeated, the fight was over.

Lycans aren't wolves. There's no such thing as a symbolic defeat.

The rat bastard would kill me. Maybe Shaggy didn't want to be there at the end, but my mind suddenly burst through just in time to understand this was the end. The evil thing leered down at me, savoring victory. Amber eyes glowed with a wicked light. The room was a bouquet of blood smells, a lot of it mine. I heard him growling, the smack of his tongue running over his lips and... something else.

The other Lycan cocked his head. The sound was really two different noises. We both made out a high-pitched scream and running footsteps across the cement. Something headed our way. On the run. Over Kozlov's shoulder, I could make out someone approaching, but not who it was.

"Where the fuck are you going?" Sweet Lou's voice echoed in the room. That meant the other figure had to be—but it couldn't be—Jerry.

Holding the Anubis Disk in his hand and emitting a battle cry, the little guy charged us. Kozlov spun to face him, releasing me. I squirmed away into the farthest corner. Johnny took more and more control as Shaggy receded and my vision cleared to watch the scene unfold.

The beast wheeled around to face his new enemy and roared its indignation. His arm arced in a vicious swipe that caught Jerry across the chest, ripping him open to expose the white bones of his ribs. Blood and torn flesh erupted in a nightmarish geyser. The poor bastard was dead, but sheer momentum carried his body into the Lycan and they fell to the ground, rolling over twice before coming to a stop.

In one gruesome motion, Kozlov's claws and teeth separated the blond head from the rest of the man's body. The corpse twitched twice before collapsing chest first on the floor. Someone screamed. It might have been Lou. Could have been me.

In fact, the scream came from Kozlov. In his headfirst charge, Jerry trapped the Anubis Disk between their bodies, and now as the beast scrambled to its feet something glowed dimly in the dark. The metal circle was welded to the center of his chest.

Without my brain telling them to, my legs pushed my body as far into a corner as it could get. I had seen what the damned thing could do and wanted no part of it. There was no avoiding the sight, however.

Kozlov bellowed his agony and confusion, swiping blade-like talons at the bronze circle adhered to his chest. As I knew it would, the cursed thing refused to detach until it had completed its work. My ears picked out that horrible *whompwhomp* pulsating sound and then a distinct stomach-churning, siphoning. A hideous, thirsty, slurp. From somewhere in the dark, Lou screamed too.

Shaggy, or maybe it was me, let out a hysterical, barking laugh.

Gotcha, dickweed.

It took less time for the beast to die than poor Badri. Blood spewed from every scratch and puncture, puddling on the metal surface for only a moment, then disappearing into its starving, bottomless depths. The metal glowed in the dark—or maybe it was just my Lycan-enhanced vision—but the damned thing seemed to shine brighter and brighter until the Russian stopped twitching and lay deathly still. Eventually the light faded to nothing and became just another inert hunk of metal on top of the dry, empty husk that used to be Maxim Kozlov.

I pushed Shaggy down deep and claimed control of my body, which turned out to be a terrible idea. The first thing I saw through my own eyes was Jerry's lifeless head staring up at me accusingly. Kozlov's hollow corpse, still dressed in torn rags, lay on the ground. The pain erupted behind my eyes and I grabbed my head in my hands and rolled on the concrete floor.

It was the combination of odors that finally did me in. The coppery smell of blood, Jerry's body covered in every body fluid there was, the fetid smell that emanated from Kozlov. I emptied my guts onto the concrete, retching and heaving until my stomach and lungs were empty. Then I laid my head against the cool concrete. Pain seared through every inch of my body and I allowed my arms and legs return to Lycan form just to make the agony stop.

I sensed, more than saw, Lou timidly approach. "Johnny, is that you?"

In my current form, there wasn't much I could do but lift my arm and wave.

"Oh, Jesus. Jerry. Oh, shit." Poor, lovable, Lou had a tenuous grip on reality at the best of times and it was clear he struggled to make sense of the carnage. The poor guy would need a lot of help to escape alive and sane, but Shaggy wouldn't be any use to him. It would hurt like a sonofabitch, and my wounds would bleed far worse in human form, but there was no justification for leaving Sweet Lou to deal with this on his own. Drawing on what little strength I had left, I willed myself all the way back to plain old Johnny.

Each muscle and ligament screamed as my body twitched and morphed. The Change occurred in stages as the pain became unbearable after a few moments, so I paused and caught my breath, then changed a little more. When I could finally speak, I coughed out, "I'm sorry about Jerry."

He was calm as hell. Either it was shock or too many years in the street to be surprised by anything, no matter how awful. "That was some weird shit. You okay?" Even though it was a silly-ass question, he meant well. Lou bent over me and reached out his dark, callused hand that I waved away. "What do you want me to do?"

It hurt to even think the words, let alone say them. "Do me a solid, make that call. Oh, and hand me my pants."

CHAPTER 34

Through the comforting mist of unconsciousness, Sweet Lou's voice drifted through the fog and pinged off my brain two or three times before finally registering. "Johnny, man. Someone's coming." I opened one eye, at least as far as I could, to see him hovering over me. "There's a car outside."

"What did you stay for? You should get the hell out while you can." While touching, I was a little pissed because I'd tried so hard to keep him out of this. Jerry too. I said something else, but he didn't hear me the first time.

"Huh? What did you say?"

I shouted at him, as much as my abused lungs and chest would allow. "Run. You don't want any part of what happens next." Shit, I didn't want any of it, but a promise was a promise.

He didn't have time to argue because flashlight beams danced around the building and an authoritative voice shouted, "Lupul, you in here?"

The bouncing light grew stronger, nearly frying my circuits when it hit my eyes, and the voices got louder. Three figures came through the door.

The first was Justin, the meathead door guy, holding an automatic rifle with a TAC flashlight mounted on the barrel. Behind him was another guy, just as big, carrying a black plastic bag along with the most impressive handgun I'd ever seen. A third figure was about three steps behind, but I couldn't make him out.

"Holy crap. What happened here?" The second guy was so busy staring at Kozlov's body, he nearly tripped over Jerry's head.

Justin didn't answer. He swung his weapon, sweeping the room end to end, side to side, until it satisfied him the only living things in it were Lou and me.

The third person stepped closer, and I heard a voice say, "Christ, Johnny."

Two things occurred to me in rapid succession.

One — that bastard Cromwell sent Francine Ball to pick up Kozlov's body.

And two, I'd only gotten my pants as far up as my knees.

In the blinding white halo of the flashlight's beam, Nurse Ball bent over me. A moment of revulsion and confusion crossed her face. Then the experienced emergency nurse took control. She "tsk tsked," a time or two and ordered the second guy to get the first aid kit out of the car in a way that only those who've worked together a long time could get away with.

She poked and prodded me while I grimaced and whined. Shaggy wanted to take a nip at her fingers when they found one particularly deep scratch. I nearly let him.

"Some of these gashes are deep. We need to get you to a hospital," she said.

"That's a terrible idea."

"Why's that?"

"Because they'd ask a lot of questions that neither Cromwell nor I want to answer." I tried lifting my ass just enough to try squirming into my jeans, but gave up on the second attempt.

She slapped my hands away. "Here, let me. I've seen it." Justin nearly dropped his gun along with his jaw, but before there was any further conversation, the other guy returned with the medical kit.

Francine's voice was colder than the floor under my butt. "You two extract the bodies and start cleaning up. You know the drill."

There's a drill? Who are these people?

The guy who wasn't Justin looked confused. "We only brought one body bag." Then he saw the look on her face and offered a weak, "Yes, ma'am."

"Where are you taking him?" I'd forgotten about poor Lou. The old guy had been squatting beside his friend's body, and his black face showed shiny tracks down his cheeks.

I tried to help. "He's a friend of mine. Give him a ride home, will you? Make sure he gets there safe." My face hurt as I formed the words with a swollen mouth.

Justin looked to Nurse Ball for approval. She nodded.

Lou stood and backed away while the two ex-Marines placed both pieces of Jerry in the body bag and carried it out. The man lifted a hand in farewell, then followed them into the echoing darkness. The hairy and smelly remains of Max Kozlov lay curled in a filthy bloodless ball on the concrete.

Francine tried not to sneak looks at it while swabbing stitching and basically reassembling my body. To keep her focus on me, I asked, "Why does Cromwell want the body?"

She tugged harder than necessary on the suture. "To study it, I suppose. Add it to his weirdo collection. The disk really did that?"

"Oh yeah." It sure as hell did. "Do yourself a favor and don't touch it."

"That's why you wouldn't let me pick it up the other night." I ignored her, trying hard as I could not to call her obscene names as she disinfected my wounds.

"And that, thing?" she asked.

I took one last good look at the hairy, desiccated body. During his death throes, Kozlov kept morphing back and forth between himself and his Lycan form. One minute, claws waved as his human face screamed, then tattooed hands scratched at his wolf-like snout and eyes. The moment he finally gave up the ghost, he had the beast's head but his own hands balled up into fists. A man's body with an animal's head. The same image stared up at me from the Anubis disk and I shivered like someone drove a Zamboni over my grave.

"Would you believe me if I said he was a Russian gangster with a case of rabies?"

"Not even a little bit."

Too bad. It was the only explanation she would get. I drew on some of Shaggy's strength to tug on her arm. I pulled myself to my feet without dragging us both to the ground. Odds were, I'd live.

Justin and the other guy reemerged carrying a blue plastic tarp. With expertise born of battle, they swaddled the corpse. The disk fell from the drained body to the ground, the bronze ringing against the floor in the darkness. Justin bent to pick it up.

"Don't." I shouted, "That thing's a biohazard. Use gloves. Better yet, tongs if you have'm. The case is over in the corner."

"Really? What is it?"

"If I told you, I'd have to kill you." Nobody else thought that was as funny as I did.

My eyes turned to Francine. "Make sure Jerry gets decently buried, will you?"

"Who's... oh. We'll handle it. What about you?"

What about me? I needed time to think and clear my head. The deer population of Cook County was in for a bad night. "I can drive myself. Besides, I have to make a stop and blow off some steam."

"Whoa, boy. I think you better give it a day or two."

That made me laugh. Then I grabbed my side and let out a groan. "Not that kind of steam."

The two men counted, "one... two... three" and lifted Kozlov's corpse. They shuffled out of the room, Justin in the lead and walking backward. Francine watched them leave like she'd have to do their performance review at the end of it all.

When we were alone, she dropped her voice and said, "That could have been you, couldn't it?"

She was a smart lady, she'd figure it out if she really wanted to put in the effort. There was a more pressing mystery that needed addressing. "Why'd he send you?"

"It's what I do. Mister Cromwell sometimes needs things done that don't fit the, uh, normal parameters. I handle them." She ran her hand over my face, her soft touch only slightly less than professional. "Work for him long enough and you'll see."

That was probably true. "I don't know if I can."

"You sound like you have a choice."

"You mean I don't?" She shrugged, her failure to answer telling me everything I needed to know. "Do you?"

"Not really. We'll talk about it some other time. Maybe in a week or two. You know, when you need to blow off some steam."

CHAPTER 35

One day after the full moon- waning gibbous.

l woke up to find Bill sitting in my recliner, playing on his phone. "What are you doing here?"

"It was my shift. That's what happens when you sleep for twenty-four hours, people take turns making sure you're not dead. You're not, are you?"

l tried to sit up, but every muscle in my body exploded and l abandoned that plan. "Definitely alive. They say the pain stops when you die." When the room stopped spinning, l made a second, more successful effort. "Twenty-four hours? You've been here the whole time?"

He put his phone down. "It was mostly Meaghan, but she's gone. Gramma says to just leave you alone and you'll come crawling upstairs for breakfast when you're good and ready."

The way l felt, crawling was about right. "Thanks."

"Want to talk about it?"

"Not yet."

Maybe never.

"Is it over? Is he..." Bill's eyes were watery, and l was in no condition for another teary heart to heart.

"Yeah. Kozlov's dead, yeah."

Relief drew the last of the tension from Bill's body like a poultice, and he slumped back in the chair. "I'm glad you're okay."

"That's kind of a relative term. You said Gramma was making breakfast?"

He used his crutch to escape my chair and clomped over to the bottom of the stairs, cupped his hand to his mouth, and shouted, "He's alive. Put the coffee on."

I gently flipped open the covers and swung my legs over the edge, avoiding the look on Bill's face when he saw my scabs and sutures. Sitting up had gone so well I tried standing, which wasn't nearly as successful. Bill offered his arm, but I waved him off.

Walk it off. Rub a little dirt on it. Don't be a wuss. Jim McPherson's voice reverberated in my ears. Can't say I didn't learn a little something from the son of a bitch.

"Wait, Meaghan's not cooking, is she?"

"Nah, I told you she went home."

"Home? Like her parent's house?"

Bill gave me a gentle shove toward the stairs. "No. It's a sober-living place. Gramma signed for her. As long as she has a part-time job and stays clean, they'll let her stay."

"What part-time job? How the hell long have I been unconscious?"

"I'll explain over breakfast. But let's just say you have an administrative assistant."

"What do I need an assistant for? I'm a one-man show. Besides, I have you."

"That was before. Your email's blowing up. Seems Neil O'Rourke's been telling everyone what a badass you are, and you're getting all kinds of inquiries about collection work. Face it, buddy, you could use the help. When it comes to computers and such, you can't find your ass with both hands."

Bill seemed to have made peace with having Meaghan around. No one was asking how I felt about it.

"Not to mention your number one client, who's already wondering why you haven't got back to him yet. He said something about a shopping list. Whatever the hell that means."

Damn. No rest for the wicked.

I fell back on my pillow. "I'll talk to him tomorrow."

I remembered what Francine said. Then I thought of the money, and the people asking for help, and Cromwell's mysterious list. It was a kind of choice. It's more than most people had.

But old man Cromwell could wait until tomorrow. Pancakes first.

OBLIGATORY AUTHOR STUFF

I hope you enjoyed *Johnny Lycan & the Anubis Disk*. Please leave a review wherever you found it. I know authors beg for reviews and it's tiresome, but it makes a difference, so thank you in advance. It's like applauding the author.

If Johnny Lycan is your introduction to my work, thanks for joining me and I hope you'll read some of my other books, which you can find on my Amazon page. If you've been a reader of my business books or my historical fiction and suddenly found yourself face to face with a werewolf detective and wondering "what the heck happened and when did Wayne snap?" Here's an explanation of sorts.

When I was thirteen years old, I used to babysit my cousins on Friday nights. Not only did that give me money for the movies, but I got to stay up late and watch the KIRO Count on Channel 7 out of Seattle. That's when I saw Oliver Reed in *The Curse of the Werewolf.* Since that was about the age when a feral, snarling teenager was trying to burst out of my own scrawny body, it left a mark. I've been fascinated by werewolves ever since. They are way cooler than zombies, although the living dead get all the press, and vampires get all the chicks. It hardly seems fair. Just saying.

I created the Anubis Disk in a short story that originally ran on Storgy.com in 2019. Check out *The Forger of Cairo.* And support magazines like Storgy who give writers a chance to find their tribe.

The idea for a Johnny Lycan series has been kicking around for a while, and I resisted writing it because I was worried about my "author brand."

After all, I was a grown-up; writing business books. Then I got it into my head to write historical novels (which at least sounds classy.) Now here I was thinking about moving into Urban Fantasy (or whatever micro-niche this falls into. Book marketing makes my head hurt.) Not the most traditional career arc, especially when my ego chafes at the idea of pen names.

I'm the first to admit that the Venn diagram of people who like adventure stories set in the Crusades, werewolf detectives, and how to do effective Skype meetings is microscopic. So, if you're here, a thousand blessings upon you.

If you're a little curious about some of my other work, please join me on my website at www.WayneTurmel.com, sign up for my newsletter and follow me on *Twitter* @Wturmel or on *Goodreads* or my *Amazon* Author Page. I love hearing from readers. Heck, snap a picture of yourself with the book or hugging your Kindle and let me know where in the world you are. You don't know how little it takes to make an author's day. Seriously.

It's a little sad, really.

Of course, thanks must go to Reagan and the team at Black Rose Writing for seeing the possibilities of Johnny and his friends and saving me from the spiral of doubt and despair that is self-publishing. Wayne works better with adult supervision, and this book is better because of their guidance. Also to Stephanie Caruso at Paste Creative for being my guide through the launch promotion mishegas.

This is the first book conceived and written entirely since The Duchess and I moved to Las Vegas in 2018. Huge thanks must be offered to the lunatics in the Sin City Writers Group, for their encouragement and good fellowship.

My beta readers, who definitely helped craft this thing, include Jeremy Brown, Drea Casali, Phillip Sturgeon, Starr Hoffman, Victoria Tokar, and Her Serene Highness.

Johnny will return shortly in a new adventure: *Johnny Lycan & the Vegas Berserker*. Join my newsletter to learn exactly when and be the first cool kid on your block to get it.

As we used to say in my standup days, "If you enjoy it, tell your friends. Word of mouth matters more than anything else. If you hate it, keep your @%@$^ mouth shut. Nobody cares what you think."

Don't let the weasels get you down.

WWT

Las Vegas, Nevada, November 2020.

OTHER NOVELS BY WAYNE TURMEL

The Count of the Sahara (2015)

In 1926 "Count" Byron de Prorok was the most famous archaeologist in the world, splashed across headlines and beloved by audiences. By the end of that year his career, his reputation and his life lay in ruins. From the scorching Saharan desert to the frigid American Midwest, this tale is based on the real life of one of the 1920s most colorful characters.

Acre's Bastard: Part 1 of the Lucca Le Pou Stories (2017)

The Holy Land-1187. Lucca the Louse is a ten-year-old orphan running the streets of Acre—the wickedest city in the world. When a horrific attack forces him to flee his orphanage, he finds himself thrust into a world of leper knights, Saracen spies, and holy war. Can one lone boy save the Kingdom of Jerusalem from defeat at the Horns of Hattin?

Acre's Orphans: Part 2 of the Lucca Le Pou Stories (2019)

Lucca narrowly survives the worst disaster ever to befall the Crusader army, but he's not safe. His beloved city of Acre is about to fall to the Saracens. With the help of a determined Druze girl, a leprous nun, and a Hospitaler knight with a tragic secret, Lucca must get a message to the last Crusader holdout at Tyre. Can he and his friends fetch help before it's too late?

ABOUT THE AUTHOR

Wayne Turmel is a former standup comedian, car salesman and corporate drone who writes to save what's left of his sanity. Originally from Canada, he writes and lives in Las Vegas with his bride, The Duchess. This is his fourth novel, and his introduction to Urban Fantasy/ Noir after 3 award-winning historical novels.

www.wayneturmel.com

NOTE FROM THE AUTHOR

Word-of-mouth is crucial for any author to succeed. If you enjoyed *Johnny Lycan & the Anubis Disk*, please leave a review online—anywhere you are able. Even if it's just a sentence or two. It would make all the difference and would be very much appreciated.

Thanks!
Wayne

Thank you so much for reading one of our **Paranormal Fantasy** novels.
If you enjoyed the experience, please check out our
recommended title for your next great read!

My Travels with a Dead Man by Steven Searls

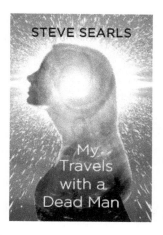

"A compulsive page-turner that contains elements of romance,
tragedy, adventure, journeys through space and time, terror,
mysticism, and meditation. It's a high-octane, multilayered
odyssey that is perfect for readers looking
for a little bit of everything."
-INDIEREADER

CPSIA information can be obtained
at www.ICGtesting.com
Printed in the USA
BVHW071141141120
593257BV00001B/26